Mark Bryant spent ... hamlet, Georgian Bristol and suburban Kent. He was educated at St Albans School, Hertfordshire, whose celebrated alumni include Nicholas Breakspear, the only English Pope, and *A Brief History of Time* scientist Stephen Hawking. The author/compiler of a number of books, he is also the editor of *Cat Tales for Christmas* and *Country Tales for Christmas*.

Also available from Headline

Dog Tales for Christmas
Murder for Christmas
Ghosts for Christmas
Chillers for Christmas
Mystery for Christmas
Cat Tales for Christmas
Country Tales for Christmas

Childhood Tales for Christmas

edited by

Mark Bryant

HEADLINE

First published in 1995
by HEADLINE BOOK PUBLISHING

10 9 8 7 6 5 4 3 2 1

ISBN 0 7472 5153 3

Typeset by Keyboard Services, Luton, Beds

Printed and bound in Great Britain by
Cox & Wyman Ltd, Reading, Berks

HEADLINE BOOK PUBLISHING
A division of Hodder Headline PLC
338 Euston Road
London NW1 3BH

For Angela

Contents

Introduction

There is a special magic about Christmas which somehow never wears off, no matter how old we are. It is one of those timeless events, a fixed point in the calendar that seems to link the past, present and future for everyone. And in particular it evokes nostalgic memories of childhood and the cosy festive gatherings of our youth. The rural homestead on Christmas Eve with a row of tiny stockings hung on the chimney breast; the Christmas-tree's lights glimmering, its base festooned with gaily coloured presents; an old golden retriever dog asleep on the hearth; mince-pies and port wine laid out for Santa. Upstairs, rocking-horses come to rest, lead soldiers return to their barracks, and weary but happy children – tucked up in cots and bunks in readiness for Christmas Day – listen drowsily to Nanny's stories of when she was a girl on just such a night as this, long, long ago . . .

But of course, childhood is more than just Christmas. It is also sunny days of happy wonder chasing butterflies and rabbits across fields of clover, of secret gardens and sparkling rock-pools, of donkey-rides and ice-cream, skipping-ropes and hopscotch, of kittens, fairies and cuddly toys. And then there are the autumnal joys of scuffing leaves and stamping in puddles, of bonfires and conkers, woolly hats and mittens, of Harvest Festival, hot soup and the first days of school.

In winter come snowballs and snowmen, toboggans and ice-skating, roasted chestnuts and log-fires, carol-singing and cocoa. And then daffodils herald the spring, bringing with it the delights of new-born lambs, Easter eggs and pancakes, of daisy-chains and buttercups, warmth and light.

Later, as the first stirrings of adolescence approach, tiny shadows cross the picture. Life, we realize, is not all sugar mice and sticky buns: Peter Pan and Wendy are only make-believe. But somehow the grazed knees and growing pains, homesickness and nightmares, pulled pig-tails and rapped knuckles fade from our memories as our school uniforms shrink ever smaller. And in hindsight it is only the romance and adventure of this period that colours our recollections of the 'best years of our lives'.

This book is an anthology of some of the very best stories of childhood in the British Isles over the last two centuries – tales not written for children but for adults. Most areas of Britain are included, from Scotland and Ireland to the various regions of England, and every aspect of childhood is represented, from Boy Scouts to doll's houses, from wicked step-parents to kindly guardians, from classroom capers to seaside holidays and featuring both girls and boys of all ages, good and bad, in sickness and in health. All the stories are fictional and self-contained, not extracts, and I have tried to make the book as balanced as the limitations of length and copyright availability have allowed. *Childhood Tales for Christmas* includes stories by both men and women, from the nineteenth century to the present day, and covers every imaginable subject; from comedy, tragedy and the macabre to romance, melodrama and mystery.

So, open up the aged photo album, dig out the box of dusty school reports from the attic, and settle the ragged old teddy-bear with its missing ear on the sofa. Then as the sounds of sleeping children drift through the night, slip back in time to the days when you too were a little child, with curly blonde hair and wide blue eyes, with so many dreams and so much to tell . . .

Mark Bryant

Childhood Tales
for Christmas

Great Uncle Crow

H. E. BATES

Once in the summer-time, when the water-lilies were in bloom and the wheat was new in ear, his grandfather took him on a long walk up the river, to see his Uncle Crow. He had heard so much of Uncle Crow, so much that was wonderful and to be marvelled at, and for such a long time, that he knew him to be, even before that, the most remarkable fisherman in the world.

'Masterpiece of a man, your Uncle Crow,' his grandfather said. 'He could git a clothes-line any day and tie a brick on it and a mossel of cake and go out and catch a pike as long as your arm.'

When he asked what kind of cake his grandfather seemed irritated and said it was just like a boy to ask questions of that sort.

'Any kind o' cake,' he said. 'Plum cake. Does it matter? Caraway cake. Christmas cake if you like. Anything. I shouldn't wonder if he could catch a pretty fair pike with a cold baked tater.'

'Only a pike?'

'Times,' his grandfather said, 'I've seen him sittin' on the bank on a sweltering hot day like a furnace, when nobody was gittin' a bite not even off a bloodsucker. And there your Uncle Crow'd be a-pullin' 'em out by the dozen, like a man shellin' harvest beans.'

'And how does he come to be my Uncle Crow?' he said, 'if my mother hasn't got a brother? Nor my father.'

'Well,' his grandfather said, 'he's really your mother's own cousin, if everybody had their rights. But all on us call him Uncle Crow.'

'And where does he live?'

'You'll see,' his grandfather said. 'All by hisself. In a little titty bit of a house, by the river.'

The little titty bit of a house, when he first saw it, surprised him very much. It was not at all unlike a black tarred boat that had either slipped down a slope and stuck there on its way to launching or one that had been washed up and left there in a flood. The roof of brown tiles had a warp in it and the sides were mostly built, he thought, of tarred beer-barrels.

The two windows with their tiny panes were about as large as chessboards and Uncle Crow had nailed underneath each of them a sill of sheet tin that was still a brilliant blue, each with the words 'Backache Pills' in white lettering on it, upside down.

On all sides of the house grew tall feathered reeds. They enveloped it like gigantic whispering corn. Some distance beyond the great reeds the river went past in a broad slow arc, on magnificent kingly currents, full of long white islands of water-lilies, as big as china breakfast cups, shining and yellow-hearted in the sun.

He thought, on the whole, that that place, the river with the water-lilies, the little titty bit of a house, and the great forest of reeds talking between soft brown beards, was the nicest place he had ever seen.

'Anybody about?' his grandfather called. 'Crow! – anybody at home?'

The door of the house was partly open, but at first there was no answer. His grandfather pushed open the door still farther with his foot. The reeds whispered down by the river and were answered, in the house, by a sound like the creak of bed springs.

'Who is't?'

'It's me, Crow,' his grandfather called. 'Lukey. Brought the boy over to have a look at you.'

A big gangling red-faced man with rusty hair came to the door. His trousers were black and very tight. His eyes were a smeary vivid blue, the same colour as the stripes of his shirt, and his trousers were kept up

2

by a leather belt with brass escutcheons on it, like those on horses' harness.

'Thought very like you'd be out a-pikin',' his grandfather said.

'Too hot. How's Lukey boy? Ain't seed y' lately, Lukey boy.'

His lips were thick and very pink and wet, like cow's lips. He made a wonderful erupting jolly sound somewhat between a belch and a laugh.

'Comin' in it a minute?'

In the one room of the house was an iron bed with an old red check horse-rug spread over it and a stone copper in one corner and a bare wooden table with dirty plates and cups and a tin kettle on it. Two osier baskets and a scythe stood in another corner.

Uncle Crow stretched himself full length on the bed as if he was very tired. He put his knees in the air. His belly was tight as a bladder of lard in his black trousers, which were mossy green on the knees and seat.

'How's the fishin?' his grandfather said. 'I bin tellin' the boy –'

Uncle Crow belched deeply. From where the sun struck full on the tarred wall of the house there was a hot whiff of baking tar. But when Uncle Crow belched there was a smell like the smell of yeast in the air.

'It ain't bin all that much of a summer yit,' Uncle Crow said. 'Ain't had the rain.'

'Not like that summer you catched the big 'un down at Archer's Mill. I recollect you a-tellin' on me –'

'Too hot and dry by half,' Uncle Crow said. 'Gits in your gullet like chaff.'

'You recollect that summer?' his grandfather said. 'Nobody else a-fetching on 'em out only you –'

'Have a drop o' neck-oil,' Uncle Crow said.

The boy wondered what neck-oil was and presently, to his surprise, Uncle Crow and his grandfather were drinking it. It came out of a dark-green bottle and it was a clear bright amber, like cold tea, in the two glasses.

'The medder were yeller with 'em,' Uncle Crow said. 'Yeller as a guinea.'

He smacked his lips with a marvellously juicy, fruity sound. The

3

boy's grandfather gazed at the neck-oil and said he thought it would be a corker if it was kept a year or two, but Uncle Crow said:

'Trouble is, Lukey boy, it's a terrible job to keep it. You start tastin' it to see if it'll keep and then you taste on it again and you go on tastin' on it until they ain't a drop left as'll keep.'

Uncle Crow laughed so much that the bed springs cackled underneath his bouncing trousers.

'Why is it called neck-oil?' the boy said.

'Boy,' Uncle Crow said, 'when you git older, when you git growed-up, you know what'll happen to your gullet?'

'No.'

'It'll git sort o' rusted up inside. Like an old gutter pipe. So's you can't swaller very easy. Rusty as old Harry it'll git. You know that, boy?'

'No.'

'Well, it will. I'm tellin' on y'. And you know what y' got to do then?'

'No.'

'Every now and then you gotta git a drop o' neck-oil down it. So's to ease it. A drop o' neck-oil every once in a while – that's what you gotta do to keep the rust out.'

The boy was still contemplating the curious prospect of his neck rusting up inside in later years when Uncle Crow said: 'Boy, you go outside and jis' round the corner you'll see a bucket. You bring a handful o' cresses out on it. I'll bet you're hungry, ain't you?'

'A little bit.'

He found the watercresses in the bucket, cool in the shadow of the little house, and when he got back inside with them Uncle Crow said:

'Now you put the cresses on that there plate there and then put your nose inside that there basin and see what's inside. What is't, eh?'

'Eggs.'

'Ought to be fourteen on 'em. Four-apiece and two over. What sort are they, boy?'

'Moor-hens'.'

'You got a knowin' boy here, Lukey,' Uncle Crow said. He dropped

4

the scaly red lid of one eye like an old cockerel going to sleep. He took another drop of neck-oil and gave another fruity, juicy laugh as he heaved his body from the bed. 'A very knowin' boy.'

Presently he was carving slices of thick brown bread with a great horn-handled shut-knife and pasting each slice with summery golden butter. Now and then he took another drink of neck-oil and once he said:

'You get the salt pot, boy, and empty a bit out on that there saucer, so's we can all dip in.'

Uncle Crow slapped the last slice of bread on to the buttered pile and then said:

'Boy, you take that there jug there and go a step or two up the path and dip yourself a drop o' spring water. You'll see it. It comes out of a little bit of a wall, jist by a doddle-willer.'

When the boy got back with the jug of spring water Uncle Crow was opening another bottle of neck-oil and his grandfather was saying: 'God a-mussy man, goo steady. You'll have me agooin' one way and another–'

'Man alive,' Uncle Crow said, 'and what's wrong with that?'

Then the watercress, the salt, the moor-hens' eggs, the spring water, and the neck-oil were all ready. The moor-hens' eggs were hard-boiled. Uncle Crow lay on the bed and cracked them with his teeth, just like big brown nuts, and said he thought the watercress was just about as nice and tender as a young lady.

'I'm sorry we ain't got the gold plate out though. I had it out a-Sunday.' He closed his old cockerel-lidded eye again and licked his tongue backwards and forwards across his lips and dipped another peeled egg in salt. 'You know what I had for my dinner a-Sunday, boy?'

'No.'

'A pussy-cat on a gold plate. Roasted with broad-beans and new taters. Did you ever heerd talk of anybody eatin' a roasted pussy-cat, boy?'

'Yes.'

'You did?'

'Yes,' he said, 'that's a hare.'

'You got a very knowin' boy here, Lukey,' Uncle Crow said. 'A very knowin' boy.'

Then he screwed up a big dark-green bouquet of watercress and dipped it in salt until it was entirely frosted and then crammed it in one neat wholesale bite into his soft pink mouth.

'But not on a gold plate?' he said.

He had to admit that.

'No, not on a gold plate,' he said.

All that time he thought the fresh watercress, the moor-hens' eggs, the brown bread-and-butter, and the spring water were the most delicious, wonderful things he had ever eaten in the world. He felt that only one thing was missing. It was that whenever his grandfather spoke of fishing Uncle Crow simply took another draught of neck-oil.

'When are you goin' to take us fishing?' he said.

'You et up that there egg,' Uncle Crow said. 'That's the last one. You et that there egg up and I'll tell you what.'

'What about gooin' as far as that big deep hole where the chub lay?' grandfather said. 'Up by the back-brook—'

'I'll tell you what, boy,' Uncle Crow said, 'you git your grandfather to bring you over September time, of a morning afore the steam's off the winders. Mushroomin' time. You come over and we'll have a bit o' bacon and mushroom for breakfast and then set into the pike. You see, boy, it ain't the pikin' season now. It's too hot. Too bright. It's too bright of an afternoon, and they ain't a-bitin'.'

He took a long rich swig of neck-oil.

'Ain't that it, Lukey? That's the time, ain't it, mushroom time?'

'Thass it,' his grandfather said.

'Tot out,' Uncle Crow said. 'Drink up. My throat's jist easin' orf a bit.'

He gave another wonderful belching laugh and told the boy to be sure to finish up the last of the watercress and the bread-and-butter. The little room was rich with the smell of neck-oil, and the tarry sun-baked odour of the beer-barrels that formed its walls. And through the door came, always, the sound of reeds talking in their beards, and the scent of summer meadows drifting in from beyond the great curl of the river with its kingly currents and its islands of full blown lilies, white and yellow in the sun.

'I see the wheat's in ear,' his grandfather said. 'Ain't that the time for tench, when the wheat's in ear?'

'Mushroom time,' Uncle Crow said. 'That's the time. You git mushroom time here, and I'll fetch you a tench out as big as a cricket bat.'

He fixed the boy with an eye of wonderful, watery, glassy blue and licked his lips with a lazy tongue, and said:

'You know what colour a tench is, boy?'

'Yes,' he said.

'What colour?'

'The colour of the neck-oil.'

'Lukey,' Uncle Crow said, 'you got a very knowin' boy here. A very knowin' boy.'

After that, when there were no more cresses or moor-hens' eggs or bread-and-butter to eat, and his grandfather said he'd get hung if he touched another drop of neck-oil, he and his grandfather walked home across the meadows.

'What work does Uncle Crow do?' he said.

'Uncle Crow? Work? – well, he ain't – Uncle Crow? Well, he works, but he ain't what you'd call a reg'lar worker –'

All the way home he could hear the reeds talking in their beards. He could see the water-lilies that reminded him so much of the gold and white inside the moor-hens' eggs. He could hear the happy sound of Uncle Crow laughing and sucking at the neck-oil, and crunching the fresh salty cresses into his mouth in the tarry little room.

He felt happy, too, and the sun was a gold plate in the sky.

The Doll's House

KATHERINE MANSFIELD

When dear old Mrs Hay went back to town after staying with the Burnells she sent the children a doll's house. It was so big that the carter and Pat carried it into the courtyard, and there it stayed, propped up on two wooden boxes beside the feed-room door. No harm could come to it; it was summer. And perhaps the smell of paint would have gone off by the time it had to be taken in. For, really, the smell of paint coming from that doll's house ('Sweet of old Mrs Hay, of course; most sweet and generous!') – but the smell of paint was quite enough to make anyone seriously ill, in Aunt Beryl's opinion. Even before the sacking was taken off. And when it was . . .

There stood the doll's house, a dark, oily, spinach green, picked out with bright yellow. Its two solid little chimneys, glued on to the roof, were painted red and white, and the door, gleaming with yellow varnish, was like a little slab of toffee. Four windows, real windows, were divided into panes by a broad streak of green. There was actually a tiny porch, too, painted yellow, with big lumps of congealed paint hanging along the edge.

But perfect, perfect little house! Who could possibly mind the smell. It was part of the joy, part of the newness.

'Open it quickly, someone!'

The hook at the side was stuck fast. Pat prised it open with his penknife, and the whole house front swung back, and – there you were, gazing at one and the same moment into the drawing-room and dining-room, the kitchen and two bedrooms. That is the way for a house to open! Why don't all houses open like that? How much more exciting than peering through the slit of a door into a mean little hall with a hat-stand and two umbrellas! That is – isn't it? – what you long to know about a house when you put your hand on the knocker. Perhaps it is the way God opens houses at the dead of night when He is taking a quiet turn with an angel . . .

'Oh-oh!' The Burnell children sounded as though they were in despair. It was too marvellous; it was too much for them. They had never seen anything like it in their lives. All the rooms were papered. There were pictures on the walls, painted on the paper, with gold frames complete. Red carpet covered all the floors except the kitchen; red plush chairs in the drawing-room, green in the dining-room; tables, beds with real bedclothes, a cradle, a stove, a dresser with tiny plates and one big jug. But what Kezia liked more than anything, what she liked frightfully, was the lamp. It stood in the middle of the dining-room table, an exquisite little amber lamp with a white globe. It was even filled all ready for lighting, though, of course, you couldn't light it. But there was something inside that looked like oil and moved when you shook it.

The father and mother dolls, who sprawled very stiff as though they had fainted in the drawing-room, and their two little children asleep upstairs, were really too big for the doll's house. They didn't look as though they belonged. But the lamp was perfect. It seemed to smile at Kezia, to say, 'I live here.' The lamp was real.

The Burnell children could hardly walk to school fast enough the next morning. They burned to tell everybody, to describe, to – well – to boast about their doll's house before the school-bell rang.

'I'm to tell,' said Isabel, 'because I'm the eldest. And you two can join in after. But I'm to tell first.'

There was nothing to answer. Isabel was bossy, but she was always right, and Lottie and Kezia knew too well the powers that went with being eldest. They brushed through the thick buttercups at the road edge and said nothing.

'And I'm to choose who's to come and see it first. Mother said I might.'

For it had been arranged that while the doll's house stood in the courtyard they might ask the girls at school, two at a time, to come and look. Not to stay to tea, of course, or to come traipsing through the house. But just to stand quietly in the courtyard while Isabel pointed out the beauties, and Lottie and Kezia looked pleased . . .

But hurry as they might, by the time they had reached the tarred palings of the boys' playground the bell had begun to jangle. They only just had time to whip off their hats and fall into line before the roll was called. Never mind. Isabel tried to make up for it by looking very important and mysterious and by whispering behind her hand to the girls near her, 'Got something to tell you at playtime.'

Playtime came and Isabel was surrounded. The girls of her class nearly fought to put their arms round her, to walk away with her, to beam flatteringly, to be her special friend. She held quite a court under the huge pine trees at the side of the playground. Nudging, giggling together, the little girls pressed up close. And the only two who stayed outside the ring were the two who were always outside, the little Kelveys. They knew better than to come anywhere near the Burnells.

For the fact was, the school the Burnell children went to was not at all the kind of place their parents would have chosen if there had been any choice. But there was none. It was the only school for miles. And the consequence was all the children of the neighbourhood, the Judge's little girls, the doctor's daughters, the store-keeper's children, the milkman's, were forced to mix together. Not to speak of there being an equal number of rude, rough little boys as well. But the line had to be drawn somewhere. It was drawn at the Kelveys. Many of the children, including the Burnells, were not allowed even to speak to them. They walked past the Kelveys with their heads in the air, and as they set the fashion in all matters of behaviour, the Kelveys were shunned by everybody. Even the teacher had a special voice for them, and a special smile for the other children when Lil Kelvey came up to the desk with a bunch of dreadfully common-looking flowers.

11

They were the daughters of a spry, hard-working little washer-woman, who went about from house to house by the day. This was awful enough. But where was Mr Kelvey? Nobody knew for certain. But everybody said he was in prison. So they were the daughters of a washerwoman and a gaolbird. Very nice company for other people's children! And they looked it. Why Mrs Kelvey made them so conspicuous was hard to understand. The truth was they were dressed in 'bits' given to her by the people for whom she worked. Lil, for instance, who was a stout, plain child, with big freckles, came to school in a dress made from a green art-serge tablecloth of the Burnells', with red plush sleeves from the Logans' curtains. Her hat, perched on top of her high forehead, was a grown-up woman's hat, once the property of Miss Lecky, the postmistress. It was turned up at the back and trimmed with a large scarlet quill. What a little guy she looked! It was impossible not to laugh. And her little sister, our Else, wore a long white dress, rather like a nightgown, and a pair of little boy's boots. But whatever our Else wore she would have looked strange. She was a tiny wishbone of a child, with cropped hair and enormous solemn eyes — a little white owl. Nobody had ever seen her smile; she scarcely ever spoke. She went through life holding on to Lil, with a piece of Lil's skirt screwed up in her hand. Where Lil went, our Else followed. In the playground, on the road going to and from school, there was Lil marching in front and our Else holding on behind. Only when she wanted anything, or when she was out of breath, our Else gave Lil a tug, a twitch, and Lil stopped and turned round. The Kelveys never failed to understand each other.

Now they hovered at the edge; you couldn't stop them listening. When the little girls turned round and sneered, Lil, as usual, gave her silly, shamefaced smile, but our Else only looked.

And Isabel's voice, so very proud, went on telling. The carpet made a great sensation, but so did the beds with real bedclothes, and the stove with an oven door.

When she finished Kezia broke in. 'You've forgotten the lamp, Isabel.'

'Oh yes,' said Isabel, 'and there's a teeny little lamp, all made of yellow glass, with a white globe, that stands on the dining-room table. You couldn't tell it from a real one.'

'The lamp's best of all,' cried Kezia. She thought Isabel wasn't making half enough of the little lamp. But nobody paid any attention. Isabel was choosing the two who were to come back with them that afternoon and see it. She chose Emmie Cole and Lena Logan. But when the others knew they were all to have a chance, they couldn't be nice enough to Isabel. One by one they put their arms round Isabel's waist and walked her off. They had something to whisper to her, a secret. 'Isabel's *my* friend.'

Only the little Kelveys moved away forgotten; there was nothing more for them to hear.

Days passed, and as more children saw the doll's house, the fame of it spread. It became the one subject, the rage. The one question was, 'Have you seen Burnells' doll's house? Oh, ain't it lovely!' 'Haven't you seen it? Oh, I say!'

Even the dinner hour was given up to talking about it. The little girls sat under the pines eating their thick mutton sandwiches and big slabs of johnny cake spread with butter. While always, as near as they could get, sat the Kelveys, our Else holding on to Lil, listening too, while they chewed their jam sandwiches out of a newspaper soaked with large red blobs.

'Mother,' said Kezia, 'can't I ask the Kelveys just once?'

'Certainly not, Kezia.'

'But why not?'

'Run away, Kezia; you know quite well why not.'

At last everybody had seen it except them. On that day the subject rather flagged. It was the dinner hour. The children stood together under the pine trees, and suddenly, as they looked at the Kelveys eating out of their paper, always by themselves, always listening, they wanted to be horrid to them. Emmie Cole started the whisper.

'Lil Kelvey's going to be a servant when she grows up.'

'O-oh, how awful!' said Isabel Burnell, and she made eyes at Emmie.

Emmie swallowed in a very meaning way and nodded to Isabel as she'd seen her mother do on those occasions.

'It's true – it's true – it's true,' she said.

Then Lena Logan's little eyes snapped. 'Shall I ask her?' she whispered.

'Bet you don't,' said Jessie May.

'Pooh, I'm not frightened,' said Lena. Suddenly she gave a little squeal and danced in front of the other girls. 'Watch! Watch me! Watch me now!' said Lena. And sliding, gliding, dragging one foot, giggling behind her hand, Lena went over to the Kelveys.

Lil looked up from her dinner. She wrapped the rest quickly away. Our Else stopped chewing. What was coming now?

'Is it true you're going to be a servant when you grow up, Lil Kelvey?' shrilled Lena.

Dead silence. But instead of answering, Lil only gave her silly, shamefaced smile. She didn't seem to mind the question at all. What a sell for Lena! The girls began to titter.

Lena couldn't stand that. She put her hands on her hips; she shot forward. 'Yah, yer father's in prison!' she hissed spitefully.

This was such a marvellous thing to have said that the little girls rushed away in a body, deeply, deeply excited, wild with joy. Someone found a long rope, and they began skipping. And never did they skip so high, run in and out so fast, or do such daring things as on that morning.

In the afternoon Pat called for the Burnell children with the buggy and they drove home. There were visitors. Isabel and Lottie, who liked visitors, went upstairs to change their pinafores. But Kezia thieved out at the back. Nobody was about; she began to swing on the big white gates of the courtyard. Presently, looking along the road, she saw two little dots. They grew bigger; they were coming towards her. Now she could see that one was in front and one close behind. Now she could see that they were the Kelveys. Kezia stopped swinging. She slipped off the gate as if she was going to run away. Then she hesitated. The Kelveys came nearer, and beside them walked their shadows, very long, stretching right across the road with their heads in the buttercups. Kezia clambered back on the gate; she had made up her mind; she swung out.

'Hullo,' she said to the passing Kelveys.

They were so astounded that they stopped. Lil gave her silly smile. Our Else stared.

'You can come and see our doll's house if you want to,' said Kezia, and she dragged one toe on the ground. But at that Lil turned red and shook her head quickly.

'Why not?' asked Kezia.

Lil gasped, then she said, 'Your ma told our ma you wasn't to speak to us.'

'Oh, well,' said Kezia. She didn't know what to reply. 'It doesn't matter. You can come and see our doll's house all the same. Come on. Nobody's looking.'

But Lil shook her head still harder.

'Don't you want to?' asked Kezia.

Suddenly there was a twitch, a tug at Lil's skirt. She turned round. Our Else was looking at her with big, imploring eyes; she was frowning; she wanted to go. For a moment Lil looked at our Else very doubtfully. But then our Else twitched her skirt again. She started forward. Kezia led the way. Like two little stray cats they followed across the courtyard to where the doll's house stood.

'There it is,' said Kezia.

There was a pause. Lil breathed loudly, almost snorted; our Else was still as stone.

'I'll open it for you,' said Kezia kindly. She undid the hook and they looked inside.

'There's the drawing-room and the dining-room, and that's the—'

'Kezia!'

Oh, what a start they gave!

'Kezia!'

It was Aunt Beryl's voice. They turned round. At the back door stood Aunt Beryl, staring as if she couldn't believe what she saw.

'How dare you ask the little Kelveys into the courtyard!' said her cold, furious voice. 'You know as well as I do, you're not allowed to talk to them. Run away, children, run away at once. And don't come back again,' said Aunt Beryl. And she stepped into the yard and shooed them out as if they were chickens.

'Off you go immediately!' she called, cold and proud.

They did not need telling twice. Burning with shame, shrinking together, Lil huddling along like her mother, our Else dazed, somehow they crossed the big courtyard and squeezed through the white gate.

'Wicked, disobedient little girl!' said Aunt Beryl bitterly to Kezia, and she slammed the doll's house to.

The afternoon had been awful. A letter had come from Willie Brent, a terrifying, threatening letter, saying if she did not meet him that evening in Pulman's Bush, he'd come to the front door and ask the reason why! But now that she had frightened those little rats of Kelveys and given Kezia a good scolding, her heart felt lighter. That ghastly pressure was gone. She went back to the house humming.

When the Kelveys were well out of sight of the Burnells', they sat down to rest on a big red drainpipe by the side of the road. Lil's cheeks were still burning; she took off the hat with the quill and held it on her knee. Dreamily they looked over the hay paddocks, past the creek, to the group of wattles where Logan's cows stood waiting to be milked. What were their thoughts?

Presently our Else nudged up close to her sister. By now she had forgotten the cross lady. She put out a finger and stroked her sister's quill; she smiled her rare smile.

'I seen the little lamp,' she said softly.

Then both were silent once more.

The Schoolboy's Story

CHARLES DICKENS

Being rather young at present – I am getting on in years, but still I am rather young – I have no particular adventures of my own to fall back upon. It wouldn't much interest anybody here, I suppose, to know what a screw the Reverend is, or what a griffin *she* is, or how they do stick it into parents – particularly hair-cutting, and medical attendance. One of our fellows was charged in his half's account twelve and sixpence for two pills – tolerably profitable at six and threepence a-piece, I should think – and he never took them either, but put them up the sleeve of his jacket.

As to the beef, it's shameful. It's not beef. Regular beef isn't veins. You can chew regular beef. Besides which, there's gravy to regular beef, and you never see a drop to ours. Another of our fellows went home ill, and heard the family doctor tell his father that he couldn't account for his complaint unless it was the beer. Of course it was the beer, and well it might be!

However, beef and Old Cheeseman are two different things. So is beer. It was old Cheeseman I meant to tell about; not the manner in which our fellows get their constitutions destroyed for the sake of profit.

Why, look at the pie-crust alone. There's no flakiness in it. It's solid – like damp lead. Then our fellows get nightmares, and are bolstered for calling out and waking other fellows. Who can wonder!

17

Old Cheeseman one night walked in his sleep, put his hat on over his nightcap, got hold of a fishing-rod and a cricket-bat, and went down into the parlour, where they naturally thought from his appearance he was a ghost. Why, he never would have done that if his meals had been wholesome. When we all begin to walk in our sleep, I suppose they'll be sorry for it.

Old Cheeseman wasn't second Latin Master then; he was a fellow himself. He was first brought here, very small, in a post-chaise, by a woman who was always taking snuff and shaking him – and that was the most he remembered about it. He never went home for the holidays. His accounts (he never earnt any extras) were sent to a bank, and the bank paid them; and he had a brown suit twice a-year, and went into boots at twelve. They were always too big for him, too.

In the Midsummer holidays, some of our fellows who lived within walking distance, used to come back and climb the trees outside the playground wall, on purpose to look at Old Cheeseman reading there by himself. He was always as mild as the tea – *that*'s pretty mild, I should hope! – so when they whistled to him, he looked up and nodded; and when they said, 'Halloa, Old Cheeseman, what have you had for dinner?' he said, 'Boiled mutton'; and when they said, 'An't it solitary, Old Cheeseman?' he said, 'It is a little dull sometimes'; and then they said, 'Well, good-bye, Old Cheeseman!' and climbed down again. Of course it was imposing on Old Cheeseman to give him nothing but boiled mutton through a whole vacation, but that was just like the system. When they didn't give him boiled mutton, they gave him rice pudding, pretending it was a treat. And saved the butcher.

So Old Cheeseman went on. The holidays brought him into other trouble besides the loneliness; because when the fellows began to come back, not wanting to, he was always glad to see them; which was aggravating when they were not at all glad to see him, and so he got his head knocked against walls, and that was the way his nose bled. But he was a favourite in general. Once a subscription was raised for him; and, to keep up his spirits, he was presented before the holidays with two white mice, a rabbit, a pigeon, and a beautiful puppy. Old Cheeseman cried about it – especially soon afterwards, when they all ate one another.

Of course Old Cheeseman used to be called by the names of all sorts of cheeses – Double Glo'sterman, Family Cheshireman, Dutchman, North Wiltshireman, and all that. But he never minded it. And I don't mean to say he was old in point of years – because he wasn't – only he was called from the first, Old Cheeseman.

At last, Old Cheeseman was made second Latin Master. He was brought in one morning at the beginning of a new half, and presented to the school in that capacity as 'Mr Cheeseman', Then our fellows all agreed that Old Cheeseman was a spy, and a deserter who had gone over to the enemy's camp, and sold himself for gold. It was no excuse for him that he had sold himself for very little gold – two pound ten a quarter and his washing, as was reported. It was decided by a Parliament which sat about it, that Old Cheeseman's mercenary motives could alone be taken into account, and that he had 'coined our blood for drachmas'. The Parliament took the expression out of the quarrel scene between Brutus and Cassius.

When it was settled in this strong way that Old Cheeseman was a tremendous traitor, who had wormed himself into our fellows' secrets on purpose to get himself into favour by giving up everything he knew, all courageous fellows were invited to come forward and enrol themselves in a Society for making a set against him. The President of the Society was First Boy, named Bob Tarter. His father was in the West Indies, and he owned, himself, that his father was worth millions. He had great power among our fellows, and he wrote a parody, beginning –

> 'Who made believe to be so meek
> That we could hardly hear him speak,
> Yet turned out an Informing Sneak?
> Old Cheeseman.'

– and on in that way through more than a dozen verses, which he used to go and sing, every morning, close by the new master's desk. He trained one of the low boys, too, a rosy-cheeked little Brass who didn't care what he did, to go up to him with his Latin Grammar one morning, and say it so: *Nominativus pronominum* – Old Cheeseman, *raro exprimitur* – was never suspected, *nisi distinctionis* – of being an informer, *aut emphasis gratia* – until he proved one. *Ut* – for instance, *vos damnastis* – when he sold the boys. *Quasi* – as though, *dicat* – he should say, *præterea nemo* – I'm a Judas! All this produced a great effect on Old Cheeseman. He had never had much hair; but what he had, began to get thinner and thinner every day. He grew paler and more worn; and sometimes of an evening he was seen sitting at his desk with a precious long snuff to his candle, and his hands before his face, crying. But no member of the Society could pity him, even if he felt inclined, because the President said it was Old Cheeseman's conscience.

So Old Cheeseman went on, and didn't he lead a miserable life! Of course the Reverend turned up his nose at him, and of course *she* did – because both of them always do that at all the masters – but he suffered from the fellows most, and he suffered from them constantly. He never told about it, that the Society could find out; but he got no credit for that, because the President said it was Old Cheeseman's cowardice.

He had only one friend in the world, and that one was almost as powerless as he was, for it was only Jane. Jane was a sort of wardrobe-woman to our fellows, and took care of the boxes. She had come at first, I believe, as a kind of apprentice – some of our fellows say from a charity, but *I* don't know – and after her time was out, had stopped at so much year. So little a year, perhaps I ought to say, for it is far more likely. However, she had put some pounds in the Savings' Bank, and she was a very nice young woman. She was not quite pretty; but she had a very frank, honest, bright face, and all our fellows were fond of her. She was uncommonly neat and cheerful, and uncommonly comfortable and kind. And if anything was the matter with a fellow's mother, he always went and showed the letter to Jane.

Jane was Old Cheeseman's friend. The more the Society went against him, the more Jane stood by him. She used to give him a good-humoured look out of her still-room window, sometimes, that seemed to set him up for the day. She used to pass out of the orchard and the kitchen garden (always kept locked, I believe you!), through the playground, when she might have gone the other way, only to give a turn of her head, as much as to say, 'Keep up your spirits!' to Old Cheeseman. His slip of a room was so fresh and orderly that it was well known who looked after it while he was at his desk; and when our fellows saw a smoking hot dumpling on his plate at dinner, they knew with indignation who had sent it up.

Under these circumstances, the Society resolved, after a quantity of meeting and debating, that Jane should be requested to cut Old Cheeseman dead; and that if she refused, she must be sent to Coventry herself. So a deputation, headed by the President, was appointed to wait on Jane, and inform her of the vote the Society had been under the painful necessity of passing. She was very much respected for all her good qualities, and there was a story about her having once waylaid the Reverend in his own study, and got a fellow off from severe punishment, of her own kind comfortable heart. So the deputation didn't much like the job. However, they went up, and the President told Jane all about it. Upon which Jane turned very red, burst into tears, informed the President and the deputation, in a way not at all like her usual way, that they were a parcel of malicious young savages, and turned the whole respected body out of the room. Consequently it was entered in the Society's book (kept in astronomical cypher for fear of detection), that all communication with Jane was interdicted: and the President addressed the members on this convincing instance of Old Cheeseman's undermining.

But Jane was as true to Old Cheeseman as Old Cheeseman was false to our fellows – in their opinion, at all events – and steadily continued to be his only friend. It was a great exasperation to the Society, because Jane was as much a loss to them as she was a gain to him; and being more inveterate against him than ever, they treated him worse than ever. At last, one morning, his desk stood empty, his room was peeped into, and found to be vacant, and a whisper went about among the pale faces of our fellows that Old Cheeseman, unable to bear it any longer, had got up early and drowned himself.

The mysterious looks of the other masters after breakfast, and the evident fact that Old Cheeseman was not expected, confirmed the Society in this opinion. Some began to discuss whether the President was liable to hanging or only transportation for life, and the President's face showed a great anxiety to know which. However, he said that a jury of his country should find him game; and that in his address he should put it to them to lay their hands upon their hearts and say whether they as Britons approved of informers, and how they thought they would like it themselves. Some of the Society considered that he had better run away until he found a forest where he might change clothes with a wood-cutter, and stain his face with blackberries; but the majority believed that if he stood his ground, his father – belonging as he did to the West Indies, and being worth millions – could buy him off.

All our fellows' hearts beat fast when the Reverend came in, and made a sort of a Roman, or a Field-Marshal, of himself with the ruler; as he always did before delivering an address. But their fears were nothing to their astonishment when he came out with the story that Old Cheeseman, 'so long our respected friend and fellow-pilgrim in the pleasant plains of knowledge', he called him – O yes, I dare say! much of that! – was the orphan child of a disinherited young lady who had married against her father's wish, and whose young husband had died, and who had died of sorrow herself, and whose unfortunate baby (Old Cheeseman) had been brought up at the cost of a grandfather who would never consent to see it, baby, boy, or man: which grandfather was now dead, and serve him right – that's *my* putting in – and which grandfather's large property, there being no will, was now, and all of a sudden and for ever, Old Cheeseman's! Our so long respected friend and fellow-pilgrim in the pleasant plains of knowledge, the Reverend wound up a lot of bothering quotations by saying, would 'come among us once more' that day fortnight, when he desired to take leave of us himself, in a more particular manner. With these words, he stared severely round at our fellows, and went solemnly out.

There was precious consternation among the members of the Society, now. Lots of them wanted to resign, and lots more began to try to make out that they had never belonged to it. However, the President stuck up, and said that they must stand or fall together, and that if a breach was made it should be over his body – which was meant to encourage the Society: but it didn't. The President further said, he would consider the position in which they stood, and would give them his best opinion and advice in a few days. This was eagerly looked for, as he knew a good deal of the world on account of his father's being in the West Indies.

After days and days of hard thinking, and drawing armies all over his slate, the President called our fellows together, and made the matter clear. He said it was plain that when Old Cheeseman came on the appointed day, his first revenge would be to impeach the Society, and have it flogged all round. After witnessing with joy the torture of his enemies, and gloating over the cries which agony would extort from them, the probability was that he would invite the Reverend, on pretence of conversation, into a private room – say the parlour into which parents were shown, where the two great globes were which were never used – and would there reproach him with various frauds and oppressions he had endured at his hands. At the close of his observations he would make a signal to a Prizefighter concealed in the passage, who would then appear and pitch into the Reverend, till he was left insensible. Old Cheeseman would then make Jane a present of from five to ten pounds, and would leave the establishment in fiendish triumph.

The President explained that against the parlour part, or the Jane part, of these arrangements he had nothing to say; but, on the part of the Society, he counselled deadly resistance. With this view he recommended that all available desks should be filled with stones, and that the first word of the complaint should be the signal to every fellow to let fly at Old Cheeseman. The bold advice put the Society in better spirits, and was unanimously taken. A post about Old Cheeseman's size was put up in the playground, and all our fellows practised at it till it was dinted all over.

When the day came, and Places were called, every fellow sat down in a tremble. There had been much discussing and disputing as to how Old Cheeseman would come; but it was the general opinion that he would appear in a sort of triumphal car drawn by four horses, with two livery servants in front, and the Prizefighter in disguise up behind. So, all our fellows sat listening for the sound of wheels. But no wheels were heard, for Old Cheeseman walked after all, and came into the school without any preparation. Pretty much as he used to be, only dressed in black.

'Gentlemen,' said the Reverend, presenting him, 'our so long respected friend and fellow-pilgrim in the pleasant plains of knowledge, is desirous to offer a word or two. Attention, gentlemen, one and all!'

Every fellow stole his hand into his desk and looked at the President.

23

The President was all ready, and taking aim at Old Cheeseman with his eyes.

What did Old Cheeseman then, but walk up to his old desk, look round him with a queer smile as if there was a tear in his eye, and begin in a quavering mild voice, 'My dear companions and old friends!'

Every fellow's hand came out of his desk, and the President suddenly began to cry.

'My dear companions and old friends,' said Old Cheeseman, 'you have heard of my good fortune. I have passed so many years under this roof – my entire life so far, I may say – that I hope you have been glad to hear of it for my sake. I would never enjoy it without exchanging congratulations with you. If we have ever misunderstood one another at all, pray, my dear boys, let us forgive and forget. I have a great tenderness for you, and I am sure you return it. I want in the fullness of a grateful heart to shake hands with you every one. I have come back to do it, if you please, my dear boys.'

Since the President had begun to cry, several other fellows had broken out here and there: but now, when Old Cheeseman began with him as First Boy, laid his left hand affectionately on his shoulder and gave him his right; and when the President said 'Indeed, I don't deserve it, sir; upon my honour I don't', there was sobbing and crying all over the school. Every other fellow said he didn't deserve it, much in the same way; but Old Cheeseman, not minding that a bit, went cheerfully round to every boy, and wound up with every master – finishing off the Reverend last.

Then a snivelling little chap in a corner, who was always under some punishment or other, set up a shrill cry of 'Success to Old Cheeseman! Hooray!' The Reverend glared upon him, and said, '*Mr* Cheeseman, sir.' But, Old Cheeseman protesting that he liked his old name a great deal better than his new one, all our fellows took up the cry; and, for I don't know how many minutes, there was such a thundering of feet and hands, and such a roaring of 'Old Cheeseman', as never was heard.

After that, there was a spread in the dining-room of the most magnificent kind. Fowls, tongues, preserves, fruits, confectioneries, jellies, neguses, barley-sugar temples, trifles, crackers – eat all you can and pocket what you like – all at Old Cheeseman's expense. After that, speeches, whole holiday, double and treble sets of all manner of things for all manners of games, donkeys, pony-chaises and drive yourself, dinner for all the masters at the Seven Bells (twenty pounds a-head our fellows estimated it at), an annual holiday and feast fixed for that day every year, and another on Old Cheeseman's birthday – the Reverend bound down before the fellows to allow it, so that he could never back out – all at Old Cheeseman's expense.

And didn't our fellows go down in a body and cheer outside the Seven Bells? O no!

But there's something else besides. Don't look at the next story-teller for there's more yet. Next day, it was resolved that the Society should make it up with Jane, and then be dissolved. What do you think of Jane being gone, though? 'What? Gone for ever?' said our fellows, with long faces. 'Yes, to be sure,' was all the answer they could get. None of the people about the house would say anything more. At length, the First Boy took upon himself to ask the Reverend whether our old friend Jane was really gone? The Reverend (he has got a daughter at home – turned-up nose, and red) replied severely, 'Yes, sir, Miss Pitt is gone.' The idea of calling Jane, 'Miss Pitt'! Some said she had been sent away in disgrace for taking money from Old Cheeseman; others said she had gone into Old Cheeseman's service at a rise of ten pounds a year. All that our fellows knew was, she was gone.

It was two or three months afterwards, when, one afternoon, an open carriage stopped at the cricket field, just outside bounds, with a lady and gentleman in it, who looked at the game for a long time and stood up to see it played. Nobody thought much about them, until the same snivelling chap came in, against all rules, from the post where he was Scout, and said, 'It's Jane!' Both Elevens forgot the game directly, and ran crowding round the carriage. It *was* Jane! In such a bonnet! And if you'll believe me, Jane was married to Old Cheeseman.

It soon became quite a regular thing when our fellows were hard at it in the playground, to see a carriage at the low part of the wall where it joins the high part, and a lady and gentleman standing up in it, looking over. The gentleman was always Old Cheeseman, and the lady was always Jane.

The first time I ever saw them, I saw them in that way. There had been a good many changes among our fellows then, and it had turned out that Bob Tarter's father wasn't worth millions! He wasn't worth anything. Bob had gone for a soldier, and Old Cheeseman had purchased his discharge. But that's not the carriage. The carriage stopped, and all our fellows stopped as soon as it was seen.

'So you have never sent me to Coventry after all!' said the lady, laughing, as our fellows swarmed up the wall to shake hands with her. 'Are you never going to do it?'

'Never! never! never!' on all sides.

I didn't understand what she meant then, but of course I do now. I was very much pleased with her face though, and with her good way, and I couldn't help looking at her – and at him too – with all our fellows clustering so joyfully about them.

They soon took notice of me as a new boy, so I thought I might as well swarm up the wall myself, and shake hands with them as the rest did. I was quite as glad to see them as the rest were, and was quite as familiar with them in a moment.

'Only a fortnight now,' said Old Cheeseman, 'to the holidays. Who stops? Anybody?'

A good many fingers pointed at me, and a good many voices cried 'He does!' For it was the year when you were all away; and rather low I was about it, I can tell you.

'Oh!' said Old Cheeseman. 'But it's solitary here in the holiday time. He had better come to us.'

So I went to their delightful house, and was as happy as I could possibly be. They understand how to conduct themselves towards boys, *they* do. When they take a boy to the play, for instance, they *do* take him. They don't go in after it's begun, or come out before it's over. They know how to bring a boy up, too. Look at their own! Though he is very little as yet, what a capital boy he is! Why my next favourite to Mrs Cheeseman and Old Cheeseman, is Young Cheeseman.

So, now I have told you all I know about Old Cheeseman. And it's not much after all, I am afraid. Is it?

26

So On He Fares

GEORGE MOORE

His mother had forbidden him to stray about the roads and, standing at the garden gate, little Ulick Burke often thought he would like to run down to the canal and watch the boats passing. His father used to take him for walks along the towing path, but his father had gone away to the wars two years ago, and standing by the garden gate he remembered how his father used to stop to talk to the lock-keepers. Their talk turned often upon the canals and its business, and Ulick remembered that the canal ended in the Shannon, and that the barges met ships coming up from the sea.

He was a pretty child with bright blue eyes, soft curls, and a shy winning manner, and he stood at the garden gate thinking how the boats rose up in the locks, how the gate opened and let the boats free, and he wondered if his father had gone away to the war in one of the barges. He felt sure if he were going away to the wars he would go in a barge. And he wondered if the barge went as far as the war. Or only as far as the Shannon. He would like to ask his mother, but she would say he was troubling her with foolish questions, or she would begin to think again that he wanted to run away from home. He wondered if he were to hide himself in one of the barges whether it would take him to a battlefield where he would meet his father walking about with a gun upon his shoulder.

27

And leaning against the gate-post, he swung one foot across the other, though he had been told by his mother that he was like one of the village children when he did it. But his mother was always telling him not to do something, and he could not remember everything he must not do. He had been told not to go to the canal lest he should fall in, nor into the field lest he should tear his trousers. He had been told he must not run about in the garden lest he should tread on the flowers, and his mother was always telling him he was not to talk to the schoolchildren as they came back from school, though he did not want to talk to them. There was a time when he would have liked to talk to them: now he ran to the other side of the garden when they were coming home from school; but there was no place in the garden where he could hide himself from them, unless he got into the dry ditch. The schoolchildren were very naughty children; they climbed up the bank, and, holding on to the paling, they mocked at him; and their mockery was to ask him the way to 'Hill Cottage'; for his mother had had the name painted on the gate, and no one else in the parish had given their cottage a name.

However, he liked the dry ditch, and under the branches, where the wren had built her nest, Ulick was out of his mother's way, and out of the way of the boys; and lying among the dead leaves he would think of the barges floating away, and of his tall father who wore a red coat and let him pull his moustache. He was content to lie in the ditch for hours, thinking he was a bargeman and that he would like to use a sail. His father had told him that the boats had sails on the Shannon – if so, it would be easy to sail to the wars; and, breaking off in the middle of some wonderful war adventure, some tale about his father and his father's soldiers, he would grow interested in the life of the ditch, in the coming and going of the wren, in the chirrup of a bird in the tall larches that grew beyond the paling.

Beyond the paling there was a wood full of moss-grown stones and trees overgrown with ivy, and Ulick thought that if he only dared to get over the paling and face the darkness of the hollow on the other side of the paling, he could run across the meadow and call from the bank to a steersman. The steersman might take him away! But he was afraid his mother might follow him on the next barge, and he dreamed a story of barges drawn by the swiftest horses in Ireland.

But dreams are but a makeshift life. He was very unhappy, and though he knew it was wrong he could not help, laying plans for escape. Sometimes he thought that the best plan would be to set fire to the house, for while his mother was carrying pails of water from the backyard, he would run away; but he did not dare to think out his plan of setting fire to the house, lest one of the spirits which dwelt in the hollow beyond the paling should come and drag him down a hole.

One day he forgot to hide himself in the ditch, and the big boy climbed up the bank, and asked him to give him some gooseberries, and though Ulick would have feared to gather gooseberries for himself, he did not like to refuse the boy, and he gave him some, hoping that the big boy would not laugh at him again. And they became friends, and very soon he was friends with them all, and they had many talks clustered in the corner, the children holding on to the palings, and Ulick hiding behind the hollyhocks ready to warn them.

'It's all right, she's gone to the village,' Ulick said.

One day the big boy asked him to come with them; they were going to spear eels in the brook, and he was emboldened to get over the fence, and to follow across the meadow, through the hazels, and very soon it seemed to him that they had wandered to the world's end. At last they came to the brook and the big boy turned up his trousers, and Ulick saw him lifting the stones with his left hand and plunging a fork into the water with his right. When he brought up a struggling eel at the end of the fork, Ulick clapped his hands and laughed, and he had never been so happy in his life before.

After a time there were no more stones to raise, and sitting on the bank they began to tell stories. His companions asked him when his father was coming back from the wars, and he told them how his father used to take him for walks up the canal, and how they used to meet a man who had a tame rat in his pocket. Suddenly the boys and girls started up, crying, 'Here's the farmer', and they ran wildly across the fields. However, they got to the high road long before the farmer could catch them and his escape enchanted Ulick. Then the children went their different ways, the big boy staying with Ulick, who thought he must offer him some gooseberries. So they crossed the fence together and crouched under the bushes, and ate the gooseberries till they wearied of them. Afterwards they went to look at the bees, and while looking at the insects crawling in and out of their little door, Ulick caught sight of his mother coming towards them. Ulick cried out, but the big boy was caught before he could reach the fence, and Ulick saw that, big as the boy was, he could not save himself from a slapping. He kicked out, and then blubbered, and at last got away. In a moment it would be Ulick's turn, and he feared she would beat him more than she had beaten the boy, for she hated him, whereas she was only vexed with the boy; she would give him bread and water; he had often had a beating and bread and water for a lesser wickedness than the bringing of one of the village boys into the garden to eat gooseberries.

He put up his right hand and saved his right cheek, and then she tried to slap him on the left, but he put up his left hand, and this went on until she grew so angry that Ulick thought he had better allow her to slap him, for if she did not slap him at once she might kill him.

'Down with your hands, sir, down with your hands, sir,' she cried, but before he had time to let her slap him, she said, 'I will give you enough of bees', and she caught one that had just rested on a flower and put it down his neck. The bee stung him in the neck where the flesh is softest, and he ran away screaming, unable to rid himself of the bee. He broke through the hedges of sweet pea, and he dashed through the poppies, trampling through the flowerbeds, until he reached the dry ditch.

There is something frightful in feeling a stinging insect on one's back, and Ulick lay in the dry ditch, rolling among the leaves in anguish. He thought he was stung all over; he heard his mother laughing and she called him a coward through an opening in the bushes, but he knew she could not follow him down the ditch. His neck had already begun to swell, but he forgot the pain of the sting in hatred. He felt he must hate his mother, however wicked it might be to do so. His mother had often slapped him; he had heard of boys being slapped, but no one had ever put a bee down a boy's back before; he felt he must always hate her, and creeping up through the brambles to where he could get a view of the garden, he waited until he saw her walk up the path into the house;

and then, stealing back to the bottom of the ditch, he resolved to get over the paling. A few minutes after he heard her calling him, and then he climbed the paling, and he crossed the dreaded hollow, stumbling over the old stones.

As he crossed the meadow he caught sight of a boat coming through the lock, but the lock-keeper knew him by sight, and would tell the bargeman where he came from, and he would be sent home to his mother. He ran on, trying to get ahead of the boat, creeping through hedges, frightened lest he should not be able to find the canal! Now he stopped, sure that he had lost it; his brain seemed to be giving way, and he ran like a mad child up the bank. Oh, what joy! The canal flowed underneath the bank. The horse had just passed, the barge was coming, and Ulick ran down the bank calling to the bargeman. He plunged into the water, getting through the bulrushes. Half of the barge had passed him, and he held out his hands. The ground gave way and he went under the water; green light took the place of day, and when he struggled to the surface he saw the rudder moving. He went under again, and remembered no more until he opened his eyes and saw the bargeman leaning over him.

'Now, what ails you to be throwing yourself into the water in that way?'

Ulick closed his eyes; he had no strength for answering him, and a little while after he heard someone come on board the barge, and he guessed it must be the man who drove the horse. He lay with his eyes closed, hearing the men talking of what they should do with him. He heard a third voice, and guessed it must be a man come up from the cabin. This man said it would be better to take him back to the last lock, and they began to argue about who should carry him. Ulick was terribly frightened, and he was just going to beg of them not to bring him back when he heard one of them say, 'It will be easier to leave him at the next lock.' Soon after, he felt the boat start again, and when Ulick opened his eyes, he saw hedges gliding past, and he hoped the next lock was a long way off.

'Now,' said the steersman, 'since you are awaking out of your faint, you'll be telling us where you come from, because we want to send you home again.'

'Oh,' he said, 'from a long way off, the Shannon.'

'The Shannon!' said the bargeman. 'Why, that is more than seventy miles away. How did you come up here?'

It was a dreadful moment. Ulick knew he must give some good answer or he would find himself in his mother's keeping very soon. But what answer was he to give? It was half accident, half cunning that made him speak of the Shannon. The steersman said again, 'The Shannon is seventy miles away, how did you get up here?' and by this time Ulick was aware that he must make the bargemen believe he had hidden himself on one of the boats coming up from the Shannon, and that he had given the bargeman some money, and then he burst into tears and told them he had been very unhappy at home, and when they asked him why he had been unhappy, he did not answer, but he promised he would not be a naughty boy any more if they would take him back to the Shannon. He would be a good boy and not run away again. His pretty face and speech persuaded the bargemen to bring him back to the Shannon; it was decided to say nothing about him to the lock-keeper, and he was carried down to the cabin. He had often asked his father if he might see the bargemen's cabin; and his father had promised him that the next time they went to the canal he should go on board a barge and see the cabin; but his father had gone away to the wars. Now he was in the bargemen's cabin, and he wondered if they were going to give him supper and if he would be a bargeman himself when he grew up to be a man.

Some miles further the boat bumped the edge of the bridge, and on the other side of the bridge there was the lock, and he heard the lock gate shut behind the boat and the water pour into the lock; the lock seemed a long time filling, and he was frightened lest the lock-man might come down to the cabin, for there was no place where he could hide.

After passing through the lock one of the men came down to see him, and he was taken on deck, and in the calm of the evening Ulick came to look upon the bargemen as his good angels. They gave him some of their supper, and when they arrived at the next lock they made their beds on the deck, the night being so warm. It seemed to Ulick that he had never seen the night before, and he watched the sunset fading streak by streak, and imagined he was the captain of a ship sailing in the Shannon. The stars were so bright that he could not sleep, and it amused him to make up a long story about the bargemen snoring by his side. The story ended with the sunset and then the night was blue all over, and raising himself out of his blanket he watched the moonlight rippling down the canal. Then the night grew grey. He began to feel very cold, and wrapped himself in his blanket tightly, and the world got so white that Ulick grew afraid, and he was not certain whether it would not be better to escape from the boat and run away while everybody slept.

He lay awake maturing his little plan, seeing the greyness pass away and the sky fill up with pink and fleecy clouds.

One of the men roused, and, without saying a word, went to fetch a horse from the stables, and another went to boil the kettle in the cabin, and Ulick asked if he might help him; and while he blew the fire he heard the water running into the lock, and thought what a fool they were making of the lock-keeper, and when the boat was well on its way towards the next lock the steersman called him to come up, and they breakfasted together. Ulick would have wished this life to go on for ever, but the following day the steersman said:

'There is only one lock more between this and our last stopping-place. Keep a look-out for your mother's cottage.'

He promised he would, and he beguiled them all the evening with pretended discoveries. That cabin was his mother's cabin. No, it was farther on, he remembered those willow trees. Ulick's object was to get as far away from his home as possible; to get as near to the Shannon as he could.

'There's not a mile between us and the Shannon now,' said the steersman. 'I believe you've been telling us a lot of lies, my young man.'

Ulick said his mother lived just outside the town, they would see the house when they passed through the last lock, and he planned to escape that night, and about an hour before the dawn he got up, and, glancing at the sleeping men, he stepped ashore and ran until he felt very tired. And when he could go no farther he lay down in the hay in an outhouse.

A woman found him in the hay some hours after, and he told her his story, and as the woman seemed very kind he laid some stress on his mother's cruelty. He mentioned that his mother had put a bee down his neck, and bending down his head he showed her where the bee had stung him. She stroked his pretty curls and looked into his blue eyes, and she said that anyone who could put a bee down a boy's neck must be a she-devil.

She was a lone widow longing for someone to look after, and in a very short time Ulick was as much loved by his chance mother as he had been hated by his real mother.

Three years afterwards she died, and Ulick had to leave the cottage.

He was now a little over thirteen, and knew the ships and their sailors, and he went away in one of the ships that came up the river, and sailed many times round the coast of Ireland, and up all the harbours of Ireland. He led a wild, rough life, and his flight from home was remembered like a tale heard in infancy, until one day, as he was steering his ship up the Shannon, a desire to see what they were doing at home came over him. The ship dropped anchor, and he went to the canal to watch the boats going home. And it was not long before he was asking one of the bargemen if he could take him on board. He knew what the rules were, and he knew they could be broken, and how, and he said if they would take him he would be careful the lock-men did not see him, and the journey began.

The month was July, so the days were as endless and the country was as green and as full of grass as they were when he had come down the canal, and the horse strained along the path, sticking his toes into it just as he had done ten years ago; and when they came to a dangerous place Ulick saw the man who was driving the horse take hold of his tail, just as he had seen him do ten years ago.

'I think those are the rushes, only there are no trees, and the bank doesn't seem so high.' And then he said as the bargeman was going to stop his horse, 'No, I am wrong. It isn't there.'

They went on a few miles farther, and the same thing happened again. At last he said, 'Now I am sure it is there.'

And the bargeman called to the man who was driving the horse and stopped him, and Ulick jumped from the boat to the bank.

'That was a big leap you took,' said a small boy who was standing on the bank. 'It is well you didn't fall in.'

'Why did you say that?' said Ulick, 'is your mother telling you not to go down to the canal?'

'Look at the frog! He's going to jump into the water,' said the little boy.

He was the same age as Ulick was when Ulick ran away, and he was dressed in the same little trousers and little boots and socks, and he had a little grey cap. Ulick's hair had grown darker now, but it had been as fair and as curly as this little boy's, and he asked him if his mother forbade him to go down to the canal.

'Are you a bargeman? Do you steer the barge or do you drive the horse?'

'I'll tell you about the barge if you'll tell me about your mother. Does she tell you not to come down to the canal?'

The boy turned away his head and nodded it.

'Does she beat you if she catches you here?'

'Oh, no, mother never beats me.'

'Is she kind to you?'

'Yes, she's very kind, she lives up there, and there's a garden to our cottage, and the name "Hill Cottage" is painted up on the gate-post.'

'Now,' said Ulick, 'tell me your name.'

'My name is Ulick.'

'Ulick! And what's your other name?'

'Ulick Burke.'

'Ulick Burke!' said the big Ulick. 'Well, my name is the same. And I used to live at Hill Cottage too.'

The boy did not answer.

'Whom do you live with?'

'I live with Mother.'

'And what's her name?'

'Well, Burke is her name,' said the boy.

'But her front name?'

'Catherine.'

'And where's your father?'

'Oh, Father's a soldier; he's away.'

'But my father was a soldier too, and I used to live in that cottage.'

'And where have you been ever since?'

'Oh,' he said, 'I've been a sailor. I think I will go in the cottage with you.'

'Yes,' said little Ulick, 'come up and see Mother, and you'll tell me where you've been sailing,' and he put his hand into the seafarer's.

And now the seafarer began to lose his reckoning; the compass no longer pointed north. He had been away for ten years, and coming back he had found his own self, the self that had jumped into the water at this place ten years ago. Why had not the little boy done as he had done, and been pulled into the barge and gone away? If this had happened Ulick would have believed he was dreaming or that he was mad. But the little boy was leading him, yes, he remembered the way, there was the cottage, and its paling, and its hollyhocks. And there was his mother coming out of the house, and very little changed.

'Ulick, where have you been? Oh, you naughty boy,' and she caught the little boy up and kissed him. And so engrossed was her attention in her little son that she had not noticed the man he had brought home with him.

'Now who is this?' she said.

'Oh, Mother, he jumped from the boat to the bank, and he will tell you, Mother, that I was not near the bank.'

'Yes, Mother, he was ten yards from the bank, and now tell me, do you think you ever saw me before? . . .'

She looked at him.

'Oh, it's you! Why, we thought you were drowned.'

'I was picked up by a bargeman.'

'Well, come into the house and tell us what you've been doing.'

'I've been seafaring,' he said, taking a chair. 'But what about this Ulick?'

'He's your brother, that's all.'

His mother asked him what he was thinking, and Ulick told her how greatly astonished he had been to find a little boy exactly like himself, waiting at the same place.

'And Father?'

'Your father is away.'

'So,' he said, 'this little boy is my brother. I should like to see Father. When is he coming back?'

'Oh,' she said, 'he won't be back for another three years. He enlisted again.'

'Mother,' said Ulick, 'you don't seem very glad to see me.'

'I shall never forget the evening we spent when you threw yourself into the canal. You were a wicked child.'

'And why did you think I was drowned?'

'Well, your cap was picked up in the bulrushes.'

He thought that whatever wickedness he had been guilty of might have been forgiven, and he began to feel that if he had known how his mother would receive him he would not have come home.

'Well, the dinner is nearly ready. You'll stay and have some with us, and we can make you up a bed in the kitchen.'

He could see that his mother wished to welcome him, but her heart was set against him now as it had always been. Her dislike had survived ten years of absence. He had gone away and had met with a mother who loved him, and had done several years' hard seafaring. He had forgotten his real mother – forgotten everything except the bee and the hatred that had gathered in her eyes when she put it down his back; and that same ugly look he could now see gathering in her eyes, and it grew deeper every hour he remained in the cottage. His little brother asked him to tell him tales about the sailing ships, and he wanted to go down to the canal with Ulick, but their mother said he was to bide here with her. The day had begun to decline, his brother was crying, and he had to tell him a sea-story to stop his crying. 'But Mother hates to hear my voice,' he said to himself, and he went out into the garden when the story was done. It would be better to go away, and he took one turn round the garden and got over the paling at the end of the dry ditch, at the place he had got over it before, and he walked through the old wood, where the trees were overgrown with ivy, and the stones with moss. In this second experience there was neither terror nor mystery – only bitterness. It seemed to him a pity that he had ever been taken out of the canal, and he thought how easy it would be to throw himself in again, but only children drown themselves because their mothers do not love them; life had taken a hold upon him, and he stood watching the canal, though not waiting for a boat. But when a boat appeared he called to the man who was driving the horse to stop, for it was the same boat that had brought him from the Shannon.

'Well, was it all right?' the steersman said. 'Did you find the house? How were they at home?'

'They're all right at home,' he said, 'but Father is still away. I am going back. Can you take me?'

The evening sky opened calm and benedictive, and the green country flowed on, the boat passed by ruins, castles and churches, and every day was alike until they reached the Shannon.

The Pool

DAPHNE DU MAURIER

The children ran out on to the lawn. There was space all around them, and light, and air, with the trees indeterminate beyond. The gardener had cut the grass. The lawn was crisp and firm now, because of the hot sun through the day; but near the summer-house where the tall grass stood there were dew-drops like frost clinging to the narrow stems.

The children said nothing. The first moment always took them by surprise. The fact that it waited, thought Deborah, all the time they were away; that day after day while they were at school, or in the Easter holidays with the aunts at Hunstanton being blown to bits, or in the Christmas holidays with their father in London riding on buses and going to theatres – the fact that the garden waited for them was a miracle known only to herself. A year was so long. How did the garden endure the snows clamping down upon it, or the chilly rain that fell in November? Surely sometimes it must mock the slow steps of Grandpapa pacing up and down the terrace in front of the windows, or Grandmama calling to Patch? The garden had to endure month after month of silence, while the children were gone. Even the spring and the days of May and June were wasted, all those mornings of butterflies and darting birds, with no one to watch but Patch gasping for breath on a cool stone slab. So wasted was the garden, so lost.

'You must never think we forget,' said Deborah in the silent voice

39

she used to her own possessions. 'I remember, even at school, in the middle of French' – but the ache then was unbearable, that it should be the hard grain of a desk under her hands, and not the grass she bent to touch now. The children had had an argument once about whether there was more grass in the world or more sand, and Roger said that of course there must be more sand because of under the sea; in every ocean all over the world there would be sand, if you looked deep down. But there could be grass too, argued Deborah, a waving grass, a grass that nobody had ever seen, and the colour of that ocean grass would be darker than any grass on the surface of the world, in fields or prairies or people's gardens in America. It would be taller than trees and it would move like corn in a wind.

They had run in to ask somebody adult, 'What is there most of in the world, grass or sand?' both children hot and passionate from the argument. But Grandpapa stood there in his old panama hat looking for clippers to trim the hedge – he was rummaging in the drawer full of screws – and he said, 'What? What?' impatiently.

The boy turned red – perhaps it was a stupid question – but the girl thought, he doesn't know, they never know, and she made a face at her brother to show that she was on his side. Later they asked their grandmother, and she, being practical, said briskly, 'I should think sand. Think of all the grains,' and Roger turned in triumph. 'I told you so!' The grains. Deborah had not considered the grains. The magic of millions and millions of grains clinging together in the world and under the oceans made her sick. Let Roger win, it did not matter. It was better to be in the minority of the waving grass.

Now, on this first evening of summer holiday, she knelt and then lay full-length on the lawn, and stretched her hands out on either side like Jesus on the Cross, only face downwards, and murmured over and over again the words she had memorized from Confirmation preparation. 'A full, perfect and sufficient sacrifice ... a full, perfect and sufficient sacrifice ... satisfaction, and oblation, for the sins of the whole world.' To offer herself to the earth, to the garden, the garden that had waited patiently all these months since last summer, surely this must be her first gesture.

'Come on,' said Roger, rousing himself from his appreciation of how

40

Willis the gardener had mown the lawn to just the right closeness for cricket, and without waiting for his sister's answer he ran to the summer-house and made a dive at the long box in the corner where the stumps were kept. He smiled as he lifted the lid. The familiarity of the smell was satisfying. Old varnish and chipped paint, and surely that must be the same spider and the same cobweb? He drew out the stumps one by one, and the bails, and there was the ball – it had not been lost after all, as he had feared. It was worn, though, a greyish red – he smelt it and bit it, to taste the shabby leather. Then he gathered the things in his arms and went out to set up the stumps.

'Come and help me measure the pitch,' he called to his sister, and looking at her, squatting in the grass with her face hidden, his heart sank, because it meant that she was in one of her absent moods and would not concentrate on the cricket.

'Deb?' he called anxiously. 'You are going to play?'

Deborah heard his voice through the multitude of earth sounds, the heartbeat and the pulse. If she listened with her ear to the ground there was a humming much deeper than anything that bees did, or the sea at Hunstanton. The nearest to it was the wind, but the wind was reckless. The humming of the earth was patient. Deborah sat up, and her heart sank just as her brother's had done, for the same reason in reverse. The monotony of the game ahead would be like a great chunk torn out of privacy.

'How long shall we have to be?' she called.

The lack of enthusiasm dampened the boy. It was not going to be any fun at all if she made a favour of it. He must be firm, though. Any concession on his part she snatched and turned to her advantage.

'Half-an-hour,' he said, and then, for encouragement's sake, 'you can bat first.'

Deborah smelt her knees. They had not yet got the country smell, but if she rubbed them in the grass, and in the earth too, the white London look would go.

'All right,' she said, 'but no longer than half-an-hour.'

He nodded quickly, and so as not to lose time measured out the pitch and then began ramming the stumps in the ground. Deborah went into the summer-house to get the bats. The familiarity of the little wooden hut pleased her as it had her brother. It was a long time now, many years, since they had played in the summer-house, making yet another house inside this one with the help of broken deck-chairs; but, just as the garden waited for them a whole year, so did the summer-house, the windows on either side, cobweb-wrapped and stained, gazing out like eyes. Deborah did her ritual of bowing twice. If she should forget this, on her first entrance, it spelt ill-luck.

She picked out the two bats from the corner, where they were stacked with old croquet-hoops, and she knew at once that Roger would choose the one with the rubber handle, even though they could not bat at the same time, and for the whole of the holidays she must make do with the smaller one, that had half the whipping off. There was a croquet clip lying on the floor. She picked it up and put it on her nose and stood a moment, wondering how it would be if for ever more she had to live thus, nostrils pinched, making her voice like Punch. Would people pity her?

'Hurry,' shouted Roger, and she threw the clip into the corner, then quickly returned when she was half-way to the pitch, because she knew the clip was lying apart from its fellows, and she might wake in the night and remember it. The clip would turn malevolent, and haunt her. She replaced it on the floor with two others, and now she was absolved and the summer-house at peace.

'Don't get out too soon,' warned Roger as she stood in the crease he had marked for her, and with a tremendous effort of concentration Deborah forced her eyes to his retreating figure and watched him roll up his sleeves and pace the required length for his run-up. Down came the ball and she lunged out, smacking it in the air in an easy catch. The impact of ball on bat stung her hands. Roger missed the catch on purpose. Neither of them said anything.

'Who shall I be?' called Deborah.

The game could only be endured, and concentration kept, if Roger gave her a part to play. Not an individual, but a country.

'You're India,' he said, and Deborah felt herself grow dark and lean. Part of her was tiger, part of her was sacred cow, the long grass fringing the lawn was jungle, the roof of the summer-house a minaret.

Even so, the half-hour dragged, and, when her turn came to bowl, the balls she threw fell wider every time, so that Roger, flushed and self-conscious because their grandfather had come out on to the terrace and was watching them, called angrily, 'Do try.'

Once again the effort at concentration, the figure of their grand-father – a source of apprehension to the boy, for he might criticize them – acting as a spur to his sister. Grandpapa was an Indian god, and tribute must be paid to him, a golden apple. The apple must be flung to slay his enemies. Deborah muttered a prayer, and the ball she bowled came fast and true and hit Roger's off-stump. In the moment of delivery their grandfather had turned away and pottered back again through the french windows of the drawing-room.

Roger looked round swiftly. His disgrace had not been seen. 'Jolly good ball,' he said. 'It's your turn to bat again.'

But his time was up. The stable clock chimed six. Solemnly Roger drew stumps.

'What shall we do now?' he asked.

Deborah wanted to be alone, but if she said so, on this first evening of the holiday, he would be offended.

'Go to the orchard and see how the apples are coming on,' she suggested, 'and then round by the kitchen-garden in case the rasp-berries haven't all been picked. But you have to do it all without meeting anyone. If you see Willis or anyone, even the cat, you lose a mark.'

It was these sudden inventions that saved her. She knew her brother would be stimulated at the thought of outwitting the gardener. The aimless wander round the orchard would turn into a stalking exercise.

'Will you come too?' he asked.

'No,' she said, 'you have to test your skill.'

He seemed satisfied with this and ran off towards the orchard, stopping on the way to cut himself a switch from the bamboo.

As soon as he had disappeared Deborah made for the trees fringing the lawn, and once in the shrouded wood felt herself safe. She walked softly along the alley-way to the pool. The late sun sent shafts of light between the trees and on to the alley-way, and a myriad insects webbed their way in the beams, ascending and descending like angels on Jacob's ladder. But were they insects, wondered Deborah, or particles of dust, or even split fragments of light itself, beaten out and scattered by the sun?

It was very quiet. The woods were made for secrecy. They did not recognize her as the garden did. They did not care that for a whole year she could be at school, or at Hunstanton, or in London. The woods would never miss her: they had their own dark, passionate life.

Deborah came to the opening where the pool lay, with the five alley-ways branching from it, and she stood a moment before advancing to the brink, because this was holy ground and required atonement. She crossed her hands on her breast and shut her eyes. Then she kicked off her shoes. 'Mother of all things wild, do with me what you will,' she said aloud. The sound of her own voice gave her a slight shock. Then she went down on her knees and touched the ground three times with her forehead.

The first part of her atonement was accomplished, but the pool demanded sacrifice, and Deborah had come prepared. There was a stub of pencil she had carried in her pocket throughout the school term which she called her 'luck'. It had teeth marks on it, and a chewed piece of rubber at one end. This treasure must be given to the pool just as other treasures had been given in the past, a miniature jug, a crested button, a china pig. Deborah felt for the stub of pencil and kissed it. She had carried and caressed it for so many lonely months, and now the moment of parting had come. The pool must not be denied. She flung out her right hand, her eyes still shut, and heard the faint plop as the stub of pencil struck the water. Then she opened her eyes, and saw in mid-pool a ripple. The pencil had gone, but the ripple moved, gently shaking the water-lilies. The movement symbolized acceptance.

Deborah, still on her knees and crossing her hands once more, edged her way to the brink of the pool and then, crouching there beside it, looked down into the water. Her reflection wavered up at her, and it was not the face she knew, not even the looking-glass face which anyway was false, but a disturbed image, dark-skinned and ghostly. The crossed hands were like the petals of the water-lilies themselves, and the colour was not waxen white but phantom green. The hair too was not the live clump she brushed every day and tied back with ribbon, but a canopy, a shroud. When the image smiled it became more distorted still. Uncrossing her hands, Deborah leant forward, took a twig, and drew a circle three times on the smooth surface. The water shook in ever-widening ripples, and her reflection, broken into fragments, heaved and danced, a sort of monster, and the eyes were there no longer, nor the mouth.

Presently the water became still. Insects, long-legged flies and beetles with spread wings hummed upon it. A dragon-fly had all the magnificence of a lily leaf to himself. He hovered there, rejoicing. But when Deborah took her eyes off him for a moment he was gone. At the far end of the pool, beyond the clustering lilies, green scum had formed, and beneath the scum were rooted, tangled weeds. They were so thick and had lain in the pool so long, that if a man walked into them from the bank he would be held and choked. A fly, though, or a beetle, could sit upon the surface, and to him the pale green scum would not be treacherous at all, but a resting-place, a haven. And if someone threw a stone, so that the ripples formed, eventually they came to the scum, and rocked it, and the whole of the mossy surface moved in rhythm, a dancing-floor for those who played upon it.

There was a dead tree standing by the far end of the pool. He could have been fir or pine, or even larch, for time had stripped him of identity. He had no distinguishing mark upon his person, but with grotesque limbs straddled the sky. A cap of ivy crowned his naked head. Last winter a dangling branch had broken loose, and this now lay in the pool half-submerged, the green scum dripping from the withered twigs. The soggy branch made a vantage point for birds, and as Deborah watched a nestling suddenly flew from the undergrowth enveloping the dead tree, and perched for an instant on the mossy filigree. He was lost in terror. The parent bird cried warningly from some dark safety, and the nestling, pricking to the cry, took off from the branch that had offered him temporary salvation. He swerved across the pool, his flight mistimed, yet reached security. The chitter from the undergrowth told of his scolding. When he had gone silence returned to the pool.

It was, so Deborah thought, the time for prayer. The water-lilies were folding upon themselves. The ripples ceased. And that dark hollow in the centre of the pool, that black stillness where the water was deepest, was surely a funnel to the kingdom that lay below. Down that funnel had travelled the discarded treasures. The stub of pencil had lately plunged the depths. He had now been received as an equal among his fellows. This was the single law of the pool, for there were no other commandments. Once it was over, that first cold head-long flight, Deborah knew that the softness of the welcoming water took away all fear. It lapped the face and cleansed the eyes, and the plunge was not into darkness at all but into light. It did not become blacker as the pool was penetrated, but paler, more golden-green, and the mud that people told themselves was there was only a defence against strangers. Those who belonged, who knew, went to the source at once, and there were caverns and fountains and rainbow-coloured seas. There were shores of the whitest sand. There was soundless music.

Once again Deborah closed her eyes and bent lower to the pool. Her lips nearly touched the water. This was the great silence, when she had no thoughts, and was accepted by the pool. Waves of quiet ringed themselves about her, and slowly she lost all feeling, and had no knowledge of her legs, or of her kneeling body, or of her cold, clasped hands. There was nothing but the intensity of peace. It was a deeper acceptance than listening to the earth, because the earth was of the world, the earth was a throbbing pulse, but the acceptance of the pool meant another kind of hearing, a closing in of the waters, and just as the lilies folded so did the soul submerge.

'Deborah . . . ? Deborah . . . ?' Oh, no! Not now, don't let them call me back now! It was as though someone had hit her on the back, or jumped out at her from behind a corner, the sharp and sudden clamour of another life destroyed the silence, the secrecy. And then came the tinkle of the cowbells. It was the signal from their grandmother that the time had come to go in. Not imperious and ugly with authority, like the clanging bell at school summoning those at play to lessons or chapel, but a reminder, nevertheless, that Time was all-important, that life was ruled to order, that even here, in the holiday home the children loved, the adult reigned supreme.

'All right, all right,' muttered Deborah, standing up and thrusting her numbed feet into her shoes. This time the rather raised tone of 'Deborah?', and the more hurried clanging of the cowbells, brought long ago from Switzerland, suggested a more imperious Grandmama than the tolerant one who seldom questioned. It must mean their supper was already laid, soup perhaps getting cold, and the farce of washing hands, of tidying, of combing hair, must first be gone through.

'Come on, Deb,' and now the shout was close, was right at hand, privacy lost for ever, for her brother came running down the alley-way swishing his bamboo stick in the air.

'What *have* you been doing?' The question was an intrusion and a threat. She would never have asked him what he had been doing, had he wandered away wanting to be alone, but Roger, alas, did not claim privacy. He liked companionship, and his question now, asked half in irritation, half in resentment, came really from the fear that he might lose her.

'Nothing,' said Deborah.

Roger eyed her suspiciously. She was in that mooning mood. And it meant, when they went to bed, that she would not talk. One of the best things, in the holidays, was having the two adjoining rooms and calling through to Deb, making her talk.

'Come on,' he said, 'they've rung,' and the making of their grandmother into 'they', turning a loved individual into something impersonal, showed Deborah that even if he did not understand he was on her side. He had been called from play, just as she had.

They ran from the woods to the lawn, and on to the terrace. Their grandmother had gone inside, but the cowbells hanging by the french windows were still jangling.

The custom was for the children to have their supper first, at seven, and it was laid for them in the dining-room on a hot-plate. They served themselves. At a quarter-to-eight their grandparents had dinner. It was called dinner, but this was a concession to their status. They ate the same as the children, though Grandpapa had a savoury which was not served to the children. If the children were late for supper then it put out Time, as well as Agnes, who cooked for both generations, and it might mean five minutes' delay before Grandpapa had his soup. This shook routine.

The children ran up to the bathroom to wash, then downstairs to the dining-room. Their grandfather was standing in the hall. Deborah sometimes thought that he would have enjoyed sitting with them while they ate their supper, but he never suggested it. Grandmama had warned them, too, never to be a nuisance, or indeed to shout, if Grandpapa was near. This was not because he was nervous, but because he liked to shout himself.

'There's going to be a heat-wave,' he said. He had been listening to the news.

'That will mean lunch outside tomorrow,' said Roger swiftly. Lunch was the meal they took in common with the grandparents, and it was the moment of the day he disliked. He was nervous that his grand-father would ask him how he was getting on at school.

'Not for me, thank you,' said Grandpapa. 'Too many wasps.'

Roger was at once relieved. This meant that he and Deborah would have the little round garden-table to themselves. But Deborah felt sorry for her grandfather as he went back into the drawing-room. Lunch on the terrace could be gay, and would liven him up. When people grew old they had so few treats.

'What do you look forward to most in the day?' she once asked her grandmother.

'Going to bed,' was the reply, 'and filling my two hot-water bottles.' Why work through being young, thought Deborah, to this?

Back in the dining-room the children discussed what they should do during the heat-wave. It would be too hot, Deborah said, for cricket. But they might make a house, suggested Roger, in the trees by the paddock. If he got a few old boards from Willis, and nailed them together like a platform, and borrowed the orchard ladder, then they could take fruit and bottles of orange squash and keep them up there, and it would be a camp from which they could spy on Willis afterwards.

Deborah's first instinct was to say she did not want to play, but she checked herself in time. Finding the boards and fixing them would take Roger a whole morning. It would keep him employed. 'Yes, it's a good idea,' she said, and to foster his spirit of adventure she looked at his notebook, as they were drinking their soup, and approved of items necessary for the camp while he jotted them down. It was all part of the day-long deceit she practised to express understanding of his way of life.

When they had finished supper they took their trays to the kitchen and watched Agnes, for a moment, as she prepared the second meal for the grandparents. The soup was the same, but garnished. Little croûtons of toasted bread were added to it. And the butter was made into pats, not cut in a slab. The savoury tonight was to be cheese straws. The children finished the ones that Agnes had burnt. Then they went through to the drawing-room to say good-night. The older people had both changed. Grandpapa was in a smoking-jacket, and wore soft slippers. Grandmama had a dress that she had worn several years ago in London. She had a cardigan round her shoulders like a cape.

'Go carefully with the bath-water,' she said. 'We'll be short if there's no rain.'

They kissed her smooth, soft skin. It smelt of rose leaves. Grandpapa's chin was sharp and bony. He did not kiss Roger.

'Be quiet overhead,' whispered their grandmother. The children nodded. The dining-room was underneath their rooms, and any jumping about or laughter would make a disturbance.

Deborah felt a wave of affection for the two old people. Their lives must be empty and sad. 'We *are* glad to be here,' she said. Grandmama smiled. This was how she lived, thought Deborah, on little crumbs of comfort.

Once out of the room their spirits soared, and to show relief Roger chased Deborah upstairs, both laughing for no reason. Undressing, they forgot the instructions about the bath, and when they went into the bathroom – Deborah was to have first go – the water was gurgling into the overflow. They tore out the plug in a panic, and listened to the waste roaring down the pipe to the drain below. If Agnes did not have the wireless on she would hear it.

The children were too old now for boats or play, but the bathroom was a place for confidences, for a sharing of those few tastes they agreed upon, or, after quarrelling, for moody silence. The one who broke silence first would then lose face.

'Willis has a new bicycle,' said Roger. 'I saw it propped against the shed. I couldn't try it because he was there. But I shall tomorrow. It's a Raleigh.'

He liked all practical things, and the trying of the gardener's bicycle would give an added interest to the morning of the next day. Willis had a bag of tools in a leather pouch behind the saddle. These could all be felt and the spanners, smelling of oil, tested for shape and usefulness.

'If Willis died,' said Deborah, 'I wonder what age he would be.'

It was the kind of remark that Roger resented always. What had death to do with bicycles? 'He's sixty-five,' he said, 'so he'd be sixty-five.'

'No,' said Deborah, 'what age when he got *there*?'

Roger did not want to discuss it. 'I bet I can ride it round the stables if I lower the seat,' he said. 'I bet I don't fall off.'

But if Roger would not rise to death, Deborah would not rise to the wager. 'Who cares?' she said.

The sudden streak of cruelty stung the brother. Who cared indeed? ... The horror of an empty world encompassed him, and to give himself confidence he seized the wet sponge and flung it out of the window. They heard it splosh on the terrace below.

'Grandpapa will step on it, and slip,' said Deborah, aghast.

The image seized them, and choking back laughter they covered their faces. Hysteria doubled them up. Roger rolled over and over on the bathroom floor. Deborah, the first to recover, wondered why laughter was so near to pain, why Roger's face, twisted now in merriment, was yet the same crumpled thing when his heart was breaking.

'Hurry up,' she said briefly, 'let's dry the floor,' and as they wiped the linoleum with their towels the action sobered them both.

Back in their bedrooms, the door open between them, they watched the light slowly fading. But the air was warm like day. Their grandfather and the people who said what the weather was going to be were right. The heat-wave was on its way. Deborah, leaning out of the open window, fancied she could see it in the sky, a dull haze where the sun had been before; and the trees beyond the lawn, day-coloured when they were having their supper in the dining-room, had turned into night-birds with outstretched wings. The garden knew about the promised heat-wave, and rejoiced: the lack of rain was of no consequence yet, for the warm air was a trap, lulling it into a drowsy contentment.

The dull murmur of their grandparents' voices came from the dining-room below. What did they discuss, wondered Deborah. Did they make those sounds to reassure the children, or were their voices part of their unreal world? Presently the voices ceased, and then there was a scraping of chairs, and voices from a different quarter, the drawing-room now, and a faint smell of their grandfather's cigarette.

Deborah called softly to her brother but he did not answer. She went through to his room, and he was asleep. He must have fallen asleep suddenly, in the midst of talking. She was relieved. Now she could be alone again, and not have to keep up the pretence of sharing conversation. Dusk was everywhere, the sky a deepening black. 'When they've gone up to bed,' thought Deborah, 'then I'll be truly alone.' She knew what she was going to do. She waited there, by the open window, and the deepening sky lost the veil that covered it, the haze disintegrated, and the stars broke through. Where there had been nothing was life, dusty and bright, and the waiting earth gave off a scent of knowledge. Dew rose from the pores. The lawn was white.

Patch, the old dog, who slept at the end of Grandpapa's bed on a plaid rug, came out on to the terrace and barked hoarsely. Deborah leant out and threw a piece of creeper on to him. He shook his back. Then he waddled slowly to the flower-tub above the steps and cocked his leg. It was his nightly routine. He barked once more, staring blindly at the hostile trees, and went back into the drawing-room. Soon afterwards, someone came to close the windows – Grandmama, thought Deborah, for the touch was light. 'They are shutting out the best,' said the child to herself, 'all the meaning, and all the point.' Patch, being an animal, should know better. He ought to be in a kennel where he could watch, but instead, grown fat and soft, he preferred the bumpiness of her grandfather's bed. He had forgotten the secrets. So had they, the old people.

Deborah heard her grandparents come upstairs. First her grandmother, the quicker of the two, and then her grandfather, more laboured, saying a word or two to Patch as the little dog wheezed his way up. There was a general clicking of lights and shutting of doors.

Then silence. How remote, the world of the grandparents, undressing with curtains closed. A pattern of life unchanged for so many years. What went on without would never be known. 'He that has ears to hear, let him hear,' said Deborah, and she thought of the callousness of Jesus which no priest could explain. Let the dead bury their dead. All the people in the world, undressing now, or sleeping, not just in the village but in cities and capitals, they were shutting out the truth, they were burying their dead. They wasted silence.

The stable clock struck eleven. Deborah pulled on her clothes. Not the cotton frock of the day, but her old jeans that Grandmama disliked, rolled up above her knees. And a jersey. Sandshoes with a hole that did not matter. She was cunning enough to go down by the back stairs. Patch would bark if she tried the front stairs, close to the grandparents' rooms. The backstairs led past Agnes' room, which smelt of apples though she never ate fruit. Deborah could hear her snoring. She would not even wake on Judgment Day. And this led her to wonder on the truth of that fable too, for there might be so many millions by then who liked their graves – Grandpapa, for instance, fond of his routine, and irritated at the sudden riot of trumpets.

Deborah crept past the pantry and the servants' hall – it was only a tiny sitting-room for Agnes, but long usage had given it the dignity of the name – and unlatched and unbolted the heavy back door. Then she stepped outside, on to the gravel, and took the long way round by the front of the house so as not to tread on the terrace, fronting the lawns and the garden.

The warm night claimed her. In a moment it was part of her. She walked on the grass, and her shoes were instantly soaked. She flung up her arms to the sky. Power ran to her finger-tips. Excitement was communicated from the waiting trees, and the orchard, and the paddock; the intensity of their secret life caught at her and made her run. It was nothing like the excitement of ordinary looking forward, of birthday presents, of Christmas stockings, but the pull of a magnet – her grandfather had shown her once how it worked, little needles springing to the jaws – and now night and the sky above were a vast magnet, and the things that waited below were needles, caught up in the great demand.

Deborah went on to the summer-house, and it was not sleeping like the house fronting the terrace but open to understanding, sharing complicity. Even the dusty windows caught the light, and the cobwebs shone. She rummaged for the old lilo and the moth-eaten car rug that Grandmama had thrown out two summers ago, and bearing them over her shoulder she made her way to the pool. The alley-way was ghostly, and Deborah knew, for all her mounting tension, that the test was hard. Part of her was still body-bound, and afraid of shadows. If anything stirred she would jump and know true terror. She must show defiance, though. The woods expected it. Like old wise lamas they expected courage.

She sensed approval as she ran the gauntlet, the tall trees watching. Any sign of turning back, of panic, and they would crowd upon her in a choking mass, smothering protest. Branches would become arms, gnarled and knotty, ready to strangle, and the leaves of the higher trees would fold in and close like the sudden furling of giant umbrellas. The smaller undergrowth, obedient to the will, would become a briary of a million thorns where animals of no known world crouched snarling, their eyes on fire. To show fear was to show misunderstanding. The woods were merciless.

Deborah walked the alley-way to the pool, her left hand holding the lilo and the rug on her shoulder, her right hand raised in salutation. This was a gesture of respect. Then she paused before the pool and laid down her burden beside it. The lilo was to be her bed, the rug her cover. She took off her shoes, also in respect, and lay down upon the lilo. Then, drawing the rug to her chin, she lay flat, her eyes upon the sky. The gauntlet of the alley-way over, she had no more fear. The woods had accepted her, and the pool was the final resting-place, the doorway, the key.

'I shan't sleep,' thought Deborah. 'I shall just lie awake here all the night and wait for morning, but it will be a kind of introduction to life, like being confirmed.'

The stars were thicker now than they had been before. No space in the sky without a prick of light, each star a sun. Some, she thought, were newly born, white-hot, and others wise and colder, nearing completion. The law encompassed them, fixing the riotous path, but how they fell and tumbled depended upon themselves. Such peace, such stillness, such sudden quietude, excitement gone. The trees were no longer menacing but guardians, and the pool was primeval water, the first, the last.

Then Deborah stood at the wicket-gate, the boundary, and there was a woman with outstretched hand, demanding tickets. 'Pass through,' she said when Deborah reached her. 'We saw you coming.' The wicket-gate became a turnstile. Deborah pushed against it and there was no resistance, she was through.

'What is it?' she asked. 'Am I really here at last? Is this the bottom of the pool?'

'It could be,' smiled the woman. 'There are so many ways. You just happened to choose this one.'

Other people were pressing to come through. They had no faces, they were only shadows. Deborah stood aside to let them by, and in a moment they had gone, all phantoms.

'Why only now, tonight?' asked Deborah. 'Why not in the afternoon, when I came to the pool?'

'It's a trick,' said the woman. 'You seize on the moment in time. We were here this afternoon. We're always here. Our life goes on around you, but nobody knows it. The trick's easier by night, that's all.'

'Am I dreaming, then?' asked Deborah.

'No,' said the woman, 'this isn't a dream. And it isn't death, either. It's the secret world.'

The secret world . . . It was something Deborah had always known, and now the pattern was complete. The memory of it, and the relief, were so tremendous that something seemed to burst inside her heart.

'Of course . . .' she said, 'of course . . .' and everything that had ever been fell into place. There was no disharmony. The joy was indescribable, and the surge of feeling, like wings about her in the air, lifted her away from the turnstile and the woman, and she had all knowledge. That was it – the invasion of knowledge.

'I'm not myself, then, after all,' she thought. 'I knew I wasn't. It was only the task given,' and, looking down, she saw a little child who was blind trying to find her way. Pity seized her. She bent down and put her hands on the child's eyes, and they opened, and the child was herself at two years old. The incident came back. It was when her mother died and Roger was born.

'It doesn't matter after all,' she told the child. 'You are not lost. You don't have to go on crying.' Then the child that had been herself melted, and became absorbed in the water and the sky, and the joy of the invading flood intensified so that there was no body at all but only being. No words, only movements. And the beating of wings. This above all, the beating of wings.

'Don't let me go!' It was a pulse in her ear, and a cry, and she saw the woman at the turnstile put up her hands to hold her. Then there was such darkness, such dragging, terrible darkness, and the beginning of pain all over again, the leaden heart, the tears, the misunderstanding. The voice saying 'No!' was her own harsh, worldly voice, and she was staring at the restless trees, black and ominous against the sky. One hand trailed in the water of the pool.

Deborah sat up, sobbing. The hand that had been in the pool was wet and cold. She dried it on the rug. And suddenly she was seized with such fear that her body took possession, and throwing aside the rug she began to run along the alley-way, the dark trees mocking and the welcome of the woman at the turnstile turned to treachery. Safety lay in the house behind the closed curtains, security was with the grandparents sleeping in their beds, and like a leaf driven before a whirlwind Deborah was out of the woods and across the silver soaking lawn, up the steps beyond the terrace and through the garden-gate to the back door.

The slumbering solid house received her. It was like an old staid person who, surviving many trials, had learnt experience. 'Don't take any notice of them,' it seemed to say, jerking its head – did a house have a head? – towards the woods beyond. 'They've made no contribution to civilization. I'm man-made, and different. This is where you belong, dear child. Now settle down.'

Deborah went back again upstairs and into her bedroom. Nothing had changed. It was still the same. Going to the open window she saw that the woods and the lawn seemed unaltered from the moment, how long back she did not know, when she had stood there, deciding upon the visit to the pool. The only difference now was in herself. The excitement had gone, the tension too. Even the terror of those last moments, when her flying feet had brought her to the house, seemed unreal.

She drew the curtains, just as her grandmother might have done, and climbed into bed. Her mind was now preoccupied with practical difficulties, like explaining the presence of the lilo and the rug beside the pool. Willis might find them, and tell her grandfather. The feel of her own pillow, and of her own blankets, reassured her. Both were familiar. And being tired was familiar too, it was a solid bodily ache, like the tiredness after too much jumping or cricket. The thing was, though – and the last remaining conscious thread of thought decided to postpone a conclusion until the morning – which was real? This safety of the house, or the secret world?

II

When Deborah woke next morning she knew at once that her mood was bad. It would last her for the day. Her eyes ached, and her neck was stiff, and there was a taste in her mouth like magnesia. Immediately Roger came running into her room, his face refreshed and smiling from some dreamless sleep, and jumped on her bed.

'It's come,' he said, 'the heat-wave's come. It's going to be ninety in the shade.'

Deborah considered how best she could damp his day. 'It can go to a hundred for all I care,' she said. 'I'm going to read all morning.'

His face fell. A look of bewilderment came into his eyes. 'But the house?' he said. 'We'd decided to have a house in the trees, don't you remember? I was going to get some planks from Willis.'

Deborah turned over in bed and humped her knees. 'You can, if you like,' she said. 'I think it's a silly game.'

She shut her eyes, feigning sleep, and presently she heard his feet patter slowly back to his own room, and then the thud of a ball against the wall. If he goes on doing that, she thought maliciously, Grandpapa will ring his bell, and Agnes will come panting up the stairs. She hoped for destruction, for grumbling and snapping, and everyone falling out, not speaking. That was the way of the world.

The kitchen, where the children breakfasted, faced west, so it did not get the morning sun. Agnes had hung up fly-papers to catch wasps. The cereal, puffed wheat, was soggy. Deborah complained, mashing the mess with her spoon.

'It's a new packet,' said Agnes. 'You're mighty particular all of a sudden.'

'Deb's got out of bed the wrong side,' said Roger.

The two remarks fused to make a challenge. Deborah seized the nearest weapon, a knife, and threw it at her brother. It narrowly missed his eye, but cut his cheek. Surprised, he put his hand to his face and felt the blood. Hurt, not by the knife but by his sister's action, his face turned red and his lower lip quivered. Deborah ran out of the kitchen and slammed the door. Her own violence distressed her, but the power of the mood was too strong. Going on to the terrace, she saw that the worst had happened. Willis had found the lilo and the rug, and had put them to dry in the sun. He was talking to her grandmother. Deborah tried to slip back into the house, but it was too late.

'Deborah, how very thoughtless of you,' said Grandmama. 'I tell you children every summer that I don't mind your taking the things from the hut into the garden if only you'll put them back.'

Deborah knew she should apologize, but the mood forbade it. 'That old rug is full of moth,' she said contemptuously, 'and the lilo has a rainproof back. It doesn't hurt them.'

They both stared at her, and her grandmother flushed, just as Roger had done when she had thrown the knife at him. Then her grandmother turned her back and continued giving some instructions to the gardener.

Deborah stalked along the terrace, pretending that nothing had happened, and skirting the lawn she made her way towards the orchard and so to the fields beyond. She picked up a windfall, but as soon as her teeth bit into it the taste was green. She threw it away. She went and sat on a gate and stared in front of her, looking at nothing. Such deception everywhere. Such sour sadness it was like Adam and Eve being locked out of Paradise. The Garden of Eden was no more. Somewhere, very close, the woman at the turnstile waited to let her in, the secret world was all about her, but the key was gone. Why had she ever come back? What had brought her?

People were going about their business. The old man who came three days a week to help Willis was sharpening his scythe behind the toolshed. Beyond the field where the lane ran towards the main road she could see the top of the postman's head. He was pedalling his bicycle towards the village. She heard Roger calling, 'Deb? Deb . . . ?', which meant that he had forgiven her, but still the mood held sway and she did not answer. Her own dullness made her own punishment. Presently a knocking sound told her that he had got the planks from Willis and had embarked on the building of his house. He was like his grandfather; he kept to the routine set for himself.

Deborah was consumed with pity. Not for the sullen self humped upon the gate, but for all of them going about their business in the world who did not hold the key. The key was hers, and she had lost it. Perhaps if she worked her way through the long day the magic would return with evening and she would find it once again. Or even now. Even now, by the pool, there might be a clue, a vision.

Deborah slid off the gate and went the long way round. By skirting the fields, parched under the sun, she could reach the other side of the wood and meet no one. The husky wheat was stiff. She had to keep close to the hedge to avoid brushing it, and the hedge was tangled. Foxgloves had grown too tall and were bending with empty sockets, their flowers gone. There were nettles everywhere. There was no gate into the wood, and she had to climb the pricking hedge with the barbed wire tearing her knickers. Once in the wood some measure of peace returned, but the alley-ways this side had not been scythed, and the grass was long. She had to wade through it like a sea, brushing it aside with her hands.

She came upon the pool from behind the monster tree, the hybrid whose naked arms were like a dead man's stumps, projecting at all angles. This side, on the lip of the pool, the scum was carpet-thick, and all the lilies, coaxed by the risen sun, had opened wide. They basked as lizards bask on hot stone walls. But here, with stems in water, they swung in grace, cluster upon cluster, pink and waxen white. 'They're asleep,' thought Deborah. 'So is the wood. The morning is not their time,' and it seemed to her beyond possibility that the turnstile was at hand and the woman waiting, smiling. 'She said they were always there, even in the day, but the truth is that being a child I'm blinded in the day. I don't know how to see.'

She dipped her hands in the pool, and the water was tepid brown. She tasted her fingers, and the taste was rank. Brackish water, stagnant from long stillness. Yet beneath ... beneath, she knew, by night the woman waited, and not only the woman but the whole secret world. Deborah began to pray. 'Let it happen again,' she whispered. 'Let it happen again. Tonight. I won't be afraid.'

The sluggish pool made no acknowledgement, but the very silence seemed a testimony of faith, of acceptance. Beside the pool, where the imprint of the lilo had marked the moss, Deborah found a kirby-grip, fallen from her hair during the night. It was proof of the visitation. She threw it into the pool as part of the treasury. Then she walked back into the ordinary day and the heat-wave, and her black mood was softened. She went to find Roger in the orchard. He was busy with the platform. Three of the boards were fixed, and the noisy hammering was something that had to be borne. He saw her coming, and as always, after trouble, sensed that her mood had changed and mention must never be made of it. Had he called, 'Feeling better?', it would have revived the antagonism, and she might not play with him all the day. Instead, he took no notice. She must be the first to speak.

Deborah waited at the foot of the tree, then bent, and handed him up an apple. It was green, but the offering meant peace. He ate it manfully. 'Thanks,' he said. She climbed into the tree beside him and reached for the box of nails. Contact had been renewed. All was well between them.

III

The hot day spun itself out like a web. The heat haze stretched across the sky, dun-coloured and opaque. Crouching on the burning boards of the apple-tree, the children drank ginger-beer and fanned themselves with dock-leaves. They grew hotter still. When the cowbells summoned them for lunch they found that their grandmother had drawn the curtains of all the rooms downstairs, and the drawing-room was a vault and strangely cool. They flung themselves into chairs. No one was hungry. Patch lay under the piano, his soft mouth dripping saliva. Grandmama had changed into a sleeveless linen dress never before seen, and Grandpapa, in a dented panama, carried a fly-whisk used years ago in Egypt.

'Ninety-one,' he said grimly, 'on the Air Ministry roof. It was on the one o'clock news.'

Deborah thought of the men who must measure heat, toiling up and down on this Ministry roof with rods and tapes and odd-shaped instruments. Did anyone care but Grandpapa?

'Can we take our lunch outside?' asked Roger.

His grandmother nodded. Speech was too much effort, and she sank languidly into her chair at the foot of the dining-room table. The roses she had picked last night had wilted.

The children carried chicken drumsticks to the summer-house. It was too hot to sit inside, but they sprawled in the shadow it cast, their heads on faded cushions shedding kapok. Somewhere, far above their heads, an aeroplane climbed like a small silver fish, and was lost in space.

'A Meteor,' said Roger. 'Grandpapa says they're obsolete.'

Deborah thought of Icarus, soaring towards the sun. Did he know when his wings began to melt? How did he feel? She stretched out her arms and thought of them as wings. The finger-tips would be the first to curl, and then turn cloggy soft, and useless. What terror in the sudden loss of height, the drooping power . . .

Roger, watching her, hoped it was some game. He threw his picked drumstick into a flower-bed and jumped to his feet.

'Look,' he said, 'I'm a Javelin,' and he too stretched his arms and ran in circles, banking. Jet noises came from his clenched teeth. Deborah dropped her arms and looked at the drumstick. What had been clean and white from Roger's teeth was now earth-brown. Was it offended to be chucked away? Years later, when everyone was dead, it would be found, moulded like a fossil. Nobody would care.

'Come on,' said Roger.

'Where to?' she asked.

'To fetch the raspberries,' he said.

'You go,' she told him.

Roger did not like going into the dining-room alone. He was self-conscious. Deborah made a shield from the adult eyes. In the end he consented to fetch the raspberries without her on condition that she played cricket after tea. After tea was a long way off.

She watched him return, walking very slowly, bearing the plates of raspberries and clotted cream. She was seized with sudden pity, that same pity which, earlier, she had felt for all people other than herself. How absorbed he was, how intent on the moment that held him. But tomorrow he would be some old man far away, the garden forgotten, and this day long past.

'Grandmama says it can't go on,' he announced. 'There'll have to be a storm.'

But why? Why not for ever? Why not breathe a spell so that all of them could stay locked and dreaming like the courtiers in *Sleeping Beauty*, never knowing, never waking, cobwebs in their hair and on their hands, tendrils imprisoning the house itself?

'Race me,' said Roger, and to please him she plunged her spoon into the mush of raspberries but finished last, to his delight.

No one moved during the long afternoon. Grandmama went upstairs to her room. The children saw her at her window in her petticoat drawing the curtains closed. Grandpapa put his feet up in the drawing-room, a handkerchief over his face. Patch did not stir from his place under the piano. Roger, undefeated, found employment still. He first helped Agnes to shell peas for supper, squatting on the back-door step while she relaxed on a lop-sided basket chair dragged from the servants' hall. This task finished, he discovered a tin-bath, put away in the cellar, in which Patch had been washed in younger days. He carried it to the lawn and filled it with water. Then he stripped to bathing-trunks and sat in it solemnly, an umbrella over his head to keep off the sun.

Deborah lay on her back behind the summer-house, wondering what would happen if Jesus and Buddha met. Would there be discussion, courtesy, an exchange of views like politicians at summit talks? Or were they after all the same person, born at separate times? The queer thing was that this topic, interesting now, meant nothing in the secret world. Last night, through the turnstile, all problems disappeared. They were non-existent. There was only the knowledge and the joy.

She must have slept, because when she opened her eyes she saw to her dismay that Roger was no longer in the bath but was hammering the cricket-stumps into the lawn. It was a quarter-to-five.

'Hurry up,' he called, when he saw her move. 'I've had tea.'

She got up and dragged herself into the house, sleepy still, and giddy. The grandparents were in the drawing-room, refreshed from the long repose of the afternoon. Grandpapa smelt of eau-de-cologne. Even Patch had come to and was lapping his saucer of cold tea.

'You look tired,' said Grandmama critically. 'Are you feeling all right?'

Deborah was not sure. Her head was heavy. It must have been sleeping in the afternoon, a thing she never did.

'I think so,' she answered, 'but if anyone gave me roast pork I know I'd be sick.'

'No one suggested you should eat roast pork,' said her grandmother, surprised. 'Have a cucumber sandwich, they're cool enough.'

Grandpapa was lying in wait for a wasp. He watched it hover over his tea, grim, expectant. Suddenly he slammed at the air with his whisk. 'Got the brute,' he said in triumph. He ground it into the carpet with his heel. It made Deborah think of Jehovah.

'Don't rush around in the heat,' said Grandmama. 'It isn't wise. Can't you and Roger play some nice, quiet game?'

'What sort of game?' asked Deborah.

But her grandmother was without invention. The croquet mallets were all broken. 'We might pretend to be dwarfs and use the heads,' said Deborah, and she toyed for a moment with the idea of squatting to play croquet. Their knees would stiffen, though, it would be too difficult.

'I'll read aloud to you, if you like,' said Grandmama.

Deborah seized upon the suggestion. It delayed cricket. She ran out on to the lawn and padded the idea to make it acceptable to Roger.

'I'll play afterwards,' she said, 'and that ice-cream that Agnes has in the fridge, you can eat all of it. I'll talk tonight in bed.'

Roger hesitated. Everything must be weighed. Three goods to balance evil.

'You know that stick of sealing-wax Daddy gave you?' he said.

'Yes.'

'Can I have it?'

The balance for Deborah too. The quiet of the moment in opposition to the loss of the long thick stick so brightly red.

'All right,' she grudged.

Roger left the cricket stumps and they went into the drawing-room. Grandpapa, at the first suggestion of reading aloud, had disappeared, taking Patch with him. Grandmama had cleared away the tea. She found her spectacles and the book. It was *Black Beauty*. Grandmama kept no modern children's books, and this made common ground for the three of them. She read the terrible chapter where the stable-lad lets Beauty get overheated and gives him a cold drink and does not put on his blanket. The story was suited to the day. Even Roger listened entranced. And Deborah, watching her grandmother's calm face and hearing her careful voice reading the sentences, thought how strange it was that Grandmama could turn herself into Beauty with such ease. She *was* a horse, suffering there with pneumonia in the stable, being saved by the wise coachman.

After the reading, cricket was anti-climax, but Deborah must keep her bargain. She kept thinking of Black Beauty writing the book. It showed how good the story was, Grandmama said, because no child had ever yet questioned the practical side of it, or posed the picture of a horse with a pen in its hoof.

'A modern horse would have a typewriter,' thought Deborah, and she began to bowl to Roger, smiling to herself as she did so because of the twentieth-century Beauty clacking with both hoofs at a machine.

This evening, because of the heat-wave, the routine was changed. They had their baths first, before their supper, for they were hot and exhausted from the cricket. Then, putting on pyjamas and cardigans, they ate their supper on the terrace. For once Grandmama was indulgent. It was still so hot that they could not take chill, and the dew had not yet risen. It made a small excitement, being in pyjamas on the terrace. Like people abroad, said Roger. Or natives in the South Seas, said Deborah. Or beachcombers who had lost caste. Grandpapa, changed into a white tropical jacket, had not lost caste.

'He's a white trader,' whispered Deborah. 'He's made a fortune out of pearls.'

Roger choked. Any joke about his grandfather, whom he feared, had all the sweet agony of danger.

'What's the thermometer say?' asked Deborah.

Her grandfather, pleased at her interest, went to inspect it.

'Still above eighty,' he said with relish.

Deborah, when she cleaned her teeth later, thought how pale her face looked in the mirror above the wash-basin. It was not brown, like Roger's, from the day in the sun, but wan and yellow. She tied back her hair with a ribbon, and the nose and chin were peaky sharp. She yawned largely, as Agnes did in the kitchen on Sunday afternoons.

'Don't forget you promised to talk,' said Roger quickly.

Talk ... That was the burden. She was so tired she longed for the white smoothness of her pillow, all blankets thrown aside, bearing only a single sheet. But Roger, wakeful on his bed, the door between them wide, would not relent. Laughter was the one solution, and to make him hysterical, and so exhaust him sooner, she fabricated a day in the life of Willis, from his first morning kipper to his final glass of beer at the village inn. The adventures in between would have tried Gulliver. Roger's delight drew protests from the adult world below. There was the sound of a bell, and then Agnes came up the stairs and put her head round the corner of Deborah's door.

'Your Granny says you're not to make so much noise,' she said.

Deborah, spent with invention, lay back and closed her eyes. She could go no further. The children called good-night to each other, both speaking at the same time, from age-long custom, beginning with their names and addresses and ending with the world, the universe, and space. Then the final main 'Good-night', after which neither must ever speak, on pain of unknown calamity.

'Must try and keep awake,' thought Deborah, but the power was not in her. Sleep was too compelling, and it was hours later that she opened her eyes and saw her curtains blowing and the forked flash light the ceiling, and heard the trees tossing and sobbing against the sky. She was out of bed in an instant. Chaos had come. There were no stars, and the night was sulphurous. A great crack split the heavens and tore them in two. The garden groaned. If the rain would only fall there might be mercy, and the trees, imploring, bowed themselves this way and that, while the vivid lawn, bright in expectation, lay like a sheet of metal exposed to flame. Let the waters break. Bring down the rain.

Suddenly the lightning forked again, and standing there, alive yet immobile, was the woman by the turnstile. She stared up at the windows of the house, and Deborah recognized her. The turnstile was there, inviting entry, and already the phantom figures, passing through it, crowded towards the trees beyond the lawn. The secret world was waiting. Through the long day, while the storm was brewing, it had hovered there unseen beyond her reach, but now that night had come, and the thunder with it, the barriers were down. Another crack, mighty in its summons, the turnstile yawned, and the woman with her hand upon it smiled and beckoned.

Deborah ran out of the room and down the stairs. Somewhere somebody called – Roger, perhaps, it did not matter – and Patch was barking; but caring nothing for concealment she went through the dark drawing-room and opened the french window on to the terrace. The lightning searched the terrace and lit the paving, and Deborah ran down the steps on to the lawn where the turnstile gleamed.

Haste was imperative. If she did not run the turnstile might be closed, the woman vanish, and all the wonder of the sacred world be taken from her. She was in time. The woman was still waiting. She held out her hand for tickets, but Deborah shook her head. 'I have none.' The woman, laughing, brushed her through into the secret world where there were no laws, no rules, and all the faceless phantoms ran before her to the woods, blown by the rising wind. Then the rain came. The sky, deep brown as the lightning pierced it, opened, and the water hissed to the ground, rebounding from the earth in bubbles. There was no order now in the alley-way. The ferns had turned to trees, the trees to Titans. All moved in ecstasy, with sweeping limbs, but the rhythm was broken up, tumultuous, so that some of them were bent backwards, torn by the sky, and others dashed their heads to the undergrowth where they were caught and beaten.

In the world behind, laughed Deborah as she ran, this would be punishment, but here in the secret world it was a tribute. The phantoms who ran beside her were like waves. They were linked one with another, and they were, each one of them, and Deborah too, part of the night force that made the sobbing and the laughter. The lightning forked where they willed it, and the thunder cracked as they looked upwards to the sky.

The pool had come alive. The water-lilies had turned to hands, with palms upraised, and in the far corner, usually so still under the green scum, bubbles sucked at the surface, steaming and multiplying as the torrents fell. Everyone crowded to the pool. The phantoms bowed and crouched by the water's edge, and now the woman had set up her turnstile in the middle of the pool, beckoning them once more. Some remnant of a sense of social order rose in Deborah and protested.

'But we've already paid,' she shouted, and remembered a second later that she had passed through free. Must there be duplication? Was the secret world a rainbow, always repeating itself, alighting on another hill when you believed yourself beneath it? No time to think. The phantoms had gone through. The lightning, streaky white, lit the old dead monster tree with his crown of ivy, and because he had no spring now in his joints he could not sway in tribute with the trees and ferns, but had to remain there, rigid, like a crucifix.

'And now ... and now ... and now ...' called Deborah.

The triumph was that she was not afraid, was filled with such wild acceptance ... She ran into the pool. Her living feet felt the mud and the broken sticks and all the tangle of old weeds, and the water was up to her armpits and her chin. The lilies held her. The rain blinded her. The woman and the turnstile were no more.

'Take me too,' cried the child. 'Don't leave me behind!' In her heart was a savage disenchantment. They had broken their promise, they had left her in the world. The pool that claimed her now was not the pool of secrecy, but dank, dark, brackish water choked with scum.

IV

'Grandpapa says he's going to have it fenced round,' said Roger. 'It should have been done years ago. A proper fence, then nothing can ever happen. But barrow-loads of shingle tipped in it first. Then it won't be a pool, but just a dewpond. Dewponds aren't dangerous.'

He was looking at her over the edge of her bed. He had risen in status, being the only one of them downstairs, the bearer of tidings good or ill, the go-between. Deborah had been ordered two days in bed.

'I should think by Wednesday,' he went on, 'you'd be able to play cricket. It's not as if you're hurt. People who walk in their sleep are just a bit potty.'

'I did not walk in my sleep,' said Deborah.

'Grandpapa said you must have done,' said Roger. 'It was a good thing that Patch woke him up and he saw you going across the lawn . . .' Then, to show his release from tension, he stood on his hands.

Deborah could see the sky from her bed. It was flat and dull. The day was a summer day that had worked through storm. Agnes came into the room, with junket on a tray. She looked important.

'Now run off,' she said to Roger. 'Deborah doesn't want to talk to you. She's supposed to rest.'

Surprisingly, Roger obeyed, and Agnes placed the junket on the table beside the bed. 'You don't feel hungry, I expect,' she said. 'Never mind, you can eat this later, when you fancy it. Have you got a pain? It's usual, the first time.'

'No,' said Deborah.

What had happened to her was personal. They had prepared her for it at school, but nevertheless it was a shock, not to be discussed with Agnes. The woman hovered a moment, in case the child asked questions; but, seeing that none came, she turned and left the room.

Deborah, her cheek on her hand, stared at the empty sky. The heaviness of knowledge lay upon her, a strange, deep sorrow.

'It won't come back,' she thought. 'I've lost the key.'

The hidden world, like ripples on the pool so soon to be filled in and fenced, was out of her reach for ever.

Baby's Bath

ARNOLD BENNETT

Mrs Blackshaw had a baby. It would be an exaggeration to say that the baby interested the entire town, Bursley being an ancient, *blasé* sort of borough of some thirty thousand inhabitants. Babies, in fact, arrived in Bursley at the rate of more than a thousand every year. Nevertheless, a few weeks after the advent of Mrs Blackshaw's baby, when the medical officer of health reported to the Town Council that the births for the month amounted to ninety-five, and that the birth-rate of Bursley compared favourably with the birth-rates of the sister towns, Hanbridge, Knape, Longshaw, and Turnhill – when the medical officer read these memorable words at the monthly meeting of the Council, and the *Staffordshire Signal* reported them, and Mrs Blackshaw perused them, a blush of pride spread over Mrs Blackshaw's face, and she picked up the baby's left foot and gave it a little peck of a kiss. She could not help feeling that the real solid foundation of that formidable and magnificent output of babies was her baby. She could not help feeling that she had done something for the town – had caught the public eye.

As for the baby, except that it was decidedly superior to the average infant in external appearance and pleasantness of disposition, it was, in all essential characteristics, a typical baby – that is to say, it was purely sensuous and it lived the life of the senses. It was utterly selfish. It never thought of anyone but itself. It honestly imagined itself to be the centre of the created universe. It was convinced that the rest of the universe had been brought into existence solely for the convenience and pleasure of it – the baby. When it wanted anything, it made no secret of the fact, and it was always utterly unscrupulous in trying to get what it wanted. If it could have obtained the moon, it would have upset all the astronomers of Europe and made *Whitaker's Almanack* unsaleable without a pang. It had no god but its stomach. It never bothered its head about higher things. It was a bully and a coward, and it treated women as beings of a lower order than men. In a word, it was that ideal creature, sung of the poets, from which we gradually sink and fall away as we grow older.

At the age of six months it had quite a lot of hair, and a charming rosy expanse at the back of its neck, caused through lying on its back in contemplation of its own importance. It didn't know the date of the Battle of Hastings, but it knew with the certainty of absolute knowledge that it was master of the house, and that the activity of the house revolved round it.

Now, the baby loved its bath. In any case its bath would have been an affair of immense and intricate pomp; but the fact that it loved its bath raised the interest and significance of the bath to the nth power. The bath took place at five o'clock in the evening, and it is not too much to say that the idea of the bath was immanent in the very atmosphere of the house. When you have an appointment with the dentist at five o'clock in the afternoon, the idea of the appointment is immanent in your mind from the first moment of your awakenings. Conceive that an appointment with the dentist implies heavenly joy instead of infernal pain, and you will have a notion of the daily state of Mrs Blackshaw and Emmie (the nurse) with regard to the baby's bath.

Even at ten in the morning Emmie would be keeping an eye on the kitchen fire, lest the cook might let it out. And shortly after noon Mrs Blackshaw would be keeping an eye on the thermometer in the bedroom where the bath occurred. From four o'clock onwards the clocks in the house were spied on and overlooked like suspected persons; but they were used to that, because the baby had his sterilized milk every two hours: I have at length allowed you to penetrate the secret of his sex.

And so at five o'clock precisely the august and exciting ceremony began in the best bedroom. A bright fire was burning (the month being December), and the carefully shaded electric lights were also burning. A large bath-towel was spread in a convenient place on the floor, and on the towel were two chairs facing each other, and a table. On one chair was the bath, and on the other was Mrs Blackshaw with her sleeves rolled up, and on Mrs Blackshaw was another towel and on that towel was Roger (the baby). On the table were zinc ointment, Vaseline, scentless eau de Cologne, Castile soap, and a powder-puff.

Emmie having pretty nearly filled the bath with a combination of hot and cold waters, dropped the floating thermometer into it, and then added more waters until the thermometer indicated the precise temperature proper for a baby's bath. But you are not to imagine that Mrs Blackshaw trusted a mere thermometer. No. She put her arm in the water up to the elbow. She reckoned the sensitive skin near the elbow was worth forty thermometers.

Emmie was chiefly an audience. Mrs Blackshaw had engaged her as nurse, but she could have taught a child to do all that she allowed the nurse to do. During the bath Mrs Blackshaw and Emmie hated and scorned each other, despite their joy. Emmie was twice Mrs Blackshaw's age, besides being twice her weight, and she knew twice as much about babies as Mrs Blackshaw did. However, Mrs Blackshaw had the terrific advantage of being the mother of that particular infant, and she could always end an argument when she chose, and in her own favour. It was unjust, and Emmie felt it to be unjust; but this is not a world of justice.

Roger, though not at all precocious, was perfectly aware of the carefully concealed hostility between his mother and his nurse, and often, with his usual unscrupulousness, he used it for his own ends. He was sitting upon his mother's knees toying with the edge of the bath, already tasting its delights in advance. Mrs Blackshaw undressed the upper half of him, and then she laid him on the flat of his back and undressed the lower half of him, but keeping some wisp of a garment round his equatorial regions. And then she washed his face with a sponge and the Castile soap, very gently, but not half gently enough for Emmie, nor half gently enough for Roger, for Roger looked upon this part of the business as insulting and superfluous. He breathed hard and kicked his feet nearly off.

'Yes, it's dreadful having our face washed, isn't it?' said Mrs Blackshaw, with her sleeves up, and her hair by this time down. 'We don't like it, do we? Yes, yes.'

Emmie grunted, without a sound, and yet Mrs Blackshaw heard her, and finished that face quickly and turned to the hands.

'Potato-gardens every day,' she said. 'Evzy day-day. Enough of that, Colonel!' (For, after all, she had plenty of spirit.) 'Fat little creases! Fat little creases! There! He likes that! There! Feet! Feet! Feet and legs! Then our back! And then *whup* we shall go into the bath! That's it. Kick! Kick your mother!'

And she turned him over.

'Incredible bungler!' said the eyes of the nurse. 'Can't she turn him over neater than that?'

'Harridan!' said the eyes of Mrs Blackshaw. 'I wouldn't let you bath him for twenty thousand pounds!'

Roger continued to breathe hard, as if his mother were a horse and he were rubbing her down.

'Now! Zoop! Whup!' cried his mother, and having deprived him of his final rag, she picked him up and sat him in the bath, and he was divinely happy, and so were the women. He appeared a gross little animal in the bath, all the tints of his flesh shimmering under the electric light. His chest was superb, but the rolled and creased bigness of his inordinate stomach was simply appalling, not to mention his great thighs and calves. The truth was, he had grown so much that if he had been only a little bit bigger, he would have burst the bath. He resembled an old man who had been steadily eating too much for about forty years.

His two womenfolk now candidly and openly worshipped him, forgetting sectarian differences.

And he splashed. Oh! he splashed. You see, he had learnt how to splash, and he had certainly got an inkling that to splash was wicked and messy. So he splashed – in his mother's face, in Emmie's face, in the fire. He pretty well splashed the fire out. Ten minutes before, the bedroom had been tidy, a thing of beauty. It was now naught but a wild welter of towels, socks, binders – peninsulas of clothes nearly surrounded by water.

Finally his mother seized him again, and, rearing his little legs up out of the water, immersed the whole of his inflated torso beneath the surface.

'Hallo!' she exclaimed. 'Did the water run over his mouf? Did it?'

'Angels and ministers of grace defend us! How clumsy she is!' commented the eyes of Emmie.

'There! I fink that's about long enough for this kind of wevver,' said the mother.

'I should think it was! There's almost a crust of ice on the water now!' the nurse refrained from saying.

And Roger, full of regrets, was wrenched out of the bath. He had ceased breathing hard while in the water, but he began again immediately he emerged.

'We don't like our face wiped, do we?' said his mother on his behalf. 'We want to go back into that bath. We like it. It's more fun than anything that happens all day long! Eh? That old dandruff's coming up in fine style. It's a-peeling off like anything.'

And all the while she wiped him, patted eau de Cologne into him with the flat of her hand, and rubbed zinc ointment into him, and massaged him, and powdered him, and turned him over and over and over, till he was thoroughly well basted and cooked. And he kept on breathing hard.

Then he sneezed, amid general horror!

'I told you so!' the nurse didn't say, and she rushed to the bed where all the idol's beautiful, clean, aired things were lying safe from splashings, and handed a piece of flannel shirt, about two inches in length, to Mrs Blackshaw. And Mrs Blackshaw rolled the left sleeve of it into a wad and stuck it over his arm, and his poor little vaccination marks were hidden from view till next morning. Roger protested.

'We don't like clothes, do we?' said his mother. 'We want to tumble back into our tub. We aren't much for clothes anyway. We're a little Hottentot, aren't we?'

And she gradually covered him with one garment or another until there was nothing left of him but his head and his hands and feet. And she sat him up on her knees, so as to fasten his things behind. And then it might have been observed that he was no longer breathing hard, but giving vent to a sound between a laugh and a cry, while sucking his thumb and gazing round the room.

'That's our little affected cry that we start for our milk, isn't it?' his mother explained to him.

And he agreed that it was.

And before Emmie could fly across the room for the bottle, all ready and waiting, his mouth, in the shape of a perfect rectangle, had monopolized five-sixths of his face and he was scarlet and bellowing with impatience.

He took the bottle like a tiger his prey, and seized his mother's hand that held the bottle, and he furiously pumped the milk into that insatiable gulf of a stomach. But he found time to gaze about the room too. A tear stood in each roving eye, caused by the effort of feeding.

'Yes, that's it,' said his mother. 'Now look round and see what's happening, Curiosity! Well, if you *will* bob your head, I can't help it.'

'Of course you can!' the nurse didn't say.

Then he put his finger into his mouth side by side with the bottle, and gagged himself, and choked, and gave a terrible – excuse the word – hiccough. After which he seemed to lose interest in the milk, and the pumping operations slackened and then ceased.

'Goosey!' whispered his mother, 'getting seepy? Is the Sandman throwing sand in our eyes? Old Sandman at it? Sh—' He had gone.

Emmie took him. The women spoke in whispers. And Mrs Blackshaw, after a day spent in being a mother, reconstituted herself a wife, and began to beautify herself for her husband.

II

Yes, there was a Mr Blackshaw, and with Mr Blackshaw the tragedy of the bath commences. Mr Blackshaw was a very important young man. Indeed, it is within the mark to say that, next to his son, he was the most important young man in Bursley. For Mr Blackshaw was the manager of the newly opened Municipal Electricity Works. And the Municipal Electricity had created more excitement and interest than anything since the 1887 Jubilee, when an ox was roasted whole in the market-place and turned bad in the process. Had Bursley been a Swiss village, or a French country town, or a hamlet in Arizona, it would have had its electricity fifteen years ago, but being only a progressive English borough, with an annual value of a hundred and fifty thousand pounds, it struggled on with gas till well into the twentieth century. Its great neighbour Hanbridge had become acquainted with electricity in the nineteenth century.

All the principal streets and squares, and every decent shop that Hanbridge competition had left standing, and many private houses, now lighted themselves by electricity, and the result was splendid and glaring and coldly yellow. Mr Blackshaw developed into the hero of the hour. People looked at him in the street as though he had been the discoverer and original maker of electricity. And if the manager of the gasworks had not already committed murder, it was because the manager of the gasworks had a right sense of what was due to his position as vicar's churchwarden at St Peter's Church.

But greatness has its penalties. And the chief penalty of Mr Blackshaw's greatness was that he could not see Roger have his nightly bath. It was impossible for Mr Blackshaw to quit his arduous and responsible post before seven o'clock in the evening. Later on, when things were going more smoothly, he might be able to get away; but then, later on, his son's bath would not be so amusing and agreeable as it then, by all reports, was. The baby was, of course, bathed on Sunday nights, but Sunday afternoon and evening Mr Blackshaw was obliged to spend with his invalid mother at Longshaw. It was on the sole condition of his weekly presence thus in her house that she had consented not to live with the married pair. And so Mr Blackshaw could not witness Roger's bath. He adored Roger. He understood Roger. He weighed, nursed, and fed Roger. He was 'up' in all the newest theories of infant rearing. In short, Roger was his passion, and he knew everything of Roger except Roger's bath. And when his wife met him at the front door of a night at seven-thirty and launched instantly into a description of the wonders, delights, and excitations of Roger's latest bath, Mr Blackshaw was ready to tear his hair with disappointment and frustration.

'I suppose you couldn't put it off for a couple of hours one night, May?' he suggested at supper on the evening of the particular bath described above.

'Sidney!' protested Mrs Blackshaw, pained.

Mr Blackshaw felt that he had gone too far, and there was a silence.

'Well!' said Mr Blackshaw at length, 'I have just made up my mind. I'm going to see that kid's bath, and, what's more, I'm going to see it tomorrow. I don't care what happens.'

'But how shall you manage to get away, darling?'

'You will telephone to me about a quarter of an hour before you're ready to begin, and I'll pretend it's something very urgent; and scoot off.'

'Well, that will be lovely, darling!' said Mrs Blackshaw.

'I *would* like you to see him in the bath, just once! He looks so—' And so on.

The next day, Mr Blackshaw, that fearsome autocrat of the Municipal Electricity Works, was saying to himself all day that at five o'clock he was going to assist at the spectacle of his wonderful son's bath. The prospect inspired him. So much so that every hand in the place was doing its utmost in fear and trembling, and the whole affair was running with the precision and smoothness of a watch.

From four o'clock onwards, Mr Blackshaw, in the solemn, illuminated privacy of the managerial office, safe behind glass partitions, could no more contain his excitement. He hovered in front of the telephone, waiting for it to ring. Then, at a quarter to five just when he felt he couldn't stand it any longer, and was about to ring up his wife instead of waiting for her to ring him up, he saw a burly shadow behind the glass door, and gave a desolate sigh. That shadow could only be thrown by one person, and that person was His Worship the Mayor of Bursley. His Worship entered the private office with mayoral assurance, pulling in his wake a stout old lady whom he introduced as his aunt from Wolverhampton, And he calmly proposed that Mr Blackshaw should show the mayoral aunt over the new Electricity Works!

Mr Blackshaw was sick of showing people over the Works. More-over, he naturally despised the Mayor. All permanent officials of municipalities thoroughly despise their mayors (up their sleeves). A mayor is here today and gone tomorrow, whereas a permanent official is permanent. A mayor knows nothing about anything except his chain and the rules of debate, and he is, further, a tedious and meddlesome person – in the opinion of permanent officials.

So Mr Blackshaw's fury at the inept appearance of the Mayor and the mayoral aunt at this critical juncture may be imagined. The worst of it was he didn't know how to refuse the Mayor.

Then the telephone-bell rang.

'Excuse me,' said Mr Blackshaw, with admirably simulated polite-ness, going to the instrument. 'Are you there? Who is it?'

'It's me, darling,' came the thin voice of his wife far away at Bleakridge. 'The water's just getting hot. We're nearly ready. Can you come now?'

'By Jove! Wait a moment!' exclaimed Mr Blackshaw, and then turning to his visitors, 'Did you hear that?'

'No,' said the Mayor.

'All those three new dynamos that they've got at the Hanbridge Electricity Works have just broken down. I knew they would. I told them they would!'

'Dear, dear!' said the Mayor of Bursley, secretly delighted by this disaster to a disdainful rival. 'Why! They'll have the town in darkness. What are they going to do?'

'They want me to go over at once. But, of course, I can't. At least, I must give myself the pleasure of showing you and this lady over our Works, first.'

'Nothing of the kind, Mr Blackshaw!' said the Mayor. 'Go at once. Go at once. If Bursley can be of any assistance to Hanbridge in such a crisis, I shall be only too pleased, we will come tomorrow, won't we, auntie?'

Mr Blackshaw addressed the telephone.

'The Mayor is here, with a lady, and I was just about to show them over the Works, but His Worship insists that I come at once.'

'Certainly,' the Mayor put in pompously.

'Wonders will never cease,' came the thin voice of Mrs Blackshaw through the telephone. 'It's very nice of the old thing! What's the lady friend like?'

'Not like anything. Unique!' replied Mr Blackshaw.

'Young?' came the voice.

'Dates from the 'thirties,' said Mr Blackshaw. 'I'm coming.' And rang off.

'I didn't know there was any electric machinery as old as that,' said the mayoral aunt.

'We'll just look about us a bit,' the Mayor remarked. 'Don't lose a moment, Mr Blackshaw.'

And Mr Blackshaw hurried off, wondering vaguely how he should explain the lie when it was found out, but not caring much. After all, he could easily ascribe the episode to the trick of some practical joker.

III

He arrived at his commodious and electrically lit residence in the very nick of time, and full to overflowing with innocent paternal glee. Was he not about to see Roger's tub? Roger was just ready to be carried upstairs as Mr Blackshaw's latchkey turned in the door.

'Wait a sec!' cried Mr Blackshaw to his wife, who had the child in her arms, 'I'll carry him up.'

And he threw away his hat, stick, and overcoat and grabbed ecstatically at the infant. And he got perhaps half-way up the stairs, when lo! the electric light went out. Every electric light in the house went out.

'Great Scott!' breathed Mr Blackshaw, aghast.

He pulled aside the blind of the window at the turn of the stairs, and peered forth. The street was as black as your hat, or nearly so.

'Great Scott!' he repeated. 'May, get the candles.'

Something had evidently gone wrong at the Works. Just his luck! He had quitted the Works for a quarter of an hour, and the current had failed!

Of course, the entire house was instantly in uproar, turned upside down, startled out of its life. But a few candles soon calmed its transports. And at length Mr Blackshaw gained the bedroom in safety, with the offspring of his desires comfortable in a shawl.

'Give him to me,' said May shortly. 'I suppose you'll have to go back to the Works at once?'

Mr Blackshaw paused, and then nerved himself; but while he was pausing, May, glancing at the two feeble candles, remarked: 'It's very tiresome. I'm sure I shan't be able to see properly.'

'No!' almost shouted Mr Blackshaw. 'I'll watch this kid have his bath or I'll die for it! I don't care if all the Five Towns are in darkness. I don't care if the Mayor's aunt has got caught in a dynamo and is suffering horrible tortures. I've come to see this bath business, and dashed if I don't see it!'

'Well, don't stand between the bath and the fire, dearest,' said May coldly.

Meanwhile, Emmie, having pretty nearly filled the bath with a combination of hot and cold waters, dropped the floating thermometer into it, and then added more waters until the thermometer indicated the precise temperature proper for a baby's bath. But you are not to imagine that Mrs Blackshaw trusted a mere thermometer –

She did not, however, thrust her bared arm into the water this time. No! Roger, who never cried before his bath, was crying, was indubitably crying. And he cried louder and louder.

'Stand where he can't see you, dearest. He isn't used to you at bath-time,' said Mrs Blackshaw still coldly. 'Are you, my pet? There! There!'

Mr Blackshaw effaced himself, feeling a fool. But Roger continued to cry. He cried himself purple. He cried till the veins stood out on his forehead and his mouth was like a map of Australia. He cried himself into a monster of ugliness. Neither mother nor nurse could do anything with him at all.

'I think you've upset him, dearest,' said Mrs Blackshaw even more coldly. 'Hadn't you better go?'

'Well—' protested the father.

'I think you had better go,' said Mrs Blackshaw, adding no term of endearment, and visibly controlling herself with difficulty.

And Mr Blackshaw went. He had to go. He went out into the

unelectric night. He headed for the Works, not because he cared twopence, at that moment, about the accident at the Works, whatever it was; but simply because the Works was the only place to go to. And even outside in the dark street he could hear the rousing accents of his progeny.

People were talking to each other as they groped about in the road, and either making jokes at the expense of the new Electricity Department, or frankly cursing it with true Five Towns directness of speech. And as Mr Blackshaw went down the hill into the town his heart was as black as the street itself with rage and disappointment. He had made his child cry!

Someone stopped him.

'Eh, Mester Blackshaw!' said a voice, and under the voice a hand struck a match to light a pipe. 'What's th' maning o' this eclipse as you'm treating uz to?'

Mr Blackshaw looked right through the inquirer – a way he had when his brain worked hard. And suddenly he smiled by the light of the match.

'*That child wasn't crying because I was there,*' said Mr Blackshaw with solemn relief. '*Not at all! He was crying because he didn't understand the candles. He isn't used to candles, and they frightened him.*'

And he began to hurry towards the Works.

At the same instant the electric light returned to Bursley.

The current was resumed.

'That's better,' said Mr Blackshaw, sighing.

The Lumber-Room

SAKI

The children were to be driven, as a special treat, to the sands at Jagborough. Nicholas was not to be of the party; he was in disgrace. Only that morning he had refused to eat his wholesome bread-and-milk on the seemingly frivolous ground that there was a frog in it. Older and wiser and better people had told him that there could not possibly be a frog in his bread-and-milk and that he was not to talk nonsense; he continued, nevertheless, to talk what seemed the veriest nonsense, and described with much detail the coloration and markings of the alleged frog. The dramatic part of the incident was that there really was a frog in Nicholas' basin of bread-and-milk; he had put it there himself, so he felt entitled to know something about it. The sin of taking a frog from the garden and putting it into a bowl of wholesome bread-and-milk was enlarged on at great length, but the fact that stood out clearest in the whole affair, as it presented itself to the mind of Nicholas, was that the older, wiser and better people had been proved to be profoundly in error in matters about which they had expressed the utmost assurance.

'You said there couldn't possibly be a frog in my bread-and-milk; there *was* a frog in my bread-and-milk,' he repeated, with the insistence of a skilled tactician who does not intend to shift from favourable ground.

So his boy-cousin and girl-cousin and his quite uninteresting younger brother were to be taken to Jagborough Sands that afternoon and he was to stay at home. His cousins' aunt, who insisted, by an unwarranted stretch of imagination, in styling herself his aunt also, had hastily invented the Jagborough expedition in order to impress on Nicholas the delights that he had justly forfeited by his disgraceful conduct at the breakfast-table. It was her habit, whenever one of the children fell from grace, to improvise something of a festival nature from which the offender would be rigorously debarred; if all the children sinned collectively they were suddenly informed of a circus in a neighbouring town, a circus of unrivalled merit and uncounted elephants, to which, but for their depravity, they would have been taken that very day.

A few decent tears were looked for on the part of Nicholas when the moment for the departure of the expedition arrived. As a matter of fact, however, all the crying was done by his girl-cousin, who scraped her knee rather painfully against the step of the carriage as she was scrambling in.

'How she did howl,' said Nicholas cheerfully, as the party drove off without any of the elation or high spirits that should have characterized it.

'She'll soon get over that,' said the *soi-disant* aunt; 'it will be a glorious afternoon for racing about over those beautiful sands. How they will enjoy themselves!'

'Bobby won't enjoy himself much, and he won't race much either,' said Nicholas with a grim chuckle; 'his boots are hurting him. They're too tight.'

'Why didn't he tell me they were hurting?' asked the aunt with some asperity.

'He told you twice, but you weren't listening. You often don't listen when we tell you important things.'

'You are not to go into the gooseberry garden,' said the aunt, changing the subject.

'Why not?' demanded Nicholas.

'Because you are in disgrace,' said the aunt loftily.

Nicholas did not admit the flawlessness of the reasoning; he felt perfectly capable of being in disgrace and in a gooseberry garden at the same moment. His face took on an expression of considerable obstinacy. It was clear to his aunt that he was determined to get into the gooseberry garden, 'Only,' as she remarked to herself, 'because I have told him he is not to.'

Now the gooseberry garden had two doors by which it might be entered, and once a small person like Nicholas had slipped in there he could effectually disappear from view amid the masking growth of artichokes, raspberry canes and fruit bushes. The aunt had many other things to do that afternoon, but she spent an hour or two in trivial gardening operations among flower-beds and shrubberies, whence she could keep a watchful eye on the two doors that led to the forbidden paradise. She was a woman of few ideas, but with immense powers of concentration.

Nicholas made one or two sorties into the front garden, wriggling his way with obvious stealth of purpose towards one or other of the doors, but never able for a moment to evade the aunt's watchful eye. As a matter of fact, he had no intention of trying to get into the gooseberry garden, but it was extremely convenient for him that his aunt should believe that he had; it was a belief that would keep her on self-imposed sentry-duty for the greater part of the afternoon. Having thoroughly confirmed and fortified her suspicions, Nicholas slipped back into the house and rapidly put into execution a plan of action that had long germinated in his brain. By standing on a chair in the library one could reach a shelf on which reposed a fat, important-looking key. The key was as important as it looked; it was the instrument which kept the mysteries of the lumber-room secure from unauthorized intrusion, which opened a way only for aunts and such-like privileged persons. Nicholas had not much experience of the art of fitting keys into keyholes and turning locks, but for some days past he had practised with the key of the school-room door; he did not believe in trusting too much to luck and accident. The key turned stiffly in the lock, but it turned. The door opened, and Nicholas was in an unknown land, compared with which the gooseberry garden was a stale delight, a mere material pleasure.

Often and often Nicholas had pictured to himself what the lumber-room might be like, that region that was so carefully sealed from youthful eyes and concerning which no questions were ever answered. It came up to his expectations. In the first place it was large and dimly lit, one high window opening on to the forbidden garden being its only source of illumination. In the second place it was a storehouse of unimagined treasures. The aunt-by-assertion was one of those people who think that things spoil by use and consign them to dust and damp by way of preserving them. Such parts of the house as Nicholas knew best were rather bare and cheerless, but here there were wonderful things for the eye to feast on. First and foremost there was a piece of framed tapestry that was evidently meant to be a fire-screen. To Nicholas it was a living, breathing story; he sat down on a roll of Indian hangings, glowing in wonderful colours beneath a layer of dust, and took in all the details of the tapestry picture. A man, dressed in the hunting costume of some remote period, had just transfixed a stag with an arrow; it could not have been a difficult shot because the stag was only one or two paces away from him; in the thickly growing vegetation that the picture suggested it would not have been difficult to creep up to a feeding stag, and the two spotted dogs that were springing forward to join in the chase had evidently been trained to keep to heel till the arrow was discharged. That part of the picture was simple, if interesting, but did the huntsman see, what Nicholas saw, that four galloping wolves were coming in his direction through the wood? There might be more than four of them hidden behind the trees, and in any case would the man and his dogs be able to cope with the four wolves if they made an attack? The man had only two arrows left in his quiver, and he might miss with one or both of them; all one knew about his skill in shooting was that he could hit a large stag at a ridiculously short range. Nicholas sat for many golden minutes revolving the possibilities of the scene; he was inclined to think that there were more than four wolves and that the man and his dogs were in a tight corner.

But there were other objects of delight and interest claiming his instant attention: here were quaint twisted candlesticks in the shape of snakes, and a teapot fashioned like a china duck, out of whose open beak the tea was supposed to come. How dull and shapeless the nursery teapot seemed in comparison! And there was a carved sandal-wood box packed tight with aromatic cotton-wool, and between the layers of cotton-wool were little brass figures, hump-necked bulls, and peacocks and goblins, delightful to see and to handle. Less promising in appearance was a large square book with plain black covers; Nicholas peeped into it, and, behold, it was full of coloured pictures of birds. And such birds! In the garden, and in the lanes when he went for a walk, Nicholas came across a few birds, of which the largest were an occasional magpie or woodpigeon; here were herons and bustards, kites, toucans, tiger-bitterns, brush-turkeys, ibises, golden pheasants, a whole portrait gallery of undreamed-of creatures. And as he was admiring the colouring of the mandarin duck and assigning a life-history to it, the voice of his aunt in shrill vociferation of his name came from the gooseberry garden without. She had grown suspicious at his long disappearance, and had leapt to the conclusion that he had climbed over the wall behind the sheltering screen of the lilac bushes; she was now engaged in energetic and rather hopeless search for him among the artichokes and raspberry canes.

'Nicholas, Nicholas!' she screamed, 'you are to come out of this at once. It's no use trying to hide there; I can see you all the time.' It was probably the first time for twenty years that anyone had smiled in that lumber-room.

Presently the angry repetitions of Nicholas' name gave way to a shriek, and a cry for somebody to come quickly. Nicholas shut the book, restored it carefully to its place in a corner, and shook some dust from a neighbouring pile of newspapers over it. Then he crept from the room, locked the door, and replaced the key exactly where he had found it. His aunt was still calling his name when he sauntered into the front garden.

'Who's calling?' he asked.

'Me,' came the answer from the other side of the wall, 'didn't you hear me? I've been looking for you in the gooseberry garden, and I've slipped into the rain-water tank. Luckily there's no water in it, but the sides are slippery and I can't get out. Fetch the little ladder from under the cherry tree –'

'I was told I wasn't to go into the gooseberry garden,' said Nicholas promptly.

'I told you not to, and now I tell you that you may,' came the voice from the rain-water tank, rather impatiently.

'Your voice doesn't sound like aunt's,' objected Nicholas; 'you may be the Evil One tempting me to be disobedient. Aunt often tells me that the Evil One tempts me and that I always yield. This time I'm not going to yield.'

'Don't talk nonsense,' said the prisoner in the tank; 'go and fetch the ladder.'

'Will there be strawberry jam for tea?' asked Nicholas innocently.

'Certainly there will be,' said the aunt, privately resolving that Nicholas should have none of it.

'Now I know that you are the Evil One and not aunt,' shouted Nicholas gleefully; 'when we asked aunt for strawberry jam yesterday she said there wasn't any. I know there are four jars of it in the store cupboard, because I looked, and of course you know it's there, but *she* doesn't, because she said there wasn't any. Oh, Devil, you *have* sold yourself!'

There was an unusual sense of luxury in being able to talk to an aunt as though one was talking to the Evil One, but Nicholas knew, with childish discernment, that such luxuries were not to be over-indulged in. He walked noisily away, and it was a kitchenmaid, in search of parsley, who eventually rescued the aunt from the rain-water tank.

Tea that evening was partaken of in a fearsome silence. The tide had been at its highest when the children had arrived at Jagborough Cove, so there had been no sands to play on – a circumstance that the aunt had overlooked in the haste of organizing her punitive expedition. The tightness of Bobby's boots had had a disastrous effect on his temper the whole of the afternoon, and altogether the children could not have been said to have enjoyed themselves. The aunt maintained the frozen muteness of one who has suffered undignified and unmerited detention in a rain-water tank for thirty-five minutes. As for Nicholas, he, too, was silent, in the absorption of one who has much to think about; it was just possible, he considered, that the huntsman would escape with his hounds while the wolves feasted on the stricken stag.

The Library Window

MARGARET OLIPHANT

I was not aware at first of the many discussions which had gone on about that window. It was almost opposite one of the windows of the large old-fashioned drawing-room of the house in which I spent that summer, which was of so much importance in my life. Our house and the library were on opposite sides of the broad High Street of St Rule's, which is a fine street, wide and ample, and very quiet, as strangers think who come from noisier places; but on a summer evening there is much coming and going, and the stillness is full of sound – the sound of footsteps and pleasant voices, softened by the summer air. There are even exceptional moments when it is noisy: the time of the fair, and on Saturday nights sometimes, and when there are excursion trains. Then even the softest sunny air of the evening will not smooth the harsh tones and the stumbling steps; but at these unlovely moments we shut the windows, and even I, who am so fond of that deep recess where I can take refuge from all that is going on inside, and make myself a spectator of all the varied story out of doors, withdraw from my watch-tower. To tell the truth, there never was very much going on inside. The house belonged to my aunt, to whom (she says, 'Thank God!') nothing ever happens. I believe that many things have happened to her in her time; but that was all over at the period of which I am speaking, and she was old, and very quiet. Her life went on in a routine never broken. She got up at the same hour every day, and did the same things in the same rotation, day by day the same. She said that this was the greatest support in the world, and that routine is a kind of salvation. It may be so; but it is a very dull salvation, and I used to feel that I would rather have incident, whatever kind of incident it might be. But then at that time I was not old, which makes all the difference.

At the time of which I speak the deep recess of the drawing-room window was a great comfort to me. Though she was an old lady (perhaps because she was so old) she was very tolerant, and had a kind of feeling for me. She never said a word, but often gave me a smile when she saw how I had built myself up, with my books and my basket of work. I did very little work, I fear – now and then a few stitches when the spirit moved me, or when I had got well afloat in a dream, and was more tempted to follow it out than to read my book, as sometimes happened. At other times, and if the book were interesting, I used to get through volume after volume sitting there, paying no attention. Aunt Mary's old ladies came in to call, and I heard them talk, though I very seldom listened; but for all that, if they had anything to say that was interesting, it is curious how I found it in my mind afterwards, as if the air had blown it to me. They came and went, and I had the sensation of their old bonnets gliding out and in, and their dresses rustling; and now and then had to jump up and shake hands with someone who knew me, and asked after my papa and mamma. Then Aunt Mary would give me a little smile again, and I slipped back to my window. She never seemed to mind. My mother would not have let me do it, I know. She would have sent me upstairs to fetch something which I was quite sure she did not want, or downstairs to carry some quite unnecessary message to the housemaid. She liked to keep me running about. Perhaps that was one reason why I was so fond of Aunt Mary's drawing-room, and the deep recess of the window, and the curtain that fell half over it, and the broad window-seat, where one could collect so many things without being found fault with for untidiness. Whenever we had anything the matter with us in these days, we were sent to St Rule's to get up our strength. And this was my case at the time of which I am going to speak.

* * *

Everybody had said, since ever I learned to speak, that I was fantastic and fanciful and dreamy, and all the other words with which a girl who may happen to like poetry, and to be fond of thinking, is so often made uncomfortable. People don't know what they mean when they say 'fantastic'. It sounds like Madge Wildfire or something of that sort. My mother thought I should always be busy, to keep nonsense out of my head. But really I was not at all fond of nonsense. I was rather serious than otherwise. I would have been no trouble to anybody if I had been left to myself. It was only that I had a sort of second-sight, and was conscious of things to which I paid no attention. Even when reading the most interesting book, the things that were being talked about blew in to me; and I heard what the people were saying in the streets as they passed under the window. Aunt Mary always said I could do two or indeed three things at once – both read and listen, and see, I am sure that I did not listen much, and seldom looked out, of set purpose – as some people do who notice what bonnets the ladies in the street have on; but I did hear what I couldn't help hearing, even when I was reading my book, and I did see all sorts of things, though often for a whole half-hour I might never lift my eyes.

This does not explain what I said at the beginning, that there were many discussions about that window. It was, and still is, the last window in the High Street. Yet it is not exactly opposite, but a little to the west, so that I could see it best from the left side of my recess. I took it calmly for granted that it was a window like any other till I first heard the talk about it which was going on in the drawing-room. 'Have you ever made up your mind, Mistress Balcarres,' said old Mr Pitmilly, 'whether that window opposite is a window or no?' He said Mistress Balcarres – and he was always called Mr Pitmilly, Morton: which was the name of his place.

'I am never sure of it, to tell the truth,' said Aunt Mary, 'all these years.'

'Bless me!' said one of the old ladies, 'and what window may it be?'

Mr Pitmilly had a way of laughing as he spoke, which did not please me; but it was true that he was not perhaps desirous of pleasing me. He said, 'Oh, just the window opposite,' with his laugh running through his words; 'our friend can never make up her mind about it, though she has been living opposite it since –'

'You need never mind the date,' said another, 'the Leebrary window! Dear me, what should it be but a window? Up at that height it could not be a door.'

'The question is,' said my aunt, 'if it is a real window with glass in it, or if it is merely painted, or if it once was a window, and has been built up. And the oftener people look at it, the less they are able to say.'

'Let me see this window,' said old Lady Carnbee, who was very active and strong-minded; and then they all came crowding upon me – three or four old ladies, very eager, and Mr Pitmilly's white hair appearing over their heads, and my aunt sitting quiet and smiling behind.

'I mind the window very well,' said Lady Carnbee; 'ay; and so do more than me. But in its present appearance it is just like any other window; but has not been cleaned, I should say, in the memory of man.'

'I see what ye mean,' said one of the others. 'It is just a very dead thing without any reflection in it; but I've seen as bad before.'

'Ay, it's dead enough,' said another, 'but that's not rule; for these hizzies of women-servants in this ill age –'

'Nay, the women are well enough,' said the softest voice of all, which was Aunt Mary's. 'I will never let them risk their lives cleaning the outside of mine. And there are no women-servants in the Old Library; there is maybe something more in it than that.'

They were all pressing into my recess, pressing upon me, a row of old faces, peering into something they could not understand. I had a sense in my mind how curious it was, the wall of old ladies in their old satin gowns all glazed with age. Lady Carnbee with her lace about her head. Nobody was looking at me or thinking of me; but I felt unconsciously the contrast of my youngness to their oldness, and stared at them as they stared over my head at the Library window. I had given it no attention up to this time. I was more taken up with the old ladies than with the thing they were looking at.

'The framework is all right at least, I can see that, and pented black –'

'And the panes are pented black too. It's no window, Mrs Balcarres. It has been filled in, in the days of the window duties you will mind, Leddy Carnbee.'

'Mind!' said that oldest lady. 'I mind when your mother was marriet, Jeanie; and that's neither the day nor yesterday. But as for the window, it's just a delusion: and that is my opinion of the matter, if you ask me.'

'There's a great want of light in that muckle room at the college,' said another. 'If it was a window, the Leebrary would have more light.'

'One thing is clear,' said one of the younger ones, 'it cannot be a window to see through. It may be filled in or it may be built up, but it is not a window to give light.'

'And whoever heard of a window that was to see through?' Lady Carnbee said. I was fascinated by the look on her face, which was a curious scornful look as of one who knew more than she chose to say: and then my wandering fancy was caught by her hand as she held it up, throwing back the lace that dropped over it. Lady Carnbee's lace was the chief thing about her – heavy black Spanish lace with large flowers. Everything she wore was trimmed with it. A large veil of it hung over her old bonnet. But her hand coming out of this heavy lace was a curious thing to see. She had very long fingers, very taper, which had been much admired in her youth; and her hand was very white, or rather more than white, pale, bleached and bloodless, with large blue veins standing up upon the back; and she wore some fine rings, among others a big diamond in an ugly old claw setting. They were too big for her, and were wound round with yellow silk to make them keep on: and this little cushion of silk, turned brown with long wearing, had twisted round so that it was more conspicuous than the jewels; while the big diamond blazed underneath in the hollow of her hand, like some dangerous thing hiding and sending out darts of light. The hand, which seemed to come almost to a point, with this strange ornament underneath, clutched at my half-terrified imagination. It too seemed to mean far more than was said. I felt as if it might clutch me with sharp claws, and the lurking, dazzling creature bite – with a sting that would go to the heart.

Presently, however, the circle of the old faces broke up, the old ladies returned to their seats, and Mr Pitmilly, small but very erect, stood up in the midst of them, talking with mild authority like a little oracle among the ladies. Only Lady Carnbee always contradicted the neat, little, old gentleman. She gesticulated, when she talked, like a Frenchwoman, and darted forth that hand of hers with the lace hanging over it, so that I always caught a glimpse of the lurking diamond. I thought she looked like a witch among the comfortable little group which gave such attention to everything Mr Pitmilly said.

'For my part, it is my opinion there is no window there at all,' he said. 'It's very like the thing that's called in scientific language an optical illusion. It arises generally, if I may use such a word in the presence of ladies, from a liver that is not just in the perfitt order and balance that organ demands – and then you will see things – a blue dog, I remember, was the thing in one case, and in another –'

'The man has gane gyte,' said Lady Carnbee; 'I mind the windows in the Auld Leebrary as long as I mind anything. Is the Leebrary itself an optical illusion too?'

'Na, na,' and 'No, no,' said the old ladies; 'a blue dogue would be a strange vagary: but the Leebrary we have all kent from our youth,' said one. 'And I mind when the Assemblies were held there one year when the Town Hall was building,' another said.

'It is just a great divert to me,' said Aunt Mary: but what was strange was that she paused there, and said in a low tone, 'now': and then went on again, 'for whoever comes to my house, there are aye discussions about that window. I have never just made up my mind about it myself. Sometimes I think it's a case of these wicked window duties, as you said, Miss Jeanie, when half the windows in our houses were blocked up to save the tax. And then, I think, it may be due to that blank kind of building like the great new buildings on the Earthen Mound in Edinburgh, where the windows are just ornaments. And then whiles I am sure I can see the glass shining when the sun catches it in the afternoon.'

'You could so easily satisfy yourself, Mrs Balcarres, if you were to –'

'Give a laddie a penny to cast a stone, and see what happens,' said Lady Carnbee.

'But I am not sure that I have any desire to satisfy myself,' Aunt Mary said. And then there was a stir in the room, and I had to come out from my recess and open the door for the old ladies and see them downstairs, as they all went away – following one another. Mr Pitmilly gave his arm to Lady Carnbee, though she was always contradicting him; and so the tea-party dispersed. Aunt Mary came to the head of the stairs with her guests in an old-fashioned gracious way, while I went down with them to see that the maid was ready at the door. When I came back Aunt Mary was still standing in the recess looking out. Returning to my seat she said, with a kind of wistful look, 'Well, honey: and what is your opinion?'

'I have no opinion. I was reading my book all the time,' I said.

'And so you were, honey, and no' very civil; but all the same I ken well you heard every word we said.'

II

It was a night in June; dinner was long over, and had it been winter the maids would have been shutting up the house, and my Aunt Mary preparing to go upstairs to her room. But it was still clear daylight, that daylight out of which the sun has been long gone, and which has no longer any rose reflections, but all has sunk into a pearly neutral tint – a light which is daylight yet is not day. We had taken a turn in the garden after dinner, and now we had returned to what we called our usual occupations. My aunt was reading. The English post had come in, and she had got her *Times*, which was her great diversion. The *Scotsman* was her morning reading, but she liked her *Times* at night.

As for me, I too was at my usual occupation, which at that time was doing nothing. I had a book as usual, and was absorbed in it: but I was conscious of all that was going on all the same. The people strolled along the broad pavement, making remarks as they passed under the open window which came up into my story or my dream, and sometimes made me laugh. The tone and the faint sing-song, or rather chant, of the accent, which was 'a wee Fifish', was novel to me, and associated with holiday, and pleasant; and sometimes they said to each other something that was amusing, and often something that suggested

93

a whole story; but presently they began to drop off, the footsteps slackened, the voices died away. It was getting late, though the clear soft daylight went on and on. All through the lingering evening, which seemed to consist of interminable hours, long but not weary, drawn out as if the spell of the light and the outdoor life might never end, I had now and then, quite unawares, cast a glance at the mysterious window which my aunt and her friends had discussed, as I felt, though I dared not say it even to myself, rather foolishly. It caught my eye without any intention on my part, as I paused, as it were, to take breath, in the flowing and current of indistinguishable thoughts and things from without and within which carried me along. First it occurred to me, with a little sensation of discovery, how absurd to say it was not a window, a living window, one to see through! Why, then, had they never *seen* it, these old folk? I saw as I looked up suddenly the faint greyness as of visible space within – a room behind, certainly – dim, as it was natural a room should be on the other side of the street – quite indefinite: yet so clear that if someone were to come to the window there would be nothing surprising in it. For certainly there was a feeling of space behind the panes which these old half-blind ladies had disputed about whether they were glass or only fictitious panes marked on the wall. How silly! when eyes that could see could make it out in a minute. It was only a greyness at present, but it was unmistakable, a space that went back into gloom, as every room does when you look into it across a street. There were no curtains to show whether it was inhabited or not; but a room – oh, as distinctly as ever room was! I was pleased with myself, but said nothing, while Aunt Mary rustled her paper, waiting for a favourable moment to announce a discovery which settled her problem at once. Then I was carried away upon the stream again, and forgot the window, till somebody threw unawares a word from the outer world, 'I'm goin' hame; it'll soon be dark.' Dark! what was the fool thinking of? it never would be dark if one waited out, wandering in the soft air for hours longer; and then my eyes, acquiring easily that new habit, looked across the way again.

Ah, now! nobody indeed had come to the window; and no light had been lighted, seeing it was still beautiful to read by – a still, clear, colourless light; but the room inside had certainly widened. I could see the grey space and air a little deeper, and a sort of vision, very dim, of a wall, and something against it; something dark, with the blackness that a solid article, however indistinctly seen, takes in the lighter darkness that is only space – a large, black, dark thing coming out into the grey. I looked more intently, and made sure it was a piece of furniture, either a writing-table or perhaps a large bookcase. No doubt it must be the last, since this was part of the old Library. I never visited the old College Library, but I had seen such places before, and I could well imagine it to myself. How curious that for all the time these old people had looked at it, they had never seen this before!

It was more silent now, and my eyes, I suppose, had grown dim with gazing, doing my best to make it out, when suddenly Aunt Mary said, 'Will you ring the bell, my dear? I must have my lamp.'

'Your lamp?' I cried, 'when it is still daylight.' But then I gave another look at my window, and perceived with a start that the light had indeed changed: for now I saw nothing. It was still light, but there was so much change in the light that my room, with the grey space and the large shadowy bookcase, had gone out, and I saw them no more: for even a Scotch night in June, though it looks as if it would never end, does darken at the last. I had almost cried out, but checked myself, and rang the bell for Aunt Mary, and made up my mind I would say nothing till next morning, when to be sure naturally it would be more clear.

Next morning I rather think I forgot all about it – or was busy: or was more idle than usual: the two things meant nearly the same. At all events I thought no more of the window, though I still sat in my own, opposite to it, but occupied with some other fancy. Aunt Mary's visitors came as usual in the afternoon; but their talk was of other things, and for a day or two nothing at all happened to bring back my thoughts into this channel. It might be nearly a week before the subject came back, and once more it was old Lady Carnbee who set me thinking; not that she said anything upon that particular theme. But she was the last of my aunt's afternoon guests to go away, and when she rose to leave she threw up her hands, with those lively gesticulations which so many old Scotch ladies have. 'My faith!' said she, 'there is that bairn there still like a dream. Is the creature bewitched, Mary Balcarres? and is she bound to sit there by night and by day for the rest of her days? You should mind that there's things about, uncanny for women of our blood.'

I was too much startled at first to recognize that it was of me she was speaking. She was like a figure in a picture, with her pale face the colour of ashes, and the big pattern of the Spanish lace hanging half over it, and her hand held up, with the big diamond blazing at me from the inside of her uplifted palm. It was held up in surprise, but it looked as if it were raised in malediction; and the diamond threw out darts of light and glared and twinkled at me. If it had been in its right place it would not have mattered; but there, in the open of the hand! I started up, half in terror, half in wrath. And then the old lady laughed, and her hand dropped. 'I've wakened you to life, and broke the spell,' she said, nodding her old head at me, while the large black silk flowers of the lace waved and threatened. And she took my arm to go downstairs, laughing and bidding me be steady, and no' tremble and shake like a broken reed. 'You should be as steady as a rock at your age. I was like a young tree,' she said, leaning so heavily that my willowy girlish frame quivered – 'I was a support to virtue, like Pamela, in my time.'

'Aunt Mary, Lady Carnbee is a witch!' I cried, when I came back.

'Is that what you think, honey? well: maybe she once was,' said Aunt Mary, whom nothing surprised.

And it was that night once more after dinner, and after the post came in, and the *Times*, that I suddenly saw the Library window again. I had seen it every day – and noticed nothing; but tonight, still in a little tumult of mind over Lady Carnbee and her wicked diamond which wished me harm, and her lace which waved threats and warnings at me, I looked across the street, and there I saw quite plainly the room opposite, far more clear than before. I saw dimly that it must be a large room, and that the big piece of furniture against the wall was a writing-desk. That in a moment, when first my eyes rested upon it, was quite clear: a large old-fashioned escritoire, standing out into the room: and I knew by the shape of it that it had a great many pigeon-holes and little drawers in the back, and a large table for writing. There was one just like it in my father's library at home. It was such a surprise to see it all so clearly that I closed my eyes, for the moment almost giddy, wondering how papa's desk could have come here – and then when I reminded myself that this was nonsense, and that there were many such writing-tables besides papa's, and looked again – lo! it had all become quite vague and indistinct as it was at first; and I saw nothing but the blank window, of which the old ladies could never be certain whether it was filled up to avoid the window-tax, or whether it had ever been a window at all.

This occupied my mind very much, and yet I did not say anything to Aunt Mary. For one thing, I rarely saw anything at all in the early part of the day; but then that is natural: you can never see into a place from the outside, whether it is an empty room or a looking-glass, or people's eyes, or anything else that is mysterious, in the day. It has, I suppose, something to do with the light. But in the evening in June in Scotland – then is the time to see. For it is daylight, yet it is not day, and there is a quality in it which I cannot describe, it is so clear, as if every object was a reflection of itself.

I used to see more and more of the room as the days went on. The large escritoire stood out more and more into the space: with sometimes white glimmering things, which looked like papers, lying on it: and once or twice I was sure I saw a pile of books on the floor close to the writing-table, as if they had gilding upon them in broken specks, like old books. It was always about the time when the lads in the street began to call to each other that they were going home, and sometimes a shriller voice would come from one of the doors, bidding somebody to 'cry upon the laddies' to come back to their suppers. That was always the time I saw best, though it was close upon the moment when the veil seemed to fall and the clear radiance became less living, and all the sounds died out of the street, and Aunt Mary said in her soft voice, 'Honey! will you ring for the lamp?' She said 'honey' as people say 'darling': and I think it is a prettier word.

Then finally, while I sat one evening with my book in my hand, looking straight across the street, not distracted by anything, I saw a little movement within. It was not anyone visible – but everybody must know what it is to see the stir in the air, the little disturbance – you cannot tell what it is, but that it indicates someone there, even though you can see no one. Perhaps it is a shadow making just one flicker in the still place. You may look at an empty room and the furniture in it for hours, and then suddenly there will be the flicker, and you know that something has come into it. It might only be a dog or a cat; it might be, if that were possible, a bird flying across; but it is someone, something living, which is so different, so completely different, in a moment, from the things that are not living. It seemed to strike quite through me, and I gave a little cry. Then Aunt Mary stirred a little, and put down the huge newspaper that almost covered her from sight, and said, 'What is it, honey?' I cried 'Nothing,' with a little gasp, quickly, for I did not want to be disturbed just at this moment when somebody was coming! But I suppose she was not satisfied, for she got up and stood behind to see what it was, putting her hand on my shoulder. It was the softest touch in the world, but I could have flung it off angrily: for that moment everything was still again, and the place grew grey and I saw no more.

'Nothing,' I repeated, but I was so vexed I could have cried. 'I told you it was nothing, Aunt Mary. Don't you believe me, that you come to look – and spoil it all!'

I did not mean of course to say these last words; they were forced out of me. I was so much annoyed to see it all melt away like a dream: for it was no dream, but as real as – as real as – myself or anything I ever saw.

She gave my shoulder a little pat with her hand. 'Honey,' she said, 'were you looking at something? Is't that? Is't that?' 'Is it what?' I wanted to say, shaking off her hand, but something in me stopped me: for I said nothing at all, and she went quietly back to her place. I suppose she must have rung the bell herself, for immediately I felt the soft flood of the light behind me, and the evening outside dimmed down, as it did every night, and I saw nothing more.

It was next day, I think, in the afternoon that I spoke. It was brought on by something she said about her fine work. 'I get a mist before my eyes,' she said; 'you will have to learn my old lace stitches, honey – for I soon will not see to draw the threads.'

'Oh, I hope you will keep your sight,' I cried, without thinking what I was saying. I was then young and very matter-of-fact. I had not found out that one may mean something, yet not half or a hundredth part of what one seems to mean: and even then probably hoping to be contradicted if it is anyhow against one's self.

'My sight!' she said, looking up at me with a look that was almost angry; 'there is no question of losing my sight – on the contrary, my eyes are very strong. I may not see to draw fine threads, but I see at a distance as well as ever I did – as well as you do.'

'I did not mean any harm, Aunt Mary,' I said. 'I thought you said – But how can your sight be as good as ever when you are in doubt about that window? I can see into the room as clear as –' My voice wavered, for I had just looked up and across the street, and I could have sworn that there was no window at all, but only a false image of one painted on the wall.

'Ah!' she said, with a little tone of keenness and of surprise: and she half rose up, throwing down her work hastily, as if she meant to come to me: then, perhaps seeing the bewildered look on my face, she paused and hesitated – 'Ay, honey!' she said, 'have you got so far ben as that?'

What did she mean? Of course I knew all the old Scotch phrases as well as I knew myself; but it is a comfort to take refuge in a little ignorance, and I know I pretended not to understand whenever I was put out. 'I don't know what you mean by "far ben",' I cried out, very impatient. I don't know what might have followed, but someone just then came to call, and she could only give me a look before she went forward, putting out her hand to her visitor. It was a very soft look, but anxious, and as if she did not know what to do: and she shook her head a very little, and I thought, though there was a smile on her face, there was something wet about her eyes. I retired into my recess, and nothing more was said.

But it was very tantalizing that it should fluctuate so; for sometimes I saw that room quite plain and clear – quite as clear as I could see papa's library, for example, when I shut my eyes. I compared it naturally to my father's study, because of the shape of the writing-table, which, as I tell you, was the same as his. At times I saw the papers on the table quite plain, just as I had seen his papers many a day. And the little pile of books on the floor at the foot – not ranged regularly in order, but put down one above the other, with all their angles going different ways, and a speck of the old gilding shining here and there. And then again at other times I saw nothing, absolutely nothing, and was no better than the old ladies who had peered over my head, drawing their eyelids together, and arguing that the window had been shut up because of the old long-abolished window tax, or else that it had never been a window at all. It annoyed me very much at those dull moments to feel that I too puckered up my eyelids and saw no better than they.

Aunt Mary's old ladies came and went day after day while June went on. I was to go back in July, and I felt that I should be very unwilling indeed to leave until I had quite cleared up – as I was indeed in the way of doing – the mystery of that window which changed so strangely and appeared quite a different thing, not only to different people, but to the same eyes at different times. Of course I said to myself it must simply be an effect of the light. And yet I did not quite like that explanation either, but would have been better pleased to make out to myself that it was some superiority in me which made it so clear to me, if it were only the great superiority of young eyes over old – though that was not quite enough to satisfy me, seeing it was a superiority which I shared with every little lass and lad in the street. I rather wanted, I believe, to think that there was some particular insight in me which gave clearness to my sight – which was a most impertinent assumption, but really did not mean half the harm it seems to mean when it is put down here in black and white. I had several times again, however, seen the room quite plain, and made out that it was a large room, with a great picture in a dim gilded frame hanging on the farther wall, and many other pieces of solid furniture making a blackness here and there, besides the great escritoire against the wall, which had evidently been placed near the window for the sake of the light. One thing became visible to me after another, till I almost thought I should end by being able to read the old lettering on one of the big volumes which projected from the others and caught the light; but this was all preliminary to the great event which happened about Midsummer Day – the day of St John, which was once so much thought of as a festival, but now means nothing at all in Scotland any more than any other of the saints' days: which I shall always think a great pity and loss to Scotland, whatever Aunt Mary may say.

III

It was about midsummer, I cannot say exactly to a day when, but near that time, when the great event happened. I had grown very well acquainted by this time with that large dim room. Not only the escritoire, which was very plain to me now, with the papers upon it, and the books at its foot, but the great picture that hung against the farther wall, and various other shadowy pieces of furniture, especially a chair which one evening I saw had been moved into the space before the escritoire – a little change which made my heart beat, for it spoke so distinctly of someone who must have been there, the someone who had already made me start, two or three times before, by some vague shadow of him or thrill of him which made a sort of movement in the silent space: a movement which made me sure that next minute I must see something or hear something which would explain the whole – if it were not that something always happened outside to stop it, at the very moment of its accomplishment. I had no warning this time of movement or shadow. I had been looking into the room very attentively a little while before, and had made out everything almost clearer than ever; and then had bent my attention again on my book, and read a chapter or two at a most exciting period of the story: and consequently had quite left St Rule's, and the High Street, and the College Library, and was really in a South American forest, almost throttled by the flowery creepers, and treading softly lest I should put my foot on a scorpion or a dangerous snake. At this moment something suddenly calling my attention to the outside, I looked across, and then, with a start, sprang up, for I could not contain myself. I don't know what I said, but enough to startle the people in the room, one of whom was old Mr Pitmilly. They all looked round upon me to ask what was the matter. And when I gave my usual answer of 'Nothing', sitting down again shamefaced but very much excited, Mr Pitmilly got up and came forward, and looked out, apparently to see what was the cause. He saw nothing, for he went back again, and I could hear him telling Aunt Mary not to be alarmed, for Missy had fallen into a doze with the heat, and had startled herself waking up, at which they all laughed: another

101

time I could have killed him for his impertinence, but my mind was too much taken up now to pay any attention. My head was throbbing and my heart beating. I was in such high excitement, however, that to restrain myself completely, to be perfectly silent, was more easy to me then than at any other time of my life. I waited until the old gentleman had taken his seat again, and then I looked back. Yes, there he was! I had not been deceived. I knew then, when I looked across, that this was what I had been looking for all the time – that I had known he was there, and had been waiting for him every time there was that flicker of movement in the room – him and no one else. And there at last, just as I had expected, he was. I don't know that in reality I ever had expected him, or anyone: but this was what I felt when, suddenly looking into that curious dim room, I saw him there.

He was sitting in the chair, which he must have placed for himself, or which someone else in the dead of night when nobody was looking must have set for him, in front of the escritoire – with the back of his head towards me, writing. The light fell upon him from the left hand and therefore upon his shoulders and the side of his head, which, however, was too much turned away to show anything of his face. Oh, how strange that there should be someone staring at him as I was doing, and he never to turn his head, to make a movement! If anyone stood and looked at me, were I in the soundest sleep that ever was, I would wake, I would jump up, I would feel it through everything. But there he sat and never moved. You are not to suppose, though I said the light fell upon him from the left hand, that there was very much light. There never is in a room you are looking into like that across the street; but there was enough to see him by – the outline of his figure dark and solid, seated in the chair, and the fairness of his head visible faintly, a clear spot against the dimness. I saw this outline against the dim gilding of the frame of the large picture which hung on the farther wall.

I sat all the time the visitors were there, in a sort of rapture, gazing at this figure. I knew no reason why I should be so much moved. In an ordinary way, to see a student at an opposite window quietly doing his work might have interested me a little, but certainly it would not have moved me in any such way. It is always interesting to have a glimpse like this of an unknown life – to see so much and yet know so little, and to wonder, perhaps, what the man is doing, and why he never turns his head. One would go to the window – but not too close, lest he should see you and think you were spying on him – and one would ask, Is he still there? is he writing, writing always? I wonder what he is writing! And it would be a great amusement – but no more. This was not my feeling at all in the present case. It was a sort of breathless watch, an absorption. I did not feel that I had eyes for anything else, or any room in my mind for another thought. I no longer heard, as I generally did, the stories and the wise remarks (or foolish) of Aunt Mary's old ladies or Mr Pitmilly. I heard only a murmur behind me, the interchange of voices, one softer, one sharper; but it was not as in the time when I sat reading and heard every word, till the story in my book, and the stories they were telling (what they said almost always shaped into stories), were all mingled into each other, and the hero in the novel became somehow the hero (or more likely heroine) of them all. But I took no notice of what they were saying now. And it was not that there was anything very interesting to look at, except the fact that he was there. He did nothing to keep up the absorption of my thoughts. He moved just so much as a man will do when he is very busily writing, thinking of nothing else. There was a faint turn of his head as he went from one side to another of the page he was writing; but it appeared to be a long, long page which never wanted turning. Just a little inclination when he was at the end of the line, outward, and then a little inclination inward when he began the next. That was little enough to keep one gazing. But I suppose it was the gradual course of events leading up to this, the finding out of one thing after another as the eyes got accustomed to the vague light: first the room itself, and then the writing-table, and then the other furniture, and last of all the human inhabitant who gave it all meaning. This was all so interesting that it was like a country which one had discovered. And then the extraordinary blindness of the other people who disputed among themselves whether it was a window at all! I did not, I am sure, wish to be disrespectful, and I was very fond of my Aunt Mary, and I liked Mr Pitmilly well enough, and I was afraid of Lady Carnbee. But yet to think of the – I know I ought not to say stupidity – the blindness of them, the foolishness, the insensibility! discussing it as if a thing that your eyes could see was a thing to discuss!

It would have been unkind to think it was because they were old and their faculties had dimmed. It is so sad to think that the faculties grow dim, that such a woman as my Aunt Mary should fail in seeing, or hearing, or feeling, that I would not have dwelt on it for a moment, it would have seemed so cruel! And then such a clever old lady as Lady Carnbee, who could see through a millstone, people said – and Mr Pitmilly, such an old man of the world. It did indeed bring tears to my eyes to think that all those clever people, solely by reason of being no longer young as I was, should have the simplest things shut out from them; and for all their wisdom and their knowledge be unable to see what a girl like me could see so easily. I was too much grieved for them to dwell upon that thought, and half ashamed, though perhaps half proud too, to be so much better off than they.

All those thoughts flitted through my mind as I sat and gazed across the street. And I felt there was so much going on in that room across the street! He was so absorbed in his writing, never looked up, never paused for a word, never turned round in his chair, or got up and walked about the room as my father did. Papa is a great writer, everybody says: but he would have come to the window and looked out, he would have drummed with his fingers on the pane, he would have watched a fly and helped it over a difficulty, and played with the fringe of the curtain, and done a dozen other nice, pleasant, foolish things, till the next sentence took shape. 'My dear, I am waiting for a word,' he would say to my mother when she looked at him, with a question why he was so idle, in her eyes; and then he would laugh, and go back again to his writing-table. But He over there never stopped at all. It was like a fascination. I could not take my eyes from him and that little scarcely perceptible movement he made, turning his head. I trembled with impatience to see him turn the page, or perhaps throw down his finished sheet on the floor, as somebody looking into a window like me once saw Sir Walter do, sheet after sheet. I should have cried out if this Unknown had done that. I should not have been able to help myself, whoever had been present; and gradually I got into such a state of suspense waiting for it to be done that my head grew hot and my hands cold. And then, just when there was a little movement of his elbow, as if he were about to do this, to be called away by Aunt

Mary to see Lady Carnbee to the door! I believe I did not hear her till she had called me three times, and then I stumbled up, all flushed and hot, and nearly crying. When I came out from the recess to give the old lady my arm (Mr Pitmilly had gone away some time before), she put up her hand and stroked my cheek. 'What ails the bairn?' she said; 'she's fevered. You must not let her sit her lane in the window, Mary Balcarres. You and me know what comes of that.' Her old fingers had a strange touch, cold like something not living, and I felt that dreadful diamond sting me on the cheek.

I do not say that this was not just a part of my excitement and suspense; and I know it is enough to make anyone laugh when the excitement was all about an unknown man writing in a room on the other side of the way, and my impatience because he never came to an end of the page. If you think I was not quite as well aware of this as anyone could be! but the worst was that this dreadful old lady felt my heart beating against her arm that was within mine. 'You are just in a dream,' she said to me, with her old voice close at my ear as we went downstairs. 'I don't know who it is about, but it's bound to be some man that is not worth it. If you were wise you would think of him no more.'

'I am thinking of no man!' I said, half crying. 'It is very unkind and dreadful of you to say so, Lady Carnbee. I never thought of – any man, in all my life!' I cried in a passion of indignation. The old lady clung tighter to my arm, and pressed it to her, not unkindly.

'Poor little bird,' she said, 'how it's strugglin' and flutterin'! I'm not sayin' but what it's more dangerous when it's all for a dream.'

She was not at all unkind; but I was very angry and excited, and would scarcely shake that old pale hand which she put out to me from her carriage window when I had helped her in. I was angry with her, and I was afraid of the diamond, which looked up from under her finger as if it saw through and through me; and whether you believe me or not, I am certain that it stung me again – a sharp malignant prick, oh full of meaning! She never wore gloves, but only black lace mittens, through which that horrible diamond gleamed.

I ran upstairs – she had been the last to go – and Aunt Mary had gone to get ready for dinner, for it was late. I hurried to my place, and looked across, with my heart beating more than ever. I made quite sure

I should see the finished sheet lying white upon the floor. But what I gazed at was only the dim blank of that window which they said was no window. The light had changed in some wonderful way during that five minutes I had been gone, and there was nothing, nothing, not a reflection, not a glimmer. It looked exactly as they all said, the blank form of a window painted on the wall. It was too much: I sat down in my excitement and cried as if my heart would break. I felt that they had done something to it, that it was not natural that I could not bear their unkindness – even Aunt Mary. They thought it not good for me! not good for me! and they had done something – even Aunt Mary herself – and that wicked diamond that hid itself in Lady Carnbee's hand. Of course I knew all this was ridiculous as well as you could tell me; but I was exasperated by the disappointment and the sudden stop to all my excited feelings, and I could not bear it. It was more strong than I.

I was late for dinner, and naturally there were some traces in my eyes that I had been crying when I came into the full light in the dining-room, where Aunt Mary could look at me at her pleasure, and I could not run away. She said, 'Honey, you have been shedding tears. I'm loth, loth that a bairn of your mother's should be made to shed tears in my house.'

'I have not been made to shed tears,' cried I; and then, to save myself another fit of crying, I burst out laughing and said, 'I am afraid of that dreadful diamond on old Lady Carnbee's hand. It bites – I am sure it bites! Aunt Mary, look here.'

'You foolish lassie,' Aunt Mary said; but she looked at my cheek under the light of the lamp, and then she gave it a little pat with her soft hand. 'Go away with you, you silly bairn. There is no bite; but a flushed cheek, my honey, and a wet eye. You must just read out my paper to me after dinner when the post is in: and we'll have no more thinking and no more dreaming for tonight.'

'Yes, Aunt Mary,' said I. But I knew what would happen; for when she opens up her *Times*, all full of the news of the world, and the speeches and things which she takes an interest in, though I cannot tell why – she forgets. And as I kept very quiet and made not a sound, she forgot tonight what she had said, and the curtain hung a little more over me than usual, and I sat down in my recess as if I had been a hundred miles away. And my heart gave a great jump, as if it would have come out of my breast; for he was there. But not as he had been in the morning – I suppose the light, perhaps, was not good enough to go on with his work without a lamp or candles – for he had turned away from the table and was fronting the window, sitting leaning back in his chair, and turning his head to me. Not to me – he knew nothing about me. I thought he was not looking at anything; but with his face turned my way. My heart was in my mouth: it was so unexpected, so strange! though why it should have seemed strange I know not, for there was no communication between him and me that it should have moved me; and what could be more natural than that a man, wearied of his work, and feeling the want perhaps of more light, and yet that it was not dark enough to light a lamp, should turn round in his own chair, and rest a little, and think – perhaps of nothing at all? Papa always says he is thinking of nothing at all. He says things blow through his mind as if the doors were open, and he has no responsibility. What sort of things were blowing through this man's mind? or was he thinking, still thinking, of what he had been writing and going on with it still? The thing that troubled me most was that I could not make out his face. It is very difficult to do so when you see a person only through two windows, your own and his. I wanted very much to recognize him afterwards if I should chance to meet him in the street. If he had only stood up and moved about the room, I should have made out the rest of his figure, and then I should have known him again; or if he had only come to the window (as Papa always did), then I should have seen his face clearly enough to have recognized him. But, to be sure, he did not see any need to do anything in order that I might recognize him, for he did not know I existed; and probably if he had known I was watching him, he would have been annoyed and gone away.

But he was as immovable there facing the window as he had been seated at the desk. Sometimes he made a little faint stir with a hand or a foot, and I held my breath, hoping he was about to rise from his chair – but he never did it. And with all the efforts I made I could not be sure of his face. I puckered my eyelids together as old Miss Jeanie did who was shortsighted, and I put my hands on each side of my face to concentrate the light on him: but it was all in vain. Either the face changed as I sat staring, or else it was the light that was not good enough, or I don't know what it was. His hair seemed to me light – certainly there was no dark line about his head, as there would have been had it been very dark – and I saw, where it came across the old gilt frame on the wall behind, that it must be fair: and I am almost sure he had no beard. Indeed I am sure that he had no beard, for the outline of his face was distinct enough; and the daylight was still quite clear out of doors, so that I recognized perfectly a baker's boy who was on the pavement opposite, and whom I should have known again whenever I had met him: as if it was of the least importance to recognize a baker's boy! There was one thing, however, rather curious about this boy. He had been throwing stones at something or somebody. In St Rule's they have a great way of throwing stones at each other, and I suppose there had been a battle. I suppose also that he had one stone in his hand left over from the battle, and his roving eye took in all the incidents of the street to judge where he could throw it with most effect and mischief. But apparently he found nothing worthy of it in the street, for he suddenly turned round with a flick under his leg to show his cleverness, and aimed it straight at the window. I remarked without remarking that it struck with a hard sound and without any breaking glass, and fell straight down on the pavement. But I took no notice of this even in my mind, so intently was I watching the figure within, which moved not nor took the slightest notice, and remained just as dimly clear, as perfectly seen, yet as undistinguishable, as before. And then the light began to fail a little, not diminishing the prospect within, but making it still less distinct than it had been.

Then I jumped up, feeling Aunt Mary's hand upon my shoulder. 'Honey,' she said, 'I asked you twice to ring the bell; but you did not hear me.'

'Oh, Aunt Mary!' I cried in great penitence, but turning again to the window in spite of myself.

'You must come away from there: you must come away from there,' she said, almost as if she were angry: and then her soft voice grew softer, and she gave me a kiss: 'never mind about the lamp, honey: I have rung myself, and it is coming; but, silly bairn, you must not aye be dreaming – your little head will turn.'

All the answer I made, for I could scarcely speak, was to give a little wave with my hand to the window on the other side of the street.

She stood there patting me softly on the shoulder for a whole minute or more, murmuring something that sounded like, 'She must go away, she must go away.' Then she said, always with her hand soft on my shoulder, 'Like a dream when one awaketh.' And when I looked again, I saw the blank of an opaque surface and nothing more.

Aunt Mary asked me no more questions. She made me come into the room and sit in the light and read something to her. But I did not know what I was reading, for there suddenly came into my mind and took possession of it, the thud of the stone upon the window, and its descent straight down, as if from some hard substance that threw it off: though I had myself seen it strike upon the glass of the panes across the way.

IV

I am afraid I continued in a state of great exaltation and commotion of mind for some time. I used to hurry through the day till the evening came, when I could watch my neighbour through the window opposite. I did not talk much to anyone, and I never said a word about my own questions and wonderings. I wondered who he was, what he was doing, and why he never came till the evening (or very rarely); and I also wondered much to what house the room belonged in which he sat. It seemed to form a portion of the old College Library, as I have often said. The window was one of the line of windows which I understood lighted the large hall; but whether this room belonged to the library itself, or how its occupant gained access to it, I could not tell. I made up my mind that it must open out of the hall, and that the gentleman must be the Librarian or one of his assistants, perhaps kept busy all the day in his official duties, and only able to get to his desk and do his own private work in the evening. One has heard of so many things like that – a man who had to take up some other kind of work for his living, and then when his leisure-time came, gave it all up to something he really loved – some study or some book he was writing. My father himself at one time had been like that. He had been in the Treasury all day, and then in the evening wrote his books, which made him famous. His daughter, however little she might know of other things, could not but know that! But it discouraged me very much when somebody pointed out to me one day in the street an old gentleman who wore a wig and took a great deal of snuff, and said, That's the Librarian of the old College. It gave me a great shock for a moment; but then I remembered that an old gentleman generally has assistants, and that he must be one of them.

Gradually I became quite sure of this. There was another small window above, which twinkled very much when the sun shone, and looked a very kindly bright little window, above that dullness of the other which hid so much. I made up my mind this was the window of his other room, and that these two chambers at the end of the beautiful hall were really beautiful for him to live in, so near all the books, and so retired and quiet, that nobody knew of them. What a fine thing for him! and you could see what use he made of his good fortune as he sat there, so constant at his writing for hours together. Was it a book he was writing, or could it be perhaps poems? This was a thought which made my heart beat; but I concluded with much regret that it could not be poems, because no one could possibly write poems like that, straight off, without pausing for a word or a rhyme. Had they been poems he must have risen up, he must have paced about the room or come to the window as Papa did – not that Papa wrote poems: he always said, 'I am not worthy even to speak of such prevailing mysteries', shaking his head – which gave me a wonderful admiration and almost awe of a poet, who was thus much greater even than Papa. But I could not believe that a poet could have kept still for hours and hours like that. What could it be then? Perhaps it was history; that is a great thing to work at, but you would not perhaps need to move nor to stride up and down, or look out upon the sky and the wonderful light.

He did move now and then, however, though he never came to the window. Sometimes, as I have said, he would turn round in his chair and turn his face towards it, and sit there for a long time musing when the light had begun to fail, and the world was full of that strange day which was night, that light without colour, in which everything was so clearly visible, and there were no shadows. 'It was between the night and the day, when the fairy folk have power.' This was the after-light of the wonderful, long, long summer evening, the light without shadows. It had a spell in it, and sometimes it made me afraid: and all manner of strange thoughts seemed to come in, and I always felt that if only we had a little more vision in our eyes we might see beautiful folk walking about in it, who were not of our world. I thought most likely he saw them from the way he sat there looking out: and this made my head expand with the most curious sensation, as if of pride that, though I could not see, he did, and did not even require to come to the window, as I did, sitting close in the depth of the recess, with my eyes upon him, and almost seeing things through his eyes.

I was so much absorbed in these thoughts and in watching him every evening – for now he never missed an evening, but was always there – that people began to remark that I was looking pale and that I could not be well, for I paid no attention when they talked to me, and did not care to go out, nor to join the other girls for their tennis, nor to do anything that others did; and some said to Aunt Mary that I was quickly losing all the ground I had gained, and that she could never send me back to my mother with a white face like that. Aunt Mary had begun to look at me anxiously for some time before that, and, I am sure, held secret consultations over me, sometimes with the doctor, and sometimes with her old ladies, who thought they knew more about young girls than even the doctors. And I could hear them saying to her that I wanted diversion, that I must be diverted, and that she must take me out more, and give a party, and that when the summer visitors began to come there would perhaps be a ball or two, or Lady Carnbee would get up a picnic. 'And there's my young lord coming home,' said the old lady whom they called Miss Jeanie, 'and I never knew the young lassie yet that would not cock up her bonnet at the sight of a young lord.'

But Aunt Mary shook her head. 'I would not lippen much to the young lord,' she said. 'His mother is sore set upon siller for him; and my poor bit honey has no fortune to speak of. No, we must not fly so high as the young lord; but I will gladly take her about the country to see the old castles and towers. It will perhaps rouse her up a little.'

'And if that does not answer we must think of something else,' the old lady said.

I heard them perhaps that day because they were talking of me, which is always so effective a way of making you hear – for latterly I had not been paying any attention to what they were saying; and I thought to myself how little they knew, and how little I cared about even the old castles and curious houses, having something else in my mind. But just about that time Mr Pitmilly came in, who was always a friend to me, and, when he heard them talking, he managed to stop them and turn the conversation into another channel. And after a while, when the ladies were gone away, he came up to my recess, and gave a glance right over my head. And then he asked my Aunt Mary if ever she had settled her question about the window opposite, 'that you thought was a window sometimes, and then not a window, and many curious things', the old gentleman said.

My Aunt Mary gave me another very wistful look; and then she said, 'Indeed, Mr Pitmilly, we are just where we were, and I am quite as unsettled as ever; and I think my niece she has taken up my views, for I see her many a time looking across and wondering, and I am not clear now what her opinion is.'

'My opinion!' I said, 'Aunt Mary.' I could not help being a little scornful, as one is when one is very young. 'I have no opinion. There is not only a window but there is a room, and I could show you–' I was going to say, 'show you the gentleman who sits and writes in it', but I stopped, not knowing what they might say, and looked from one to another. 'I could tell you – all the furniture that is in it,' I said. And then I felt something like a flame that went over my face, and that all at once my cheeks were burning. I thought they gave a little glance at each other, but that may have been folly. 'There is a great picture, in a big dim frame,' I said, feeling a little breathless, 'on the wall opposite the window–'

'Is there so?' said Mr Pitmilly, with a little laugh. And he said, 'Now I will tell you what we'll do. You know that there is a conversation party, or whatever they call it, in the big room tonight, and it will be all open and lighted up. And it is a handsome room, and two–three things well worth looking at. I will just step along after we have all got our dinner, and take you over to the party, madam – Missy and you –'

'Dear me!' said Aunt Jane. 'I have not gone to a party for more years than I would like to say – and never once to the Library Hall.' Then she gave a little shiver, and said quite low, 'I could not go there.'

'Then you will just begin again tonight, madam,' said Mr Pitmilly, taking no notice of this, 'and a proud man will I be leading in Mistress Balcarres that was once the pride of the ball!'

'Ah, once!' said Aunt Mary, with a low little laugh and then a sigh. 'And we'll not say how long ago'; and after that she made a pause, looking always at me: and then she said, 'I accept your offer, and we'll put on our braws; and I hope you will have no occasion to think shame of us. But why not take your dinner here?'

That was how it was settled, and the old gentleman went away to dress, looking quite pleased. But I came to Aunt Mary as soon as he was gone, and besought her not to make me go. 'I like the long bonnie night and the light that lasts so long. And I cannot bear to dress up and go out, wasting it all in a stupid party. I hate parties, Aunt Mary!' I cried, 'and I would far rather stay here.'

'My honey,' she said, taking both my hands, 'I know it will maybe be a blow to you – but it's better so.'

'How could it be a blow to me?' I cried; 'but I would far rather not go.'

'You'll just go with me, honey, just this once: it is not often I go out. You will go with me this one night, just this one night, my honey sweet.'

I am sure there were tears in Aunt Mary's eyes, and she kissed me between the words. There was nothing more that I could say; but how I grudged the evening! A mere party, a conversazione (when all the College was away, too, and nobody to make conversation!), instead of my enchanted hour at my window and the soft strange light, and the dim face looking out, which kept me wondering and wondering what was he thinking of, what was he looking for, who was he? all one wonder and mystery and question, through the long, long, slowly fading night!

It occurred to me, however, when I was dressing – though I was so sure that he would prefer his solitude to everything – that he might perhaps, it was just possible, be there. And when I thought of that, I took out my white frock – though Janet had laid out my blue one – and my little pearl necklace which I had thought was too good to wear. They were not very large pearls, but they were real pearls, and very even and lustrous though they were small; and though I did not think much of my appearance then, there must have been something about me – pale as I was but apt to colour in a moment, with my dress so white, and my pearls so white, and my hair all shadowy – perhaps, that was pleasant to look at: for even old Mr Pitmilly had a strange look in his eyes, as if he was not only pleased but sorry too, perhaps thinking me a creature that would have troubles in this life, though I was so young and knew them not. And when Aunt Mary looked at me, there was a little quiver about her mouth. She herself had on her pretty lace and her white hair very nicely done, and looking her best. As for Mr Pitmilly, he had a beautiful fine French cambric frill to his shirt, plaited in the most minute plaits, and with a diamond pin in it which sparkled as much as Lady Carnbee's ring; but this was a fine frank, kindly stone, that looked you straight in the face and sparkled, with the light dancing in it as if it were pleased to see you, and to be shining on that old gentleman's honest and faithful breast: for he had been one of Aunt Mary's lovers in their early days, and still thought there was nobody like her in the world.

I had got into quite a happy commotion of mind by the time we set out across the street in the soft light of the evening to the Library Hall. Perhaps, after all, I should see him, and see the room which I was so well acquainted with, and find out why he sat there so constantly and never was seen abroad. I thought I might even hear what he was working at, which would be such a pleasant thing to tell Papa when I went home. A friend of mine at St Rule's – oh, far, far more busy than you ever were, Papa – and then my father would laugh as he always did, and say he was but an idler and never busy at all.

The room was all light and bright, flowers wherever flowers could be, and the long lines of the books that went along the walls on each side, lighting up wherever there was a line of gilding or an ornament, with a little response. It dazzled me at first all that light: but I was very eager, though I kept very quiet, looking round to see if perhaps in any corner, in the middle of any group, he would be there. I did not expect to see him among the ladies. He would not be with them – he was too studious, too silent: but, perhaps among that circle of grey heads at the upper end of the room – perhaps –

No: I am not sure that it was not half a pleasure to me to make quite sure that there was not one whom I could take for him, who was at all like my vague image of him. No: it was absurd to think that he would be here, amid all that sound of voices, under the glare of that light. I felt a little proud to think that he was in his room as usual, doing his work, or thinking so deeply over it, as when he turned round in his chair with his face to the light.

I was thus getting a little composed and quiet in my mind, for now that the expectation of seeing him was over, though it was a disappointment, it was a satisfaction too – when Mr Pitmilly came up to me, holding out his arm. 'Now,' he said, 'I am going to take you to see the curiosities.' I thought to myself that after I had seen them and spoken to everybody I knew, Aunt Mary would let me go home, so I went very willingly, though I did not care for the curiosities. Something, however, struck me strangely as we walked up the room. It was the air, rather fresh and strong, from an open window at the east end of the hall. How should there be a window there? I hardly saw what it meant for the first moment, but it blew in my face as if there was some meaning in it, and I felt very uneasy without seeing why.

Then there was another thing that startled me. On that side of the wall which was to the street there seemed no windows at all. A long line of bookcases filled it from end to end. I could not see what that meant either, but it confused me. I was altogether confused. I felt as if I was in a strange country, not knowing where I was going, not knowing what I might find out next. If there were no windows on the wall to the street, where was my window? My heart, which had been jumping up and calming down again all this time, gave a great leap at this, as if it would come out of me – but I did not know what it could mean.

Then we stopped before a glass case, and Mr Pitmilly showed me some things in it. I could not pay much attention to them. My head was going round and round. I heard his voice going on, and then myself speaking with a queer sound that was hollow in my ears; but I did not know what I was saying or what he was saying. Then he took me to the very end of the room, the east end, saying something that I caught – that I was pale, that the air would do me good. The air was blowing full on me, lifting the lace of my dress, lifting my hair, almost chilly. The window opened into the pale daylight, into the little lane that ran by the end of the building. Mr Pitmilly went on talking, but I could not make out a word he said. Then I heard my own voice, speaking through it, though I did not seem to be aware that I was speaking. 'Where is my window? – where, then, is my window?' I seemed to be saying, and I turned right round, dragging him with me, still holding his arm. As I did this my eye fell upon something at last which I knew. It was a large picture in a broad frame, hanging against the farther wall.

What did it mean? Oh, what did it mean? I turned round again to the open window at the east end, and to the daylight, the strange light without any shadow, that was all round about this lighted hall, holding it like a bubble that would burst, like something that was not real. The real place was the room I knew, in which that picture was hanging, where the writing-table was, and where he sat with his face to the light. But where was the light and the window through which it came? I think my senses must have left me. I went up to the picture which I knew, and then I walked straight across the room, always dragging Mr Pitmilly, whose face was pale, but who did not struggle but allowed me to lead him, straight across to where the window was – where the window was not – where there was no sign of it. 'Where is my window? – where is my window?' I said. And all the time I was sure that I was in a dream, and these lights were all some theatrical illusion, and the people talking; and nothing real but the pale, pale, watching, lingering day standing by to wait until that foolish bubble should burst.

'My dear,' said Mr Pitmilly, 'my dear! Mind that you are in public. Mind where you are. You must not make an outcry and frighten your Aunt Mary. Come away with me. Come away, my dear young lady! and you'll take a seat for a minute or two and compose yourself; and I'll get you an ice or a little wine.' He kept patting my hand, which was on his arm, and looking at me very anxiously. 'Bless me! bless me! I never thought it would have this effect,' he said.

But I would not allow him to take me away in that direction. I went to the picture again and looked at it without seeing it: and then I went across the room again, with some kind of wild thought that if I insisted I should find it. 'My window – my window!' I said.

There was one of the professors standing there, and he heard me. 'The window!' said he. 'Ah, you've been taken in with what appears outside. It was put there to be in uniformity with the window on the stair. But it never was a real window. It is just behind that bookcase. Many people are taken in by it,' he said.

His voice seemed to sound from somewhere far away, and as if it would go on for ever; and the hall swam in a dazzle of shining and of noises round me; and the daylight through the open window grew greyer, waiting till it should be over, and the bubble burst.

V

It was Mr Pitmilly who took me home; or rather it was I who took him, pushing him on a little in front of me, holding fast to his arm, not waiting for Aunt Mary or anyone. We came out into the daylight again outside, I, without even a cloak or a shawl, with my bare arms, and uncovered head, and the pearls round my neck. There was the rush of the people about, and a baker's boy, that baker's boy, stood right in my way and cried, 'Here's a braw ane!' shouting to the others: the words struck me somehow, as his stone had struck the window, without any reason. But I did not mind the people staring, and hurried across the street, with Mr Pitmilly half a step in advance. The door was open, and Janet standing in it, looking out to see what she could see of the ladies in their grand dresses. She gave a shriek when she saw me hurrying across the street; but I brushed past her, and pushed Mr Pitmilly up the stairs, and took him breathless to the recess, where I threw myself down on the seat, feeling as if I could not have gone another step farther, and waved my hand across to the window. 'There! There!' I cried. Ah! there it was – not that senseless mob – not the theatres and the gas, and the people all in a murmur and clang of talking. Never in

117

all these days had I seen that room so clearly. There was a faint tone of light behind, as if it might have been a reflection from some of those vulgar lights in the hall, and he sat against it, calm, wrapped in his thoughts, with his face turned to the window. Nobody but must have seen him. Janet could have seen him had I called her upstairs. It was like a picture, all the things I knew, and the same attitude, and the atmosphere, full of quietness, not disturbed by anything. I pulled Mr Pitmilly's arm before I let him go – 'You see, you see!' I cried. He gave me the most bewildered look, as if he would have liked to cry. He saw nothing! I was sure of that from his eyes. He was an old man, and there was no vision in him. If I had called up Janet, she would have seen it all. 'My dear!' he said. 'My dear!' waving his hands in a helpless way.

'He has been there all these nights,' I cried, 'and I thought you could tell me who he was and what he was doing; and that he might have taken me in to that room, and showed me, that I might tell Papa. Papa would understand, he would like to hear. Oh, can't you tell me what work he is doing, Mr Pitmilly? He never lifts his head as long as the light throws a shadow, and then when it is like this he turns round and thinks, and takes a rest!'

Mr Pitmilly was trembling, whether it was with cold or I know not what. He said, with a shake in his voice, 'My dear young lady – my dear –' and then stopped and looked at me as if he were going to cry. 'It's peetiful, it's peetiful,' he said; and then in another voice, 'I am going across there again to bring your Aunt Mary home; do you understand, my poor little thing, my— I am going to bring her home – you will be better when she is here.' I was glad when he went away, as he could not see anything: and I sat alone in the dark which was not dark, but quite clear light – light like nothing I ever saw. How clear it was in that room! not glaring like the gas and the voices, but so quiet, everything so visible, as if it were in another world. I heard a little rustle behind me, and there was Janet, standing staring at me with two big eyes wide open. She was only a little older than I was. I called to her, 'Janet, come here, come here, and you will see him – come here and see him!' impatient that she should be so shy and keep behind. 'Oh, my bonnie young leddy!' she said, and burst out crying. I stamped my foot at her, in my indignation that she would not come, and she fled

118

before me with a rustle and swing of haste, as if she were afraid. None of them, none of them! not even a girl like myself, with the sight in her eyes, would understand. I turned back again, and held out my hands to him sitting there, who was the only one that knew. 'Oh,' I said, 'say something to me! I don't know who you are, or what you are: but you're lonely and so am I; and I only – feel for you. Say something to me!' I neither hoped that he would hear, nor expected any answer. How could he hear, with the street between us, and his window shut, and all the murmuring of the voices and the people standing about? But for one moment it seemed to me that there was only him and me in the whole world.

But I gasped with my breath, that had almost gone from me, when I saw him move in his chair! He had heard me, though I knew not how. He rose up, and I rose too, speechless, incapable of anything but this mechanical movement. He seemed to draw me as if I were a puppet moved by his will. He came forward to the window, and stood looking across at me. I was sure that he looked at me. At last he had seen me: at last he had found out that somebody, though only a girl, was watching him, looking for him, believing in him. I was in such trouble and commotion of mind and trembling, that I could not keep on my feet, but dropped kneeling on the window-seat, supporting myself against the window, feeling as if my heart were being drawn out of me. I cannot describe his face. It was all dim, yet there was a light on it: I think it must have been a smile; and as closely as I looked at him he looked at me. His hair was fair, and there was a little quiver about his lips. Then he put his hands upon the window to open it. It was stiff and hard to move; but at last he forced it open with a sound that echoed up along the street. I saw that people heard it, and several looked up. As for me, I put my hands together, leaning with my face against the glass, drawn to him as if I could have gone out of myself, my heart out of my bosom, my eyes out of my head. He opened the window with a noise that was heard from the West Port to the Abbey. Could anyone doubt that?

And then he leaned forward out of the window, looking out. There was not one in the street but must have seen him. He looked at me first, with a little wave of his hand, as if it were a salutation – yet not exactly that either, for I thought he waved me away; and then he looked up and down in the dim shining of the ending day, first to the east, to the old Abbey towers, and then to the west, along the broad line of the street where so many people were coming and going, but with so little noise, all like enchanted folk in an enchanted place. I watched him with such a melting heart, with such a deep satisfaction as words could not say; for nobody could tell me now that he was not there – nobody could say I was dreaming any more. I watched him as if I could not breathe – my heart in my throat, my eyes upon him. He looked up and down, and then he looked back at me. I was the first, and I was the last, though it was not for long: he did know, he did see, who it was that had recognized him and sympathized with him all the time. I was in a kind of rapture, yet stupor too; my look went with his look, following it as if I were his shadow; and then suddenly he was gone, and I saw him no more.

I dropped back again upon my seat, seeking something to support me, something to lean upon. He had lifted his hand and waved it once again to me. How he went I cannot tell, nor where he went I cannot tell; but in a moment he was away, and the window standing open, and the room fading into stillness and dimness, yet so clear, with all its space, and the great picture in its gilded frame upon the wall. It gave me no pain to see him go away. My heart was so content, and I was so worn out and satisfied – for what doubt or question could there be about him now? As I was lying back as weak as water, Aunt Mary came in behind me, and flew to me with a little rustle as if she had come on wings, and put her arms round me, and drew my head on to her breast. I had begun to cry a little, with sobs like a child. 'You saw him, you saw him!' I said. To lean upon her, and feel her so soft, so kind, gave me a pleasure I cannot describe, and her arms round me, and her voice saying 'Honey, my honey!' – as if she were nearly crying too. Lying there I came back to myself, quite sweetly, glad of everything. But I wanted some assurance from them that they had seen him too. I waved my hand to the window that was still standing open, and the room that was stealing away into the faint dark. 'This time you saw it all?' I said, getting more eager. 'My honey!' said Aunt Mary, giving me a kiss: and Mr Pitmilly began to walk about the room with short little steps behind, as if he were out of patience. I sat straight up and put away Aunt Mary's arms. 'You cannot be so blind, so blind!' I cried. 'Oh, not tonight, at least not tonight!' But neither the one nor the other made any reply. I shook myself quite free, and raised myself up. And there, in the middle of the street, stood the baker's boy like a statue, staring up at the open window, with his mouth open and his face full of wonder – breathless, as if he could not believe what he saw. I darted forward, calling to him, and beckoned him to come to me. 'Oh, bring him up! bring him, bring him to me!' I cried.

Mr Pitmilly went directly, and got the boy by the shoulder. He did not want to come. It was strange to see the little old gentleman, with his beautiful frill and his diamond pin, standing out in the street, with his hand upon the boy's shoulder, and the other boys round, all in a little crowd. And presently they came towards the house, the others all following, gaping and wondering. He came in unwillingly, almost resisting, looking as if we meant him some harm. 'Come away, my laddie, come and speak to the young lady,' Mr Pitmilly was saying. And Aunt Mary took my hands to keep me back. But I would not be kept back.

'Boy,' I cried, 'you saw it too: you saw it: tell them you saw it! It is what I want, and no more.'

He looked at me as they all did, as if he thought I was mad. 'What's she wantin' wi' me?' he said; and then, 'I did nae harm, even if I did throw a bit o' stane at it – and it's nae sin to throw a stane.'

'You rascal!' said Mr Pitmilly, giving him a shake; 'have you been throwing stones? You'll kill somebody one of these days with your stones!' The old gentleman was confused and troubled, for he did not understand what I wanted, nor anything that had happened. And then Aunt Mary, holding my hands and drawing me close to her, spoke. 'Laddie,' she said, 'answer the young lady, like a good lad. There's no intention of finding fault with you. Answer her, my man, and then Janet will give ye your supper before ye go.'

'Oh speak, speak!' I cried; 'answer them and tell them! You saw that window opened, and the gentleman look out and wave his hand?'

'I saw nae gentleman,' he said, with his head down, 'except this wee gentleman here.'

'Listen, laddie,' said Aunt Mary. 'I saw ye standing in the middle of the street staring. What were ye looking at?'

'It was naething to make a wark about. It was just yon windy yonder in the library that is nae windy. And it was open – as sure's death. Ye may laugh if ye like. Is that a' she's wantin' wi' me?'

'You are telling a pack of lies, laddie,' Mr Pitmilly said.

'I'm tellin' nae lees – it was standin' open just like ony ither windy. It's as sure's death. I couldna believe it mysel'; but it's true.'

'And there it is,' I cried, turning round and pointing it out to them with great triumph in my heart. But the light was all grey, it had faded, it had changed. The window was just as it had always been, a sombre break upon the wall.

I was treated like an invalid all that evening, and taken upstairs to bed, and Aunt Mary sat up in my room the whole night through. Whenever I opened my eyes she was always sitting there close to me, watching. And there never was in all my life so strange a night. When I would talk in my excitement, she kissed me and hushed me like a child. 'Oh, honey, you are not the only one!' she said. 'Oh whisht, whisht, bairn! I should never have let you be there!'

'Aunt Mary, Aunt Mary, you have seen him too?'

'Oh whisht whisht, honey!' Aunt Mary said: her eyes were shining – there were tears in them. 'Oh whisht, whisht! Put it out of your mind, and try to sleep. I will not speak another word,' she cried.

But I had my arms round her, and my mouth at her ear. 'Who is he there? – tell me that and I will ask no more –'

'Oh honey, rest, and try to sleep! It is just – how can I tell you? – a dream! Did you not hear what Lady Carnbee said? – the women of our blood –'

'What? what? Aunt Mary, oh Aunt Mary –'

'I canna tell you,' she cried in her agitation, 'I canna tell you! How can I tell you, when I know just what you know and no more? It is a longing all your life after – it is a looking – for what never comes.'

'He will come,' I cried. 'I shall see him tomorrow – that I know, I know!'

She kissed me and cried over me, her cheek hot and wet like mine. 'My honey, try if you can sleep – try if you can sleep: and we'll wait to see what tomorrow brings.'

'I have no fear,' said I; and then I suppose, though it is strange to think of, I must have fallen asleep – I was so worn-out, and young, and not used to lying in my bed awake. From time to time I opened my eyes, and sometimes jumped up remembering everything: but Aunt Mary was always there to soothe me, and I lay down again in her shelter like a bird in its nest.

But I would not let them keep me in bed next day. I was in a kind of fever, not knowing what I did. The window was quite opaque, without the least glimmer in it, flat and blank like a piece of wood. Never from the first day had I seen it so little like a window. 'It cannot be wondered at,' I said to myself, 'that seeing it like that, and with eyes that are old, not so clear as mine, they should think what they do.' And then I smiled to myself to think of the evening and the long light, and whether he would look out again, or only give me a signal with his hand. I decided I would like that best: not that he should take the trouble to come forward and open it again, but just a turn of his head and a wave of his hand. It would be more friendly and show more confidence – as if I wanted that kind of demonstration every night.

I did not come down in the afternoon, but kept at my own window upstairs, till the tea-party should be over. I could hear them making a great talk; and I was sure they were all in the recess staring at the window, and laughing at the silly lassie. Let them laugh! I felt above it all now. At dinner I was very restless, hurrying to get it over; and I think Aunt Mary was restless too. I doubt whether she read her *Times* when it came; she opened it up so as to shield her, and watched from a corner. And I settled myself in the recess, with my heart full of expectation. I wanted nothing more than to see him writing at his table, and to turn his head and give me a little wave of his hand, just to show that he knew I was there. I sat from half-past seven o'clock to ten o'clock: and the daylight grew softer and softer, till at last it was as if it was shining through a pearl, and not a shadow to be seen. But the window all the time was as black as night, and there was nothing, nothing there.

Well: but other nights it had been like that; he would not be there every night only to please me. There are other things in a man's life, a great learned man like that. I said to myself I was not disappointed.

Why should I be disappointed? There had been other nights when he was not there. Aunt Mary watched me, every movement I made, her eyes shining, often wet, with a pity in them that almost made me cry: but I felt as if I were more sorry for her than for myself. And then I flung myself upon her, and asked her, again and again, what it was, and who it was, imploring her to tell me if she knew? and when she had seen him, and what had happened? and what it meant about the women of our blood? She told me that how it was she could not tell, nor when: it was just at the time it had to be; and that we all saw him in our time – 'that is,' she said, 'the ones that are like you and me'. What was it that made her and me different from the rest? but she only shook her head and would not tell me. 'They say,' she said, and then stopped short. 'Oh, honey, try and forget all about it – if I had but known you were of that kind! They say – that once there was one that was a scholar, and liked his books more than any lady's love. Honey, do not look at me like that. To think I should have brought all this on you!'

'He was a scholar?' I cried.

'And one of us, that must have been a light woman, not like you and me— But maybe it was just in innocence; for who can tell? She waved to him and waved to him to come over: and yon ring was the token: but he would not come. But still she sat at her window and waved and waved – till at last her brothers heard of it, that were stirring men; and then— Oh, my honey, let us speak of it no more!'

'They killed him!' I cried, carried away. And then I grasped her with my hands, and gave her a shake, and flung away from her. 'You tell me that to throw dust in my eyes – when I saw him only last night: and he as living as I am, and as young!'

'My honey, my honey!' Aunt Mary said.

After that I would not speak to her for a long time; but she kept close to me, never leaving me when she could help it, and always with that pity in her eyes. For the next night it was the same; and the third night. That third night I thought I could not bear it any longer. I would have to do something – if only I knew what to do! If it would ever get dark, quite dark, there might be something to be done. I had wild dreams of stealing out of the house and getting a ladder, and mounting up to try if I could not open that window, in the middle of the night – if perhaps I could get the baker's boy to help me; and then my mind got into a whirl, and it was as if I had done it; and I could almost see the boy put the ladder to the window, and hear him cry out that there was nothing there. Oh, how slow it was, the night! and how light it was, and everything so clear – no darkness to cover you, no shadow, whether on one side of the street or on the other side! I could not sleep, though I was forced to go to bed. And in the deep midnight, when it is dark in every other place, I slipped very softly downstairs, though there was one board on the landing-place that creaked – and opened the door and stepped out. There was not a soul to be seen, up or down, from the Abbey to the West Port: and the trees stood like ghosts, and the silence was terrible, and everything as clear as day. You don't know what silence is till you find it in the light like that, not morning but night, no sunrising, no shadow, but everything as clear as the day.

It did not make any difference as the slow minutes went on: one o'clock, two o'clock. How strange it was to hear the clocks striking in that dead light when there was nobody to hear them! But it made no difference. The window was quite blank; even the marking of the panes seemed to have melted away. I stole up again after a long time, through the silent house, in the clear light, cold and trembling, with despair in my heart.

I am sure Aunt Mary must have watched and seen me coming back, for after a while I heard faint sounds in the house; and very early, when there had come a little sunshine into the air, she came to my bedside with a cup of tea in her hand; and she, too, was looking like a ghost. 'Are you warm, honey – are you comfortable?' she said. 'It doesn't matter,' said I. I did not feel as if anything mattered; unless if one could get into the dark somewhere – the soft, deep dark that would cover you over and hide you – but I could not tell from what. The dreadful thing was that there was nothing, nothing to look for, nothing to hide from – only the silence and the light.

That day my mother came and took me home. I had not heard she was coming; she arrived quite unexpectedly, and said she had no time to stay, but must start the same evening so as to be in London next day, Papa having settled to go abroad. At first I had a wild thought I would not go. But how can a girl say I will not, when her mother has come for her, and there is no reason, no reason in the world, to resist, and no right! I had to go, whatever I might wish or anyone might say. Aunt Mary's dear eyes were wet; she went about the house drying them quietly with her handkerchief, but she always said, 'It is the best thing for you, honey – the best thing for you!' Oh, how I hated to hear it said that it was the best thing, as if anything mattered, one more than another! The old ladies were all there in the afternoon, Lady Carnbee looking at me from under her black lace, and the diamond lurking, sending out darts from under her finger. She patted me on the shoulder, and told me to be a good bairn. 'And never lippen to what you see from the window,' she said. 'The eye is deceitful as well as the heart.' She kept patting me on the shoulder, and it felt again as if that sharp wicked stone stung me. Was that what Aunt Mary meant when she said yon ring was the token? I thought afterwards I saw the mark on my shoulder. You will say why? How can I tell why? If I had known, I should have been contented, and it would not have mattered any more.

I never went back to St Rule's, and for years of my life I never again looked out of a window when any other window was in sight. You ask me did I ever see him again? I cannot tell: the imagination is a great deceiver, as Lady Carnbee said: and if he stayed there so long, only to punish the race that had wronged him, why should I ever have seen him again? for I had received my share. But who can tell what happens in a heart that often, often, and so long as that, comes back to do its errand? If it was he whom I have seen again, the anger is gone from him, and he means good and no longer harm to the house of the woman that loved him. I have seen his face looking at me from a crowd. There was one time when I came home a widow from India, very sad, with my little children: I am certain I saw him there among all the people coming to welcome their friends. There was nobody to welcome me – for I was not expected: and very sad was I, without a face I knew: when all at once I saw him, and he waved his hand to me. My heart leaped up again: I had forgotten who he was, but only that it was a face I knew, and I landed almost cheerfully, thinking here was someone who would help me. But he had disappeared, as he did from the window, with that one wave of his hand.

And again I was reminded of it all when old Lady Carnbee died – an old, old woman – and it was found in her will that she had left me that diamond ring. I am afraid of it still. It is locked up in an old sandal-wood box in the lumber-room in the little old country-house which belongs to me, but where I never live. If anyone would steal it, it would be a relief to my mind. Yet I never knew what Aunt Mary meant when she said, 'Yon ring was the token', nor what it could have to do with that strange window in the old College Library of St Rule's.

An Encounter

JAMES JOYCE

It was Joe Dillon who introduced the Wild West to us. He had a little library made up of old numbers of *The Union Jack*, *Pluck*, and *The Halfpenny Marvel*. Every evening after school we met in his back garden and arranged Indian battles. He and his fat young brother Leo, the idler, held the loft of the stable while we tried to carry it by storm; or we fought a pitched battle on the grass. But, however well we fought, we never won siege or battle and all our bouts ended with Joe Dillon's war dance of victory. His parents went to eight o'clock mass every morning in Gardiner Street and the peaceful odour of Mrs Dillon was prevalent in the hall of the house. But he played too fiercely for us who were younger and more timid. He looked like some kind of an Indian when he capered round the garden, an old tea-cosy on his head, beating a tin with his fist and yelling:

'Ya! yaka, yaka, yaka!'

Everyone was incredulous when it was reported that he had a vocation for the priesthood. Nevertheless it was true.

A spirit of unruliness diffused itself among us and, under its influence, differences of culture and constitution were waived. We banded ourselves together, some boldly, some in jest and some almost in fear: and of the number of these latter, the reluctant Indians who were afraid to seem studious or lacking in robustness, I was one. The adventures related in the literature of the Wild West were remote from my nature but, at least, they opened doors of escape. I liked better some American detective stories which were traversed from time to time by unkempt fierce and beautiful girls. Though there was nothing wrong in these stories and though their intention was sometimes literary, they were circulated secretly at school. One day when Father Butler was hearing the four pages of Roman History, clumsy Leo Dillon was discovered with a copy of *The Halfpenny Marvel*.

'This page or this page? This page? Now, Dillon, up! "*Hardly had the day*" . . . Go on! What day? "*Hardly had the day dawned*" . . . Have you studied it? What have you there in your pocket?'

Everyone's heart palpitated as Leo Dillon handed up the paper and everyone assumed an innocent face. Father Butler turned over the pages, frowning.

'What is this rubbish?' he said. '*The Apache Chief*! Is this what you read instead of studying your Roman History? Let me not find any more of this wretched stuff in this college. The man who wrote it, I suppose, was some wretched fellow who writes these things for a drink. I'm surprised at boys like you, educated, reading such stuff. I could understand it if you were . . . National School boys. Now, Dillon, I advise you strongly, get at your work or . . .'

This rebuke during the sober hours of school paled much of the glory of the Wild West for me, and the confused puffy face of Leo Dillon awakened one of my consciences. But when the restraining influence of the school was at a distance I began to hunger again for wild sensations, for the escape which these chronicles of disorder alone seemed to offer me. The mimic warfare of the evening became at last as wearisome to me as the routine of school in the morning because I wanted real adventures to happen to myself. But real adventures, I reflected, do not happen to people who remain at home: they must be sought abroad.

The summer holidays were near at hand when I made up my mind to break out of the weariness of school life for one day at least. With Leo Dillon and a boy named Mahony I planned a day's miching. Each of us saved up sixpence. We were to meet at ten in the morning on the Canal Bridge. Mahony's big sister was to write an excuse for him and Leo

Dillon was to tell his brother to say he was sick. We arranged to go along the Wharf Road until we came to the ships, then to cross in the ferryboat and walk out to see the Pigeon House. Leo Dillon was afraid we might meet Father Butler or someone out of the college: but Mahony asked, very sensibly, what would Father Butler be doing out at the Pigeon House. We were reassured, and I brought the first stage of the plot to an end by collecting sixpence from the other two, at the same time showing them my own sixpence. When we were making the last arrangements on the eve we were all vaguely excited. We shook hands, laughing, and Mahony said:

'Till tomorrow, mates.'

That night I slept badly. In the morning I was first-comer to the bridge, as I lived nearest. I hid my books in the long grass near the ashpit at the end of the garden where nobody ever came, and hurried along the canal bank. It was a mild sunny morning in the first week of June. I sat up on the coping of the bridge, admiring my frail canvas shoes which I had diligently pipeclayed overnight and watching the docile horses pulling a tramload of business people up the hill. All the branches of the tall trees which lined the mall were gay with little light green leaves, the sunlight slanted through them on to the water. The granite stone of the bridge was beginning to be warm, and I began to pat it with my hands in time to an air in my head. I was very happy.

When I had been sitting there for five or ten minutes I saw Mahony's grey suit approaching. He came up the hill, smiling, and clambered up beside me on the bridge. While we were waiting he brought out the catapult which bulged from his inner pocket and explained some improvements which he had made in it. I asked him why he had brought it, and he told me he had brought it to have some gas with the birds. Mahony used slang freely, and spoke of Father Butler as Old Bunser. We waited on for a quarter of an hour more, but still there was no sign of Leo Dillon. Mahony, at last, jumped down and said:

'Come along. I knew Fatty'd funk it.'

'And his sixpence . . .' I said.

'That's forfeit,' said Mahony. 'And so much the better for us – a bob and a tanner instead of a bob.'

We walked along the North Strand Road till we came to the Vitriol

Works and then turned to the right along the Wharf Road. Mahony began to play the Indian as soon as we were out of public sight. He chased a crowed of ragged girls, brandishing his unloaded catapult and, when two ragged boys began, out of chivalry, to fling stones at us, he proposed that we should charge them. I objected that the boys were too small, and so we walked on, the ragged troop screaming after us *'Swaddlers! Swaddlers!'* thinking that we were Protestants because Mahony, who was dark-complexioned, wore the silver badge of a cricket club in his cap. When we came to the Smoothing Iron we arranged a siege; but it was a failure because you must have at least three. We revenged ourselves on Leo Dillon by saying what a funk he was and guessing how many he would get at three o'clock from Mr Ryan.

We came then near the river. We spent a long time walking about the noisy streets flanked by high stone walls watching the working of cranes and engines and often being shouted at for our immobility by the drivers of groaning carts. It was noon when we reached the quays and, as all the labourers seemed to be eating their lunches, we bought two big currant buns and sat down to eat them on some metal piping beside the river. We pleased ourselves with the spectacle of Dublin's commerce – the barges signalled from far away by their curls of woolly smoke, the brown fishing fleet beyond Ringsend, the big white sailing vessel which was being discharged on the opposite quay. Mahony said it would be right skit to run away to sea on one of those big ships, and even I, looking at the high masts, saw, or imagined, the geography which had been scantily dosed to me at school gradually taking substance under my eyes. School and home seemed to recede from us and their influences upon us seemed to wane.

We crossed the Liffey in the ferryboat, paying our toll to be transported in the company of two labourers and a little Jew with a bag. We were serious to the point of solemnity, but once during the short voyage our eyes met and we laughed. When we landed we watched the discharging of the graceful three-master which we had observed from the other quay. Some bystander said that she was a Norwegian vessel. I went to the stern and tried to decipher the legend upon it but, failing to do so, I came back and examined the foreign sailors to see if any of them had green eyes, for I had some confused notion . . . The sailors' eyes were blue, and grey, and even black. The only sailor whose eyes could have been called green was a tall man who amused the crowd on the quay by calling out cheerfully every time the planks fell: 'All right! All right!'

When we were tired of this sight we wandered slowly into Ringsend. The day had grown sultry, and in the windows of the grocers' shops musty biscuits lay bleaching. We bought some biscuits and chocolate, which we ate sedulously as we wandered through the squalid streets where the families of the fishermen live. We could find no dairy and so we went into a huckster's shop and bought a bottle of raspberry lemonade each. Refreshed by this, Mahony chased a cat down a lane, but the cat escaped into a wide field. We both felt rather tired, and when we reached the field we made at once for a sloping bank, over the ridge of which we could see the Dodder.

It was too late and we were too tired to carry out our project of visiting the Pigeon House. We had to be home before four o'clock, lest our adventure should be discovered. Mahony looked regretfully at his catapult, and I had to suggest going home by train before he regained any cheerfulness. The sun went in behind some clouds and left us to our jaded thoughts and the crumbs of our provisions.

There was nobody but ourselves in the field. When we had lain on the bank for some time without speaking I saw a man approaching from the far end of the field. I watched him lazily as I chewed one of those green stems on which girls tell fortunes. He came along by the bank slowly. He walked with one hand upon his hip and in the other hand he held a stick with which he tapped the turf lightly. He was shabbily dressed in a suit of greenish-black and wore what we used to call a jerry hat with a high crown. He seemed to be fairly old, for his moustache was ashen-grey. When he passed at our feet he glanced up at us quickly and then continued his way. We followed him with our eyes and saw that when he had gone on for perhaps fifty paces he turned about and began to retrace his steps. He walked towards us very slowly, always tapping the ground with his stick, so slowly that I thought he was looking for something in the grass.

He stopped when he came level with us and bade us good-day. We

133

answered him, and he sat down beside us on the slope slowly and with great care. He began to talk of the weather, saying that it would be a very hot summer and adding that the seasons had changed greatly since he was a boy – a long time ago. He said that the happiest time of one's life was undoubtedly one's schoolboy days, and that he would give anything to be young again. While he expressed these sentiments, which bored us a little, we kept silent. Then he began to talk of school and of books. He asked us whether we had read the poetry of Thomas Moore or the works of Sir Walter Scott and Lord Lytton. I pretended that I had read every book he mentioned, so that in the end he said:

'Ah, I can see you are a bookworm like myself. Now,' he added, pointing to Mahony, who was regarding us with open eyes, 'he is different; he goes in for games.'

He said he had all Sir Walter Scott's works and all Lord Lytton's works at home and never tired of reading them. 'Of course,' he said, 'there were some of Lord Lytton's works which boys couldn't read.' Mahony asked why boys couldn't read them – a question which agitated and pained me because I was afraid the man would think I was as stupid as Mahony. The man, however, only smiled. I saw that he had great gaps in his mouth between his yellow teeth. Then he asked us which of us had the most sweethearts. Mahony mentioned lightly that he had three totties. The man asked me how many I had. I answered that I had none. He did not believe me and said he was sure I must have one. I was silent.

'Tell us,' said Mahony pertly to the man, 'how many have you yourself?'

The man smiled as before and said that when he was our age he had lots of sweethearts.

'Every boy,' he said, 'has a little sweetheart.'

His attitude on this point struck me as strangely liberal in a man of his age. In my heart I thought that what he said about boys and sweethearts was reasonable. But I disliked the words in his mouth, and I wondered why he shivered once or twice as if he feared something or felt a sudden chill. As he proceeded I noticed that his accent was good. He began to speak to us about girls, saying what nice soft hair they had and how soft their hands were and how all girls were not so good as they seemed to be if one only knew. There was nothing he liked, he said, so much as looking at a nice young girl, at her nice white hands and her beautiful soft hair. He gave me the impression that he was repeating something which he had learned by heart or that, magnetized by some words of his own speech, his mind was slowly circling round and round in the same orbit. At times he spoke as if he were simply alluding to some fact that everybody knew, and at times he lowered his voice and spoke mysteriously, as if he were telling us something secret which he did not wish others to overhear. He repeated his phrases over and over again, varying them and surrounding them with his monotonous voice. I continued to gaze towards the foot of the slope, listening to him.

After a long while his monologue paused. He stood up slowly, saying that he had to leave us for a minute or so, a few minutes, and, without changing the direction of my gaze, I saw him walking slowly away from us towards the near end of the field. We remained silent when he had gone. After a silence of a few minutes I heard Mahony exclaim:

'I say! Look what he's doing!'

As I neither answered nor raised my eyes, Mahony exclaimed again:

'I say . . . He's a queer old josser!'

'In case he asks us for our names,' I said, 'let you be Murphy and I'll be Smith.'

We said nothing further to each other. I was still considering whether I would go away or not when the man came back and sat down beside us again. Hardly had he sat down when Mahony, catching sight of the cat which had escaped him, sprang up and pursued her across the field. The man and I watched the chase. The cat escaped once more and Mahony began to throw stones at the wall she had escaladed. Desisting from this, he began to wander about the far end of the field, aimlessly.

After an interval the man spoke to me. He said that my friend was a very rough boy, and asked did he get whipped often at school. I was going to reply indignantly that we were not National School boys to be whipped, as he called it; but I remained silent. He began to speak on the subject of chastising boys. His mind, as if magnetized again by his speech, seemed to circle slowly round and round its new centre. He said that when boys were that kind they ought to be whipped and well whipped. When a boy was rough and unruly there was nothing would do him any good but a good sound whipping. A slap on the hand or a box on the ear was no good: what he wanted was to get a nice warm whipping. I was surprised at this sentiment and involuntarily glanced at his face. As I did so I met the gaze of a pair of bottle-green eyes peering at me from under a twitching forehead. I turned my eyes away again.

The man continued his monologue. He seemed to have forgotten his recent liberalism. He said that if ever he found a boy talking to girls or having a girl for a sweetheart he would whip him and whip him; and that would teach him not to be talking to girls. And if a boy had a girl for a sweetheart and told lies about it, then he would give him such a whipping as no boy ever got in this world. He said that there was nothing in this world he would like so well as that. He described to me how he would whip such a boy, as if he were unfolding some elaborate mystery. He would love that, he said, better than anything in this world; and his voice, as he led me monotonously through the mystery, grew almost affectionate and seemed to plead with me that I should understand him.

I waited till his monologue paused again. Then I stood up abruptly. Lest I should betray my agitation I delayed a few moments, pretending to fix my shoe properly, and then, saying that I was obliged to go, I bade him good-day. I went up the slope calmly but my heart was beating quickly with fear that he would seize me by the ankles. When I reached the top of the slope I turned round and, without looking at him, called loudly across the field:

'Murphy!'

My voice had an accent of forced bravery in it, and I was ashamed of my paltry stratagem. I had to call the name again before Mahony saw me and hallooed in answer. How my heart beat as he came running across the field to me. He ran as if to bring me aid. And I was penitent; for in my heart I had always despised him a little.

136

Dream-Children

CHARLES LAMB

Children love to listen to stories about their elders when *they* were children; to stretch their imagination to the conception of a traditionary great-uncle, or grandame, whom they never saw. It was in this spirit that my little ones crept about me the other evening to hear about their great-grandmother Field, who lived in a great house in Norfolk (a hundred times bigger than that in which they and Papa lived), which had been the scene – so at least it was generally believed in that part of the country – of the tragic incidents which they had lately become familiar with from the ballad of the *Children in the Wood*.

Certain it is, that the whole story of the children and their cruel uncle was to be seen fairly carved out in the wood upon the chimney-piece of the great hall – the whole story down to the Robin Redbreasts – till a foolish rich person pulled it down to set up a marble one of modern invention in its stead, with no story upon it. Here Alice put out one of her dear mother's looks, too tender to be called upbraiding.

Then I went on to say how religious and how good their great-grandmother Field was, how beloved and respected by everybody, though she was not, indeed, the mistress of this great house, but had only the charge of it (and yet in some respects she might be said to be the mistress of it too), committed to her by the owner, who preferred living in a newer and more fashionable mansion, which he had

137

purchased somewhere in the adjoining county; but still she lived in it in a manner as if it had been her own, and kept up the dignity of the great house of a sort while she lived, which afterwards came to decay, and was nearly pulled down, and all its old ornaments stripped and carried away to the owner's other house, where they were set up, and looked as awkward as if someone were to carry away the old tombs they had seen lately at the Abbey, and stick them up in Lady C.'s tawdry gilt drawing-room.

Here John smiled, as much as to say, 'That would be foolish indeed.'

And then I told how, when she came to die, her funeral was attended by a concourse of all the poor, and some of the gentry too, of the neighbourhood, for many miles round, to show their respect for her memory, because she had been such a good and religious woman – so good, indeed, that she knew all the Psalter by heart, aye, and a great part of the Testament besides.

Here little Alice spread her hands. Then I told what a tall, upright, graceful person their great-grandmother Field once was; and how in her youth she was esteemed the best dancer – here Alice's little right foot played an involuntary movement, till, upon my looking grave, it desisted – the best dancer, I was saying, in the county, till a cruel disease, called a cancer, came, and bowed her down with pain; but it could never bend her good spirits, or make them stoop; but they were still upright, because she was so good and religious.

Then I told how she was used to sleep by herself in a lone chamber of the great lone house; and how she believed that an apparition of two infants was to be seen at midnight gliding up and down the great staircase near where she slept; but she said, 'Those innocents would do her no harm'; and how frightened I used to be, though in those days I had my maid to sleep with me, because I was never half so good or religious as she, and yet I never saw the infants.

Here John expanded all his eyebrows, and tried to look courageous. Then I told how good she was to all her grandchildren, having us to the great house in the holidays, where I in particular used to spend many hours by myself in gazing upon the old busts of the twelve Caesars, that had been emperors of Rome, till the old marble heads would seem to live again, or I to be turned into marble with them; how I never could be tired with roaming about that huge mansion, with its vast empty rooms, with their worn-out hangings, fluttering tapestry, and carved oaken panels, with the gilding almost rubbed out – sometimes in the spacious old-fashioned gardens, which I had almost to myself, unless when now and then a solitary gardening man would cross me – and how the nectarines and peaches hung upon the walls without my ever offering to pluck them, because they were forbidden fruit, unless now and then – and because I had more pleasure in strolling about among the old melancholy-looking yew-trees, or the firs, and picking up the red berries, and the fir-apples, which were good for nothing but to look at – or in lying about upon the fresh grass, with all the fine garden smells around me – or basking in the orangery, till I could almost fancy myself ripening too along with the oranges and the limes, in that grateful warmth – or in watching the dace that darted to and fro in the fish-pond, at the bottom of the garden, with here and there a great sulky pike hanging midway down the water in silent state, as if it mocked at their impertinent friskings – I had more pleasure in these busy-idle diversions than in all the sweet flavours of peaches, nectarines, oranges, and such-like common baits of children.

Here John slyly deposited back upon the plate a bunch of grapes, which, not unobserved by Alice, he had meditated dividing with her, and both seemed willing to relinquish them for the present as irrelevant. Then, in somewhat a more heightened tone, I told how, though their great-grandmother Field loved all her grandchildren, yet, in an especial manner, she might be said to love their uncle, John L——, because he was so handsome and spirited a youth, and a king to the rest of us; and, instead of moping about in solitary corners like some of us, he would mount the most mettlesome horse he could get, when but an imp no bigger than themselves, and make it carry him half over the county in a morning, and join the hunters when there were any out – and yet he loved the old great house and gardens too, but had too much spirit to be always pent up within their boundaries – and how their uncle grew up to man's estate as brave as he was handsome, to the admiration of everybody, but of their great-grandmother Field most especially; and how he used to carry me upon his back when I was a lame-footed boy – for he was a good bit older than me – many a mile when I could not walk for pain – and how, in after-life, he became lame-footed too, and I did not always (I fear) make allowances enough for him when he was impatient, and in pain, nor remember sufficiently how considerate he had been to me when I was lame-footed; and how, when he died, though he had not been dead an hour it seemed as if he had died a great while ago, such a distance there is betwixt life and death; and how I bore his death, as I thought, pretty well at first, but afterwards it haunted and haunted me; and though I did not cry or take it to heart as some do, and as I think he would have done if I had died, yet I missed him all day long, and I knew not till then how much I had loved him.

I missed his kindness, and I missed his crossness, and wished him to be alive again, to be quarrelling with him (for we quarrelled sometimes), rather than not have him again, and was as uneasy without him as he, their poor uncle, must have been when the doctor took off his limb.

Here the children fell a-crying, and asked if their little mourning which they had on was not for Uncle John, and they looked up, and prayed me not to go on about their uncle, but to tell them some stories about their pretty dead mother.

Then I told how, for seven long years, in hope sometimes, sometimes in despair, yet persisting ever, I courted the fair Alice W——n; and, as much as children could understand, I explained to them what coyness, and difficulty, and denial meant in maidens, when suddenly turning to Alice, the soul of the first Alice looked out at her eyes, with such a reality of representment that I became in doubt which of them stood there before me, or whose that bright hair was; and while I stood gazing, both the children gradually grew fainter to my view, receding, and still receding, till nothing at last but two mournful features were seen in the uttermost distance, which, without speech, strangely impressed upon me the effects of speech:

'We are not of Alice, nor of thee, nor are we children at all. The children of Alice call Bartrum father. We are nothing; less than nothing, and dreams. We are only what might have been, and must wait upon the tedious shores of Lethe millions of ages before we have existence and a name' – and immediately awaking, I found myself quietly seated in my bachelor arm-chair, where I had fallen asleep with the faithful Bridget unchanged by my side.

Little Mim

W. S. GILBERT

The only point on which Joe Paulby and I could ever bring ourselves to agree was that his cousin Mim was the only young lady in the world who was worth falling in love with. Joe Paulby was eight, I was seven, and his cousin Mim was six. Joe was a strong, rough, troublesome boy, and I was small and weak and delicate; and if it had not been that we were both deeply in love with the same young lady I believe I should have hated him. That solitary bond of sympathy served to bind us more or less firmly to each other, and I seldom quarrelled with him except when his regard for her showed signs of cooling down.

She was a pretty, fragile little lady, with quaint ways of her own, and a gentle frightened manner of dealing with her boisterous playmate which seldom failed to bring him to a sense of order. She loved us both very dearly, but I think Joe was her favourite. Although a rude, unpleasant boy to others, to her he was quiet and gentle enough; but perhaps this palpable submission appealed more directly to the little lady than my undemonstrative and colourless affection. But she was very fond of me for all that.

Neither Mim nor I had any parents, and we lived with Joe's papa in a great gaunt, draughty house in Bloomsbury Square. Captain Paulby was our guardian – a tall, bony, unsympathetic widower – who

143

governed his house as though it had been a regiment of soldiers. A scale of dietary was hung up in the nursery, and from it one learnt how many quarter-ounces of cocoa, how many half-pounds of bread, and how many tablespoonfuls of arrowroot we consumed in the week. An order-book was brought into the nursery every morning, in which the detail of the day's duties was carefully set out, and to the instructions it contained implicit and unmurmuring obedience was exacted. It regulated the hours of rising and going to bed, the school hours and the hours of relaxation, when and where we were to walk, and what we were to wear.

We were placed in charge of a nurse – Nurse Starke – a tall, muscular, hardened woman of forty. She had a stern unrelenting face, close lips, hard grey eyes, and a certain smooth roundness of figure, which on looking back, suggests the idea of her having been turned in a lathe. I never see the masculine old woman who lets lodgings in a pantomime without thinking of Nurse Starke. I am bound to say, however, that she was scrupulously, indeed aggravatingly, clean and neat, and in that respect of course, the analogy falls to the ground.

Nurse Starke was not actively unkind to us. Indeed, I believe she had cheated herself into a belief that she was rather weak-minded and indulgent than otherwise; but in this she was in error. I believe she was fond of us in a hard unyielding way, but she was sudden and impulsive in her movements, and never handled us without hurting us. There was a housemaid – Jane Cotter – who occasionally helped to put us to bed, and sometimes Nurse Starke undressed us while Jane put our hair into curl papers, and sometimes Nurse Starke did the curling while Jane undressed us. And the manner in which these duties were to be divided became a matter of no light speculation to us as evening approached, for it was Nurse Starke's custom to pull the locks of hair out to their full length, and then roll them round a piece of paper, twisting the ends together when the curl had been rolled well home, whereas Jane Cotter first made the curl up flat with her fingers, and then encased it gently in a triangular paper, which she pinched with the tongs. Jane Cotter's flat curls were pleasant to sleep upon, but Nurse Starke's corkscrews placed a comfortable night's rest out of the question. It is impossible to sleep in peace with a double row of balls, each as big as a large chestnut, round your head. You can't move without giving four or five of them a wrench.

I think we must have been sufficiently happy as a rule, or Sunday would not have stood out in such gaunt and desolate contrast to the other days of the week. There reigned in our nursery an unaccountable fiction that Sunday was a holiday; and in deference to this tradition we endeavoured to cheat ourselves into a belief that we were glad when that day arrived. Sunday began at a very early hour in Bloomsbury. It began to ring itself in at half-past seven when we got up, and continued to ring itself through the day at short intervals until it finally rang itself out, and us into bed, at half-past eight in the evening. There were drawbacks, however, to our enjoyment of the day. I think we were required to tackle more Collect than is good for a child of six or seven, and perhaps we did not quite understand the bearing of that Shorter Catechism which a bench of thoughtful bishops has prepared for the express use of very young children. Even Nurse Starke, a high authority on all points of Church controversy, never succeeded in placing its meaning quite beyond all question. But Nurse Starke, had a special Sunday frame of mind which discouraged close questioning, and on that day of the week she was exceptionally short and sharp in her replies. She baffled our interrogatories by pointing out to us that there was nothing so unbecoming as a tendency to ask questions; which seemed to us a little unreasonable, when we considered the inquisitive character of *her* share in the Catechism.

I believe I liked going to church, though I am sure Joe Paulby did not. That rugged boy never looked so hot or so rumpled as he did during Divine Service. As I look back upon Joe in church, I am always reminded of the appearance of restless decorum presented by a Christy Minstrel 'Bones' during the singing of a plaintive ballad. Joe occupied himself during the service in laying the foundations of a series of pains and penalties which usually lasted well into Thursday, for Nurse Starke had a quick eye for misdemeanours, and every crime had its apportioned punishment. Poor little Mim was too delicate to go to church, and used to sit at home in theological conference with Jane Cotter, whose picturesque and highly dramatic ideas of future rewards and punishments had a special interest for the poor little lady.

For Mim had been told that even children die sometimes, and both Nurse Starke and Jane had a long catalogue of stories in which good little people were cut off in their earliest years, and bad little people lived on to an evil old age. Mim was often weak and ailing, and at such times the recollection of these stories came upon her. Nurse Starke's grim, hard manner relaxed when she was speaking to the little sick child, and her kindness to Mim, gaunt and grudging as it was, seemed to increase with the trouble the child gave her – a never-ceasing source of wonderment to Joe and myself, who were only in favour when we ceased to occupy Nurse Starke's attention. Nurse Starke had a brother, a boy of twelve or thereabouts (though we believed him to be eight-and-twenty at least), who was a page at a doctor's in Charlotte Street; and Nurse Starke, as a great treat, used to allow this young gentleman to spend the afternoon with us, and entertain us with his varied social powers. Gaspar – for that was his unfortunate name – was a talented boy with a taste for acrobatics, conjuring, killing flies, and putting lob-worms down Mim's back; but notwithstanding these powerful recommendations we looked coldly upon him, and, on the whole, discouraged his visits. He had a way of challenging Joe and me to fight him with one of his hands tied behind his back, by way of a handicap, which was not what you look for in a visitor, and moreover compromised our reputation for valour in Mim's eyes. On the whole he was not popular with us, and eventually he was proscribed by Nurse Starke herself on a charge of filling the nursery candle with gunpowder, which exploded and burnt poor little Mim's eyebrows and eye-lashes. Gaspar eventually got into trouble about some original draughts of his own composition, which he supplied to his master's patients as healing waters made up in accordance with that gentleman's prescriptions, and spent several years in a reformatory.

I have a dismal impression of the wretched afternoons that Mim and Joe and I used to spend together in our great bare play-room. We were locked in by Nurse Starke at about five every afternoon, and not released until seven, when we had supper, and as the shadows deepened and the fire got lower and lower, we crowded together in a corner for warmth, and told each other strange stories of princes and noblemen who were tortured by cruel and vindictive pageboys; with an occasional touch from Joe Paulby upon caverns, demons, vampires, and other ghostly matters until poor little Mim screamed aloud with terror.

She was a pretty, fragile, sweet-tempered, clinging little soul, far too delicate for the coarse, inconsiderate treatment to which she was subjected in common with ourselves. So at last she became seriously ill, and we noticed that the poor little child grew paler and thinner in her cot, day after day, day after day. She was very cheerful, although so weak, and when the tall, grave, kind doctor came – once a day at first, and then towards the last (for she died) two or three times a day – she would say in reply to his question, 'And how is our Little Mim?' that she was much better, and hoped in a day or two to be quite well again. After a time she was removed to another room which was always darkened, and to which we were seldom admitted, and only one at a time. An odd change seemed to come over us all. Nurse Starke was quite kind now, and used to read to her (but now about good children who lived and were very happy), and tell stories, and make beef-tea for her, and turn the cold side of the pillow to her poor little fevered head. And the oddest part of the thing was that Nurse Starke was kind to us too, and used to come of her own accord to tell us how Mim was (she was always a little better), and what messages she had sent to us, and how she seemed to take a new pleasure in the toys she had once discarded. And then she would take us, one at a time, to the sick room, and we were allowed at first to speak to her, but afterwards only to sit on the edge of the bed (it was such a big bed now!), and hold her little dry hand. Joe Paulby would come back crying (it was a strange thing to see *him* cry, and it touched me as it touches me now to see a strong man in tears), and he would spend his half-pence – they were rare enough, poor fellow – on picture-books for our poor little dying wife. But a time came when even the picture-books were forbidden, and then the whole house was enjoined to silence, and the grave doctor – graver now than ever – came and went on tip-toe. And if we stole to the little girl's bedroom as we often did, we were pretty sure to find great hard Nurse Starke in tears, or with traces of tears upon her face; and once when Joe and I crept down to the room, and looked in at the half-opened door, we saw the shadow of Nurse Starke on her knees, thrown by the flickering firelight on the wall. Then we knew that the end was near.

One day Captain Paulby came home earlier than usual, looking very grave, and with him came the kind doctor, and with them another doctor, an older man, but also very kind. They went up into little Mim's room, and they stayed so long that Joe and I stole down from our old dark play-room to hear, if we could, the reason of his father's unexpected return. And Joe and I cried as if our hearts would break, for our dear little wife was dying.

Captain Paulby came out of the room, and seeing us in the passage, told us quite kindly to go back to the play-room. Joe Paulby went, but I begged Captain Paulby to let me see my dear little playmate once more and, alarmed by my excited manner and my choking sobs, he admitted me.

I had not seen her for two days, and she was greatly changed. She looked so little in that big bed that the two doctors and Captain Paulby and Nurse Starke seemed absolutely gigantic as they all bent, silently and without motion, over the little child. I think we must have remained so for nearly two hours, the silence undisturbed except by an occasional whisper from one of the doctors, and a sob from Nurse Starke. When I first went into the dark room Mim was asleep, but eventually she recognized me, and begged to be allowed to kiss me as she was nearly quite well. They laid me on the bed by her side, and her little thin arms were placed round my neck, and there we lay motionless, both of us in deep silence. At length I became conscious of a movement among the doctors, and then a loud ringing wail from Nurse Starke told me that my little wife was quite, quite well again.

The Half-Brothers

ELIZABETH GASKELL

My mother was twice married. She never spoke of her first husband, and it is only from other people that I have learnt what little I know about him. I believe she was scarcely seventeen when she was married to him: and he was barely one-and-twenty. He rented a small farm up in Cumberland, somewhere towards the sea-coast; but he was perhaps too young and inexperienced to have the charge of land and cattle; anyhow, his affairs did not prosper, and he fell into ill-health, and died of consumption before they had been three years man and wife, leaving my mother a young widow of twenty, with a little child only just able to walk, and the farm on her hands for four years more by the lease, with half the stock on it dead, or sold off one by one to pay the more pressing debts, and with no money to purchase more, or even to buy the provisions needed for the small consumption of every day. There was another child coming, too; and sad and sorry, I believe, she was to think of it.

A dreary winter she must have had in her lonesome dwelling, with never another near it for miles around; her sister came to bear her company, and the two planned and plotted how to make every penny they could raise go as far as possible. I can't tell you how it happened that my little sister, whom I never saw, came to sicken and die; but, as if my poor mother's cup was not full enough, only a fortnight before

149

Gregory was born the little girl took ill of scarlet fever, and in a week she lay dead.

My mother was, I believe, just stunned with this last blow. My aunt has told me that she did not cry; Aunt Fanny would have been thankful if she had; but she sat holding the poor wee lassie's hand, and looking in her pretty, pale, dead face, without so much as shedding a tear. And it was all the same, when they had to take her away to be buried. She just kissed the child, and sat her down in the window-seat to watch the little black train of people (neighbours – my aunt, and one far-off cousin, who were all the friends they could muster) go winding away amongst the snow, which had fallen thinly over the country the night before.

When my aunt came back from the funeral, she found my mother in the same place, and as dry-eyed as ever. So she continued until after Gregory was born; and, somehow, his coming seemed to loosen the tears, and she cried day and night, day and night, till my aunt and the other watcher looked at each other in dismay, and would fain have stopped her if they had but known how. But she bade them let her alone, and not be over-anxious, for every drop she shed eased her brain, which had been in a terrible state before for want of the power to cry. She seemed after that to think of nothing but her new little baby; she hardly appeared to remember either her husband or her little daughter that lay dead in Brigham churchyard – at least so Aunt Fanny said; but she was a great talker, and my mother was very silent by nature, and I think Aunt Fanny may have been mistaken in believing that my mother never thought of her husband and child just because she never spoke about them.

Aunt Fanny was older than my mother, and had a way of treating her like a child; but, for all that, she was a kind, warm-hearted creature, who thought more of her sister's welfare than she did of her own; and it was on her bit of money that they principally lived, and on what the two could earn by working for the great Glasgow sewing-merchants. But by-and-by my mother's eyesight began to fail. It was not that she was exactly blind, for she could see well enough to guide herself about the house, and to do a good deal of domestic work; but she could no longer do fine sewing and earn money. It must have been with the heavy crying she had had in her day, for she was but a young creature at this time, and as pretty a young woman, I have heard people say, as any in the countryside.

She took it sadly to heart that she could no longer gain anything towards the keep of herself and her child. My Aunt Fanny would fain have persuaded her that she had enough to do in managing their cottage and minding Gregory; but my mother knew that they were pinched, and that Aunt Fanny herself had not as much to eat, even of the commonest kind of food, as she could have done with; and as for Gregory, he was not a strong lad, and needed, not more food – for he always had enough, whoever went short – but better nourishment, and more flesh-meat.

One day – it was Aunt Fanny who told me all this about my poor mother, long after her death – as the sisters were sitting together, Aunt Fanny working, and my mother hushing Gregory to sleep, William Preston, who was afterwards my father, came in.

He was reckoned an old bachelor; I suppose he was long past forty, and he was one of the wealthiest farmers thereabouts, and had known my grandfather well, and my mother and my aunt in their more prosperous days. He sat down, and began to twirl his hat by way of being agreeable; my Aunt Fanny talked, and he listened and looked at my mother. But he said very little, either on that visit, or on many another that he paid before he spoke out about what had been the real purpose of his calling so often all along, and from the very first time he came to their house.

One Sunday, however, my Aunt Fanny stayed away from church, and took care of the child, and my mother went alone. When she came back, she ran straight upstairs, without going into the kitchen to look at Gregory or speak any word to her sister, and Aunt Fanny heard her cry as if her heart was breaking; so she went up and scolded her right well through the bolted door, till at last she got her to open it. And then she threw herself on my aunt's neck, and told her that William Preston had asked her to marry him, and had promised to take good charge of her boy, and to let him want for nothing, neither in the way of keep nor of education, and that she had consented.

Aunt Fanny was a good deal shocked at this; for, as I have said, she had often thought that my mother had forgotten her first husband very quickly, and now here was proof positive of it, if she could so soon think of marrying again. Besides, as Aunt Fanny used to say, she herself would have been a far more suitable match for a man of William Preston's age than Helen, who, though she was a widow, had not seen her four-and-twentieth summer.

However, as Aunt Fanny said, they had not asked her advice; and there was much to be said on the other side of the question. Helen's eyesight would never be good for much again, and as William Preston's wife she would never need to do anything, if she chose to sit with her hands before her; and a boy was a great charge to a widowed mother; and now there would be a decent, steady man to see after him. So, by-and-by, Aunt Fanny seemed to take a brighter view of the marriage than did my mother herself, who hardly ever looked up, and never smiled after the day when she promised William Preston to be his wife. But much as she had loved Gregory before, she seemed to love him more now. She was continually talking to him when they were alone, though he was far too young to understand her moaning words, or give her any comfort, except by his caresses.

At last William Preston and she were wed; and she went to be mistress of a well-stocked house, not above half an hour's walk from where Aunt Fanny lived. I believe she did all that she could to please my father; and a more dutiful wife, I have heard him himself say, could never have been. But she did not love him, and he soon found it out. She loved Gregory, and she did not love him.

Perhaps, love would have come in time, if he had been patient enough to wait; but it just turned him sour to see how her eye brightened and her colour came at the sight of that little child, while for him who had given her so much, she had only gentle words as cold as ice. He got to taunt her with the difference in her manner, as if that would bring love: and he took a positive dislike to Gregory – he was so jealous of the ready love that always gushed out like a spring of fresh water when he came near. He wanted her to love him more, and perhaps that was all well and good; but he wanted her to love her child less, and that was an evil wish.

One day, he gave way to his temper, and cursed and swore at

Gregory, who had got into some mischief, as children will; my mother made some excuse for him; my father said it was hard enough to have to keep another man's child, without having it perpetually held up in its naughtiness by his wife, who ought to be always in the same mind that he was; and so from little they got to more; and the end of it was, that my mother took to her bed before her time, and I was born that very day.

My father was glad, and proud, and sorry, all in a breath; glad and proud that a son was born to him; and sorry for his poor wife's state, and to think how his angry words had brought it on. But he was a man who liked better to be angry than sorry, so he soon found out that it was all Gregory's fault, and owed him an additional grudge for having hastened my birth.

He had another grudge against him before long. My mother began to sink the day after I was born. My father sent to Carlisle for doctors, and would have coined his heart's blood into gold to save her, if that could have been; but it could not.

My Aunt Fanny used to say sometimes, that she thought that Helen did not wish to live, and so just let herself die away without trying to take hold on life; but when I questioned her, she owned that my mother did all the doctors bade her do, with the same sort of uncomplaining patience with which she had acted through life. One of her last requests was to have Gregory laid in her bed by my side, and then she made him take hold of my little hand. Her husband came in while she was looking at us so, and when he bent tenderly over her to ask her how she felt now, and seemed to gaze on us two little half-brothers, with a grave sort of kindliness, she looked up in his face and smiled, almost her first smile at him; and such a sweet smile! as more besides Aunt Fanny have said.

In an hour she was dead. Aunt Fanny came to live with us. It was the best thing that could be done. My father would have been glad to return to his old mode of bachelor life, but what could he do with two little children? He needed a woman to take care of him, and who so fitting as his wife's elder sister? So she had the charge of me from my birth; and for a time I was weakly, as was but natural, and she was always beside me, night and day watching over me, and my father nearly as anxious as she. For his land had come down from father to son for more than three hundred years, and he would have cared for me merely as his flesh and blood that was to inherit the land after him.

But he needed something to love, for all that, to most people, he was a stern, hard man, and he took to me as, I fancy, he had taken to no human being before – as he might have taken to my mother, if she had had no former life for him to be jealous of. I loved him back again right heartily. I loved all around me, I believe, for everybody was kind to me. After a time, I overcame my original weakliness of constitution, and was just a bonny, strong-looking lad whom every passer-by noticed, when my father took me with him to the nearest town.

At home I was the darling of my aunt, the tenderly beloved of my father, the pet and plaything of the old domestic, the 'young master' of the farm-labourers, before whom I played many a lordly antic, assuming a sort of authority which sat oddly enough, I doubt not, on such a baby as I was.

Gregory was three years older than I. Aunt Fanny was always kind to him in deed and in action, but she did not often think about him, she had fallen so completely into the habit of being engrossed by me, from the fact of my having come into her charge as a delicate baby. My father never got over his grudging dislike of his stepson, who had so innocently wrestled with him for the possession of my mother's heart. I mistrust me, too, that my father always considered him as the cause of my mother's death and my early delicacy; and utterly unreasonable as this may seem, I believe my father rather cherished his feeling of alienation to my brother as a duty, than strove to repress it.

Yet not for the world would my father have grudged him anything that money could purchase. That was, as it were, in the bond when he had wedded my mother. Gregory was lumpish and loutish, awkward and ungainly, marring whatever he meddled in, and many a hard word and sharp scolding did he get from the people about the farm, who hardly waited till my father's back was turned before they rated the stepson.

I am ashamed – my heart is sore to think how I fell into the fashion of the family, and slighted my poor orphan step-brother. I don't think I ever scouted him, or was wilfully ill-natured to him; but the habit of

154

being considered in all things, and being treated as something uncommon and superior, made me insolent in my prosperity, and I exacted more than Gregory was always willing to grant, and then, irritated, I sometimes repeated the disparaging words I had heard others use with regard to him, without fully understanding their meaning. Whether he did or not I cannot tell. I am afraid he did. He used to turn silent and quiet – sullen and sulky, my father thought it; stupid, Aunt Fanny used to call it.

But everyone said he was stupid and dull, and this stupidity and dullness grew upon him. He would sit without speaking a word, sometimes, for hours; then my father would bid him rise and do some piece of work, maybe, about the farm. And he would take three or four tellings before he would go. When we were sent to school, it was all the same. He could never be made to remember his lessons; the schoolmaster grew weary of scolding and flogging, and at last advised my father just to take him away, and set him to some farmwork that might not be above his comprehension. I think he was more gloomy and stupid than ever after this, yet he was not a cross lad; he was patient and good-natured, and would try to do a kind turn for anyone, even if they had been scolding or cuffing him not a minute before. But very often his attempts at kindness ended in some mischief to the very people he was trying to serve, owing to his awkward, ungainly ways.

I suppose I was a clever lad; at any rate, I always got plenty of praise; and was, as we called it, the cock of the school. The school-master said I could learn anything I chose, but my father, who had no great learning himself, saw little use in much for me, and took me away betimes, and kept me with him about the farm. Gregory was made into a kind of shepherd, receiving his training under old Adam, who was nearly past his work. I think old Adam was almost the first person who had a good opinion of Gregory. He stood to it that my brother had good parts, though he did not rightly know how to bring them out; and, for knowing the bearings of the Fells, he said he had never seen a lad like him. My father would try to bring Adam round to speak of Gregory's faults and shortcomings; but, instead of that, he would praise him twice as much as soon as he found out what was my father's object.

One winter-time, when I was about sixteen, and Gregory nineteen, I was sent by my father on an errand to a place about seven miles distant by the road, but only about four by the Fells. He bade me return by the road, whichever way I took in going, for the evenings closed in early, and were often thick and misty; besides which, old Adam, now paralytic and bedridden, foretold a downfall of snow before long.

I soon got to my journey's end, and soon had done my business; earlier by an hour, I thought, than my father had expected, so I took the decision of the way by which I would return into my own hands, and set off back again over the Fells, just as the first shades of evening began to fall. It looked dark and gloomy enough; but everything was so still that I thought I should have plenty of time to get home before the snow came down.

Off I set at a pretty quick pace. But night came on quicker. The right path was clear enough in the daytime, although at several points two or three exactly similar diverged from the same place; but when there was a good light, the traveller was guided by the sight of distant objects – a piece of rock, a fall in the ground – which were quite invisible to me now. I plucked up a brave heart, however, and took what seemed to me the right road. It was wrong, however, and led me whither I knew not, but to some wild boggy moor where the solitude seemed painful, intense, as if never footfall of man had come thither to break the silence.

I tried to shout – with the dimmest possible hope of being heard – rather to reassure myself by the sound of my own voice; but my voice came husky and short, and it dismayed me; it seemed so weird and strange in that noiseless expanse of black darkness. Suddenly the air was filled with thick and dusky flakes, my face and hands were wet with snow. It cut me off from the slightest knowledge of where I was, for I lost every idea of the direction from which I had come, so that I could not even retrace my steps; it hemmed me in, thicker, thicker, with a darkness that might be felt. The boggy soil on which I stood quaked under me if I remained long in one place, and yet I dared not move far.

All my youthful hardiness seemed to leave me at once. I was on the point of crying, and only very shame seemed to keep it down. To save myself from shedding tears, I shouted – terrible, wild shouts for bare life they were. I turned sick as I paused to listen; no answering sound came but the unfeeling echoes. Only the noiseless, pitiless snow kept falling thicker, thicker – faster, faster! I was growing numb and sleepy. I tried to move about, but I dared not go far, for fear of the precipices which, I knew, abounded in certain places on the Fells. Now and then, I stood still and shouted again; but my voice was getting choked with tears, as I thought of the desolate, helpless death I was to die, and how little they at home, sitting round the warm, red, bright fire, wotted what was become of me – and how my poor father would grieve for me – it would surely kill him – it would break his heart, poor old man! Aunt Fanny too – was this to be the end of all her cares for me?

I began to review my life in a strange kind of vivid dream, in which the various scenes of my few boyish years passed before me like visions. In a pang of agony, caused by such remembrance of my short life, I gathered up my strength and called out once more, a long, despairing, wailing cry, to which I had no hope of obtaining any answer, save from the echoes around, dulled as the sound might be by the thickened air.

To my surprise, I heard a cry – almost as long, as wild as mine – so wild that it seemed unearthly, and I almost thought it must be the voice of some of the mocking spirits of the Fells, about whom I had heard so many tales. My heart suddenly began to beat fast and loud. I could not reply for a minute or two. I nearly fancied I had lost the power of utterance.

Just at this moment a dog barked. Was it Lassie's bark – my brother's collie? – an ugly enough brute, with a white, ill-looking face, that my father always kicked whenever he saw it, partly for its own demerits, partly because it belonged to my brother. On such occasions, Gregory would whistle Lassie away, and go off and sit with her in some outhouse.

My father had once or twice been ashamed of himself, when the poor collie had yowled out with the suddenness of the pain, and had relieved himself of his self-reproach by blaming my brother, who, he said, had no notion of training a dog, and was enough to ruin any collie in Christendom with his stupid way of allowing them to lie by the kitchen fire. To all of which Gregory would answer nothing, nor even seem to hear, but go on looking absent and moody. Yes! there again! It was Lassie's bark! Now or never! I lifted up my voice and shouted, 'Lassie! Lassie! For God's sake, Lassie!'

Another moment, and the great white-faced Lassie was curving and gambolling with delight round my feet and legs, looking, however, up in my face with her intelligent, apprehensive eyes, as if fearing lest I might greet her with a blow, as I had done oftentimes before. But I cried with gladness, as I stooped down and patted her. My mind was sharing in my body's weakness, and I could not reason, but I knew that help was at hand. A grey figure came more and more distinctly out of the thick, close-pressing darkness. It was Gregory wrapped in his maud.

'Oh, Gregory!' said I, and I fell upon his neck, unable to speak another word. He never spoke much, and made me no answer for some little time. Then he told me we must move, we must walk for dear life – we must find our road home, if possible; but we must move or we should be frozen to death.

'Don't you know the way home?' asked I.

'I thought I did when I set out, but I am doubtful now. The snow blinds me, and I am feared that in moving about just now I have lost the right gait homewards.'

He had his shepherd's staff with him, and by dint of plunging it before us at every step we took – clinging close to each other, we went on safely enough, as far as not falling down any of the steep rocks, but it was slow, dreary work. My brother, I saw, was more guided by Lassie and the way she took than anything else, trusting to her instinct. It was too dark to see far before us; but he called her back continually, and noted from what quarter she returned, and shaped our slow steps accordingly. But the tedious motion scarcely kept my very blood from freezing. Every bone, every fibre in my body seemed first to ache, and then to swell, and then to turn numb with the intense cold. My brother bore it better than I, from having been more out upon the hills. He did not speak, except to call Lassie. I strove to be brave, and not complain; but now I felt the deadly fatal sleep stealing over me.

'I can go no farther,' I said, in a drowsy tone. I remember I suddenly became dogged and resolved. Sleep I would, were it only for five minutes. If death were to be the consequence, sleep I would. Gregory stood still. I suppose he recognized the peculiar phase of suffering to which I had been brought by the cold.

'It is of no use,' said he, as if to himself. 'We are no nearer home than we were when we started, as far as I can tell. Our only chance is in Lassie. Here! roll thee in my maud, lad, and lay thee down on this sheltered side of this bit of rock. Creep close under it, lad, and I'll lie by thee, and strive to keep the warmth in us. Stay! hast gotten aught about thee they'll know at home?'

I felt him unkind thus to keep me from slumber, but on his repeating the question, I pulled out my pocket-handkerchief, of some showy pattern, which Aunt Fanny had hemmed for me – Gregory took it, and tied it round Lassie's neck.

'Hie thee, Lassie, hie thee home!' And the white-faced, ill-favoured brute was off like a shot in the darkness. Now I might lie down – now I might sleep. In my drowsy stupor I felt that I was being tenderly covered up by my brother; but what with I neither knew nor cared – I was too dull, too selfish, too numb to think and reason, or I might have known that in that bleak bare place there was naught to wrap me in, save what was taken off another. I was glad enough when he ceased his cares and lay down by me. I took his hand.

'Thou canst not remember, lad, how we lay together thus by our dying mother. She put thy small, wee hand in mine – I reckon she sees us now; and belike we shall soon be with her. Anyhow, God's will be done.'

'Dear Gregory,' I muttered, and crept nearer to him for warmth. He was talking still, and again about our mother, when I fell asleep. In an instant – or so it seemed – there were many voices about me – many faces hovering round me – the sweet luxury of warmth was stealing into every part of me. I was in my own little bed at home. I am thankful to say, my first word was 'Gregory?'

A look passed from one to another – my father's stern old face strove in vain to keep its sternness; his mouth quivered, his eyes filled slowly with unwonted tears.

'I would have given him half my land – I would have blessed him as my son – oh God! I would have knelt at his feet, and asked him to forgive my hardness of heart.'

I heard no more. A whirl came through my brain, catching me back to death. I came slowly to my consciousness, weeks afterwards. My father's hair was white when I recovered, and his hands shook as he looked into my face.

We spoke no more of Gregory. We could not speak of him; but he was strangely in our thoughts. Lassie came and went with never a word of blame; nay, my father would try to stroke her, but she shrank away; and he, as if reproved by the poor dumb beast, would sigh, and be silent and abstracted for a time.

Aunt Fanny – always a talker – told me all. How, on that fatal night, my father, irritated by my prolonged absence, and probably more anxious than he cared to show, had been fierce and imperious, even beyond his wont, to Gregory: had upbraided him with his father's poverty, his own stupidity which made his services good for nothing – for so, in spite of the old shepherd, my father always chose to consider them.

At last, Gregory had risen up, and whistled Lassie out with him – poor Lassie, crouching underneath his chair for fear of a kick or a blow. Some time before, there had been some talk between my father and my aunt respecting my return; and when Aunt Fanny told me all this, she said she fancied that Gregory might have noticed the coming storm, and gone out silently to meet me. Three hours afterwards, when all were running about in wild alarm, not knowing whither to go in search of me – not even missing Gregory, or heeding his absence, poor fellow – poor, poor fellow! – Lassie came home, with my handkerchief tied round her neck. They knew and understood, and the whole strength of the farm was turned out to follow her, with wraps, and blankets, and brandy, and everything that could be thought of. I lay in chilly sleep, but still alive, beneath the rock that Lassie guided them to. I was covered over with my brother's plaid, and his thick shepherd's coat was carefully wrapped round my feet. He was in his shirt-sleeves – his arm thrown over me – a quiet smile (he had hardly ever smiled in life) upon his still, cold face.

My father's last words were, 'God forgive me my hardness of heart towards the fatherless child!'

And what marked the depth of his feeling of repentance, perhaps more than all, considering the passionate love he bore my mother, was this: we found a paper of directions after his death, in which he desired that he might lie at the foot of the grave in which, by his desire, poor Gregory had been laid with OUR MOTHER.

A Long-Ago Affair

JOHN GALSWORTHY

Hubert Marsland, the landscape painter, returning from a day's sketching on the river in the summer of 1921, had occasion to stay the progress of his two-seater about ten miles from London for a minor repair, and while his car was being seen to, strolled away from the garage to have a look at a house where he had often spent his holidays as a boy. Walking through a gateway and passing a large gravel-pit on his left, he was soon opposite the house, which stood back a little in its grounds. Very much changed! More pretentious, not so homely as when his uncle and aunt lived there, and he used to play cricket on this warren opposite, where the cricket ground, it seemed, had been turned into a golf course. It was late – the dinner-hour, nobody playing, and passing on to the links he stood digesting the geography. Here must have been where the old pavilion was. And there – still turfed – where he had made that particularly nice stroke to leg, when he went in last and carried his bat for thirteen. Thirty-nine years ago – his sixteenth birthday. How vividly he remembered his new pads! A. P. Lucas had played against them and only made thirty-two – one founded one's style on A. P. Lucas in those days – feet in front of the bat, and pointed a little forward, elegant; you never saw it now, and a good thing too – one could sacrifice too much to style! Still, the tendency was all the other way; style was too much 'off', perhaps!

He stepped back into the sun and sat down on the grass. Peaceful – very still! The haze of the distant downs was visible between his uncle's old house and the next; and there was the clump of elms on the far side behind which the sun would be going down just as it used to then. He pressed the palms of his hands to the turf. A glorious summer – something like that summer of long ago. And warmth from the turf, or perhaps from the past, crept into his heart and made it ache a little. Just here he must have sat, after his innings, at Mrs Monteith's feet peeping out of a flounced dress. Lord! The fools boys were! How head-long and uncalculating their devotions! A softness in voice and eyes, a smile, a touch or two – and they were slaves! Young fools, but good young fools. And, standing behind her chair – he could see him now – that other idol Captain MacKay, with his face of browned ivory – just the colour of that elephant's tusk his uncle had, which had gone so yellow – and his perfect black moustache, his white tie, check suit, carnation, spats, Malacca cane – all so fascinating! Mrs Monteith, 'the grass widow' they had called her! He remembered the look in people's eyes, the tone in their voices. Such a pretty woman! He had 'fallen for her' at first sight, as the Yanks put it – her special scent, her daintiness, her voice! And that day on the river, when she made much of him, and Captain MacKay attended Evelyn Curtiss so assiduously that he was expected to propose. Quaint period! They used the word 'courting' then, wore full skirts, high stays; and himself a blue elastic belt round his white-flannelled waist. And in the evening afterwards, his aunt had said with an arch smile: 'Good-night, *silly* boy!' Silly boy indeed, with a flower the grass widow had dropped pressed by his cheek into his pillow! What folly! And that next Sunday – looking forward to Church – passionately brushing his top hat; all through the service spying at her creamy profile, two pews in front on the left, between goat-bearded old Hallgrave her uncle, and her pink, broad, white-haired aunt; scheming to get near her when she came out, lingering, lurking, getting just a smile and the rustle of her flounces. Ah, ha! A little went a long way then! And the last day of his holidays and its night with the first introduction to reality. Who said the Victorian Age was innocent?

Marsland put his palm up to his cheek. No! the dew was not yet falling! And his mind lightly turned and tossed his memories of women, as a man turns and tosses hay to air it; but nothing remembered gave him quite the feeling of that first experience.

His aunt's dance! His first white waistcoat, bought *ad hoc*, from the local tailor, his tie laboriously imitating the hero – Captain MacKay's. All came back with such freshness in the quiet of the warren – the expectancy, the humble shy excitement, the breathless asking for a dance, the writing 'Mrs Monteith' twice on his little gilt-edged programme with its tiny tasselled white pencil; her slow-moving fan, her smile. And the first dance when it came; what infinite care not to tread on her white satin toes; what a thrill when her arm pressed his in the crush – such holy rapture, about all the first part of that evening, with yet another dance to come! If only he could have twirled her and 'reversed' like his pattern, Captain MacKay! Then delirium growing as the second dance came near, making him cut his partner – the cool grass-scented air out on the dark terrace, with the chafers booming by, and in the starshine the poplars wonderously tall; the careful adjustment of his tie and waistcoat, the careful polishing of his hot face! A long breath then, and into the house to find her! Ballroom, supper-room, stairs, library, billiard-room, all drawn blank – 'Estudiantina' going on and on, and he a wandering, white-waistcoated young ghost. Ah! The conservatory – and the hurrying there! And then the moment which had always been, was even now, such a blurred confused impression. Smothered voices from between a clump of flowers: 'I saw her.' 'Who was the man?' A glimpse, gone past in a flash, of an ivory face, a black moustache! And then her voice: 'Hubert'; and her hot hand clasping his, drawing him to her; her scent, her face smiling, very set! A rustling behind the flowers, those people spying; and suddenly her lips on his cheeks, the kiss sounding in his ears, her voice saying, very softly: 'Hubert, dear boy!' The rustle receded, ceased. What a long silent minute, then, among the ferns and blossoms in the dusk with her face close to his, pale, perturbed, before she led him out into the light, while he was slowly realizing that she had made use of him to shelter her. A boy – not old enough to be her lover, but old enough to save her name and that of Captain MacKay! Her kiss – the last of many – but not upon *his* lips, *his* cheeks! Hard work realizing that! A boy – of

165

no account – a boy, who in a day would be at school again, kissed that *he* and *she* might renew their intrigue unsuspected!

How had he behaved the rest of that evening of romance bedrabbled? He hardly knew. Betrayed with a kiss! Two idols in the dust! And did they care what he was feeling? Not they! All they cared for was to cover up their tracks with him! But somehow – somehow – he had never shown her that he knew. Only, when their dance was over, and someone came and took her for the next, he escaped up to his little room, tore off his gloves, his waistcoat; lay on his bed, thought bitter thoughts. A boy! There he had stayed, with the thrum of the music in his ears, till at last it died away for good and the carriages were gone, and the night was quiet.

Squatting on the warren grass, still warm and dewless, Marsland rubbed his knees. Nothing like boys for generosity. And, with a little smile, he thought of his aunt next morning, half-arch and half-concerned: 'It isn't nice, dear, to sit out in dark corners, and – well, perhaps, it wasn't your fault, but still, it isn't nice – not – quite –' and of how suddenly she had stopped, looking in his face, where his lips were curling in his first ironic laugh. She had never forgiven him that laugh – thinking him a cynical young Lothario? And Marsland thought: 'Live and learn! Wonder what became of those two? Victorian Age! Hatches were battened down in those days! But, innocent – my hat!'

Ah! The sun was off, dew falling! He got up, rubbing his knees to take the stiffness out of them. Pigeons in the wood beyond were calling. A window in his uncle's old home blazed like a jewel in the sun's last rays between the poplar trees. Heh! dear – a little long-ago affair!

166

The Rocking-Horse Winner

D. H. LAWRENCE

There was a woman who was beautiful, who started with all the advantages, yet she had no luck. She married for love, and the love turned to dust. She had bonny children, yet she felt they had been thrust upon her, and she could not love them. They looked at her coldly, as if they were finding fault with her. And hurriedly she felt she must cover up some fault in herself. Yet what it was that she must cover up she never knew. Nevertheless, when her children were present, she always felt the centre of her heart go hard. This troubled her, and in her manner she was all the more gentle and anxious for her children, as if she loved them very much. Only she herself knew that at the centre of her heart was a hard little place that could not feel love, no, not for anybody. Everybody else said of her: 'She is such a good mother. She adores her children.' Only she herself, and her children themselves, knew it was not so. They read it in each other's eyes.

There were a boy and two little girls. They lived in a pleasant house, with a garden, and they had discreet servants, and felt themselves superior to anyone in the neighbourhood.

Although they lived in style, they felt always an anxiety in the house. There was never enough money. The mother had a small income, and the father had a small income, but not nearly enough for the social position which they had to keep up. The father went into town to some office. But though he had good prospects, these prospects never materialized. There was always the grinding sense of the shortage of money, though the style was always kept up.

At last the mother said: 'I will see if I can't make something.' But she did not know where to begin. She racked her brains, and tried this thing and the other, but could not find anything successful. The failure made deep lines come into her face. Her children were growing up, they would have to go to school. There must be more money, there must be more money. The father, who was always very handsome and expensive in his tastes, seemed as if he never *would* be able to do anything worth doing. And the mother, who had a great belief in herself, did not succeed any better, and her tastes were just as expensive.

And so the house came to be haunted by the unspoken phrase: *There must be more money! There must be more money!* The children could hear it all the time, though nobody said it aloud. They heard it at Christmas, when the expensive and splendid toys filled the nursery. Behind the shining modern rocking-horse, behind the smart doll's house, a voice would start whispering: 'There *must* be more money! There *must* be more money!' And the children would stop playing, to listen for a moment. They would look into each other's eyes, to see if they had all heard. And each one saw in the eyes of the other two that they too had heard. 'There *must* be more money! There *must* be more money!'

It came whispering from the springs of the still-swaying rocking-horse, and even the horse, bending his wooden, champing head, heard it. The big doll, sitting so pink and smirking in her new pram, could hear it quite plainly, and seemed to be smirking all the more self-consciously because of it. The foolish puppy, too, that took the place of the teddy-bear, he was looking so extraordinarily foolish for no other reason but that he heard the secret whisper all over the house: 'There *must* be more money!'

Yet nobody ever said it aloud. The whisper was everywhere, and therefore no one spoke it. Just as no one ever says: 'We are breathing!' in spite of the fact that breath is coming and going all the time.

'Mother,' said the boy Paul one day, 'why don't we keep a car of our own? Why do we always use uncle's, or else a taxi?'

'Because we're the poor members of the family,' said the mother.

'But why *are* we, Mother?'

'Well – I suppose,' she said slowly and bitterly, 'it's because your father has no luck.'

The boy was silent for some time.

'Is luck money, Mother?' he asked, rather timidly.

'No, Paul. Not quite. It's what causes you to have money.'

'Oh!' said Paul vaguely. 'I thought when Uncle Oscar said *filthy lucker*, it meant money.'

'*Filthy lucre* does mean money,' said the mother. 'But it's lucre, not luck.'

'Oh!' said the boy. 'Then what *is* luck, Mother?'

'It's what causes you to have money. If you're lucky you have money. That's why it's better to be born lucky than rich. If you're rich, you may lose your money. But if you're lucky, you will always get more money.'

'Oh! Will you? And is Father not lucky?'

'Very unlucky, I should say,' she said bitterly.

The boy watched her with unsure eyes.

'Why?' he asked.

'I don't know. Nobody ever knows why one person is lucky and another unlucky.'

'Don't they? Nobody at all? Does *nobody* know?'

'Perhaps God. But He never tells.'

'He ought to, then. And aren't you lucky either, Mother?'

'I can't be, if I married an unlucky husband.'

'But by yourself, aren't you?'

'I used to think I was, before I married. Now I think I am very unlucky indeed.'

'Why?'

'Well – never mind! Perhaps I'm not really,' she said.

The child looked at her to see if she meant it. But he saw, by the lines of her mouth, that she was only trying to hide something from him.

'Well, anyhow,' he said stoutly, 'I'm a lucky person.'

'Why?' said his mother, with a sudden laugh.

He stared at her. He didn't even know why he had said it.

'God told me,' he asserted, brazening it out.

'I hope He did, dear!' she said, again with a laugh, but rather bitter.

'He did, Mother!'

'Excellent!' said the mother, using one of her husband's exclamations.

The boy saw she did not believe him; or rather, that she paid no attention to his assertion. This angered him somewhat, and made him want to compel her attention.

He went off by himself, vaguely, in a childish way, seeking for the clue to 'luck'. Absorbed, taking no heed of other people, he went about with a sort of stealth, seeking inwardly for luck. He wanted luck, he wanted it, he wanted it. When the two girls were playing dolls in the nursery, he would sit on his big rocking-horse, charging madly into space, with a frenzy that made the little girls peer at him uneasily. Wildly the horse careered, the waving dark hair of the boy tossed, his eyes had a strange glare in them. The little girls dared not speak to him.

When he had ridden to the end of his mad little journey, he climbed down and stood in front of his rocking-horse, staring fixedly into its lowered face. Its red mouth was slightly open, its big eye was wide and glassy-bright.

'Now!' he would silently command the snorting steed. 'Now, take me to where there is luck! Now take me!'

And he would slash the horse on the neck with the little whip he had asked Uncle Oscar for. He *knew* the horse could take him to where there was luck, if only he forced it. So he would mount again and start on his furious ride, hoping at last to get there. He knew he could get there.

'You'll break your horse, Paul!' said the nurse.

'He's always riding like that! I wish he'd leave off!' said his elder sister Joan.

But he only glared down on them in silence. Nurse gave him up. She could make nothing of him. Anyhow, he was growing beyond her.

One day his mother and his Uncle Oscar came in when he was on one of his furious rides. He did not speak to them.

'Hallo, you young jockey! Riding a winner?' said his uncle.

'Aren't you growing too big for a rocking-horse? You're not a very little boy any longer, you know,' said his mother.

But Paul only gave a blue glare from his big, rather close-set eyes. He would speak to nobody when he was in full tilt. His mother watched him with an anxious expression on her face.

At last he suddenly stopped forcing his horse into the mechanical gallop and slid down.

'Well, I got there!' he announced fiercely, his blue eyes still flaring, and his sturdy long legs straddling apart.

'Where did you get to?' asked his mother.

'Where I wanted to go,' he flared back at her.

'That's right, son!' said Uncle Oscar. 'Don't you stop till you get there. What's the horse's name?'

'He doesn't have a name,' said the boy.

'Gets on without all right?' asked the uncle.

'Well, he has different names. He was called Sansovino last week.'

'Sansovino, eh? Won the Ascot. How did you know this name?'

'He always talks about horse-races with Bassett,' said Joan.

The uncle was delighted to find that his small nephew was posted with all the racing news. Bassett, the young gardener, who had been wounded in the left foot in the war and had got his present job through Oscar Cresswell, whose batman he had been, was a perfect blade of the 'turf'. He lived in the racing events, and the small boy lived with him.

Oscar Cresswell got it all from Bassett.

'Master Paul comes and asks me, so I can't do more than tell him, sir,' said Bassett, his face terribly serious, as if he were speaking of religious matters.

'And does he ever put anything on a horse he fancies?'

'Well – I don't want to give him away – he's a young sport, a fine sport, sir. Would you mind asking him himself? He sort of takes a pleasure in it, and perhaps he'd feel I was giving him away, sir, if you don't mind.'

Bassett was as serious as a church.

The uncle went back to his nephew and took him off for a ride in the car.

'Say, Paul, old man, do you ever put anything on a horse?' the uncle asked.

The boy watched the handsome man closely.

'Why, do you think I oughtn't to?' he parried.

'Not a bit of it! I thought perhaps you might give me a tip for the Lincoln.'

The car sped on into the country, going down to Uncle Oscar's place in Hampshire.

'Honour bright?' said the nephew.

'Honour bright, son!' said the uncle.

'Well, then, Daffodil.'

'Daffodil! I doubt it, sonny. What about Mirza?'

'I only know the winner,' said the boy. 'That's Daffodil.'

'Daffodil, eh?'

There was a pause. Daffodil was an obscure horse comparatively.

'Uncle!'

'Yes, son?'

'You won't let it go any further, will you? I promised Bassett.'

'Bassett be damned, old man! What's he got to do with it?'

'We're partners. We've been partners from the first. Uncle, he lent me my first five shillings, which I lost. I promised him, honour bright, it was only between me and him; only you gave me that ten-shilling note I started winning with, so I thought you were lucky. You won't let it go any further, will you?'

The boy gazed at his uncle from those big, hot, blue eyes, set rather close together. The uncle stirred and laughed uneasily.

'Right you are, son! I'll keep your tip private. Daffodil, eh? How much are you putting on him?'

'All except twenty pounds,' said the boy. 'I keep that in reserve.'

The uncle thought it a good joke.

'You keep twenty pounds in reserve, do you, you young romancer? What are you betting, then?'

'I'm betting three hundred,' said the boy gravely. 'But it's between you and me, Uncle Oscar! Honour bright?'

The uncle burst into a roar of laughter.

'It's between you and me all right, you young Nat Gould,' he said, laughing. 'But where's your three hundred?'

'Bassett keeps it for me. We're partners.'

'You are, are you! And what is Bassett putting on Daffodil?'

'He won't go quite as high as I do, I expect. Perhaps he'll go a hundred and fifty.'

'What, pennies?' laughed the uncle.

'Pounds,' said the child, with a surprised look at his uncle. 'Bassett keeps a bigger reserve than I do.'

Between wonder and amusement Uncle Oscar was silent. He pursued the matter no further, but he determined to take his nephew with him to the Lincoln races.

'Now, son,' he said, 'I'm putting twenty on Mirza, and I'll put five on for you on any horse you fancy. What's your pick?'

'Daffodil, uncle.'

'No, not the fiver on Daffodil!'

'I should if it was my own fiver,' said the child.

'Good! Good! Right you are! A fiver for me and a fiver for you on Daffodil.'

The child had never been to a race-meeting before, and his eyes were blue fire. He pursed his mouth tight and watched. A Frenchman just in front had put his money on Lancelot. Wild with excitement, he flayed his arms up and down, yelling '*Lancelot! Lancelot!*' in his French accent.

Daffodil came in first, Lancelot second, Mirza third. The child, flushed and with eyes blazing, was curiously serene. His uncle brought him four five-pound notes, four to one.

'What am I to do with these?' he cried, waving them before the boy's eyes.

'I suppose we'll talk to Bassett,' said the boy. 'I expect I have fifteen hundred now; and twenty in reserve; and this twenty.'

His uncle studied him for some moments.

'Look here, son!' he said. 'You're not serious about Bassett and that fifteen hundred, are you?'

'Yes, I am. But it's between you and me, uncle. Honour bright?'

'Honour bright all right, son! But I must talk to Bassett.'

'If you'd like to be a partner, uncle, with Bassett and me, we could all be partners. Only, you'd have to promise, honour bright, uncle, not to let it go beyond us three. Bassett and I are lucky, and you must be lucky, because it was your ten shillings I started winning with . . .'

Uncle Oscar took both Bassett and Paul into Richmond Park for an afternoon, and there they talked.

'It's like this, you see, sir,' Bassett said. 'Master Paul would get me talking about racing events, spinning yarns, you know, sir. And he was always keen on knowing if I'd made or if I'd lost. It's about a year since, now, that I put five shillings on Blush of Dawn for him: and we lost. Then the luck turned, with that ten shillings he had from you: that we put on Singhalese. And since that time, it's been pretty steady, all things considering. What do you say, Master Paul?'

'We're all right when we're sure,' said Paul. 'It's when we're not quite sure that we go down.'

'Oh, but we're careful then,' said Bassett.

'But when are you *sure*?' smiled Uncle Oscar.

'It's Master Paul, sir,' said Bassett in a secret, religious voice. 'It's as if he had it from heaven. Like Daffodil, now for the Lincoln. That was as sure as eggs.'

'Did you put anything on Daffodil?' asked Oscar Cresswell.

'Yes, sir. I made my bit.'

'And my nephew?'

Bassett was obstinately silent, looking at Paul.

'I made twelve hundred, didn't I, Bassett? I told uncle I was putting three hundred on Daffodil.'

'That's right,' said Bassett, nodding.

'But where's the money?' asked the uncle.

'I keep it safe locked up, sir. Master Paul he can have it any minute he likes to ask for it.'

'What, fifteen hundred pounds?'

'And twenty! And *forty*, that is, with the twenty he made on the course.'

'It's amazing!' said the uncle.

174

'If Master Paul offers you to be partners, sir, I would, if I were you: if you'll excuse me,' said Bassett.

Oscar Cresswell thought about it.

'I'll see the money,' he said.

They drove home again, and, sure enough, Bassett came round to the garden-house with fifteen hundred pounds in notes. The twenty pounds reserve was left with Joe Glee, in the Turf Commission deposit.

'You see, it's all right, uncle, when I'm *sure*! Then we go strong, for all we're worth. Don't we, Bassett?'

'We do that, Master Paul.'

'And when are you sure?' said the uncle, laughing.

'Oh, well, sometimes I'm *absolutely* sure, like about Daffodil,' said the boy; 'and sometimes I have an idea; and sometimes I haven't even an idea, have I, Bassett? Then we're careful, because we mostly go down.'

'You do, do you! And when you're sure, like about Daffodil, what makes you sure, sonny?'

'Oh, well, I don't know,' said the boy uneasily. 'I'm sure, you know, uncle; that's all.'

'It's as if he had it from heaven, sir,' Bassett reiterated.

'I should say so!' said the uncle.

But he became a partner. And when the Leger was coming on Paul was 'sure' about Lively Spark, which was a quite inconsiderable horse. The boy insisted on putting a thousand on the horse, Bassett went for five hundred, and Oscar Cresswell two hundred. Lively Spark came in first, and the betting had been ten to one against him. Paul had made ten thousand.

'You see,' he said, 'I was absolutely sure of him.'

Even Oscar Cresswell had cleared two thousand.

'Look here, son,' he said, 'this sort of thing makes me nervous.'

'It needn't, uncle! Perhaps I shan't be sure again for a long time.'

'But what are you going to do with your money?' asked the uncle.

'Of course,' said the boy, 'I started it for Mother. She said she had no luck, because Father is unlucky, so I thought if *I* was lucky, it might stop whispering.'

175

'What might stop whispering?'

'Our house. I *hate* our house for whispering.'

'What does it whisper?'

'Why – why' – the boy fidgeted – 'why, I don't know. But it's always short of money, you know, uncle.'

'I know it, son, I know it.'

'You know people send Mother writs, don't you, uncle?'

'I'm afraid I do,' said the uncle.

'And then the house whispers, like people laughing at you behind your back. It's awful, that is! I thought if I was lucky–'

'You might stop it,' added the uncle.

The boy watched him with big blue eyes, that had an uncanny cold fire in them, and he said never a word.

'Well, then!' said the uncle. 'What are we doing?'

'I shouldn't like Mother to know I was lucky,' said the boy.

'Why not, son?'

'She'd stop me.'

'I don't think she would.'

'Oh!' – and the boy writhed in an odd way – 'I don't *want* her to know, uncle.'

'All right, son! We'll manage it without her knowing.'

They managed it very easily. Paul, at the other's suggestion, handed over five thousand pounds to his uncle, who deposited it with the family lawyer, who was then to inform Paul's mother that a relative had put five thousand pounds into his hands, which sum was to be paid out a thousand pounds at a time, on the mother's birthday, for the next five years.

'So she'll have a birthday present of a thousand pounds for five successive years,' said Uncle Oscar. 'I hope it won't make it all the harder for her later.'

Paul's mother had her birthday in November. The house had been 'whispering' worse than ever lately, and, even in spite of his luck, Paul could not bear up against it. He was very anxious to see the effect of the birthday letter, telling his mother about the thousand pounds.

When there were no visitors, Paul now took his meals with his parents, as he was beyond the nursery control. His mother went into town nearly every day. She had discovered that she had an odd knack of sketching furs and dress materials, so she worked secretly in the studio of a friend who was the chief 'artist' for the leading drapers. She drew the figures of ladies in furs and ladies in silk and sequins for the newspaper advertisements. This young woman artist earned several thousand pounds a year, but Paul's mother only made several hundreds, and she was again dissatisfied. She so wanted to be first in something, and she did not succeed, even in making sketches for drapery advertisements.

She was down to breakfast on the morning of her birthday. Paul watched her face as she read her letters. He knew the lawyer's letter. As his mother read it, her face hardened and became more expressionless. Then a cold, determined look came on her mouth. She hid the letter under the pile of others, and said not a word about it.

'Didn't you have anything nice in the post for your birthday, Mother?' said Paul.

'Quite moderately nice,' she said, her voice cold and absent.

She went away to town without saying more.

But in the afternoon Uncle Oscar appeared. He said Paul's mother had had a long interview with the lawyer, asking if the whole five thousand could not be advanced at once, as she was in debt.

'What do you think, uncle?' said the boy.

'I leave it to you, son.'

'Oh, let her have it, then! We can get some more with the other,' said the boy.

'A bird in the hand is worth two in the bush, laddie!' said Uncle Oscar.

'But I'm sure to *know* for the Grand National; or the Lincolnshire; or else the Derby. I'm sure to know for *one* of them,' said Paul.

So Uncle Oscar signed the agreement, and Paul's mother touched the whole five thousand. Then something very curious happened. The voices in the house suddenly went mad, like a chorus of frogs on a spring evening. There were certain new furnishings, and Paul had a tutor. He was *really* going to Eton, his father's school, in the following autumn. There were flowers in the winter, and a blossoming of the luxury Paul's mother had been used to. And yet the voices in the house, behind the sprays of mimosa and almond-blossom, and from under the piles of iridescent cushions, simply trilled and screamed in a sort of ecstasy: 'There *must* be more money! Oh-h-h; there *must* be more money. Oh, now, now-w! Now-w-w – there *must* be more money! – more than ever! More than ever!'

It frightened Paul terribly. He studied away at his Latin and Greek with his tutor. But his intense hours were spent with Bassett. The Grand National had gone by: he had not 'known', and had lost a hundred pounds. Summer was at hand. He was in agony for the Lincoln. But even for the Lincoln he didn't 'know', and he lost fifty pounds. He became wild-eyed and strange, as if something were going to explode in him.

'Let it alone, son! Don't you bother about it!' urged Uncle Oscar. But it was as if the boy couldn't really hear what his uncle was saying.

'I've got to know for the Derby! I've got to know for the Derby!' the child reiterated, his big blue eyes blazing with a sort of madness.

His mother noticed how overwrought he was.

'You'd better go to the seaside. Wouldn't you like to go now to the seaside, instead of waiting? I think you'd better,' she said, looking down at him anxiously, her heart curiously heavy because of him.

But the child lifted his uncanny blue eyes.

'I couldn't possibly go before the Derby, Mother!' he said. 'I couldn't possibly!'

'Why not?' she said, her voice becoming heavy when she was opposed. 'Why not? You can still go from the seaside to see the Derby with your Uncle Oscar, if that's what you wish. No need for you to wait here. Besides, I think you care too much about these races. It's a bad sign. My family has been a gambling family, and you won't know till you grow up how much damage it has done. But it has done damage. I shall have to send Bassett away, and ask Uncle Oscar not to talk racing to you, unless you promise to be reasonable about it: go away to the seaside and forget it. You're all nerves!'

'I'll do what you like, Mother, so long as you don't send me away till after the Derby,' the boy said.

'Send you away from where? Just from this house?'

'Yes,' he said, gazing at her.

'Why, you curious child, what makes you care about this house so much, suddenly? I never knew you loved it.'

He gazed at her without speaking. He had a secret within a secret, something he had not divulged, even to Bassett or to his Uncle Oscar.

But his mother, after standing undecided and a little bit sullen for some moments, said:

'Very well, then! Don't go to the seaside till after the Derby, if you don't wish it. But promise me you won't let your nerves go to pieces. Promise you won't think so much about horse-racing and *events*, as you call them.'

'Oh no,' said the boy casually. 'I won't think much about them, Mother. You needn't worry. I wouldn't worry, Mother, if I were you.'

'If you were me and I were you,' said his mother, 'I wonder what we *should* do!'

'But you know you needn't worry, Mother, don't you?' the boy repeated.

'I should be awfully glad to know it,' she said wearily.

'Oh, well, you *can*, you know. I mean, you *ought* to know you needn't worry,' he insisted.

'Ought I? Then I'll see about it,' she said.

Paul's secret of secrets was his wooden horse, that which had no name. Since he was emancipated from a nurse and a nursery-governess, he had had his rocking-horse removed to his own bedroom at the top of the house.

'Surely you're too big for a rocking-horse!' his mother had remonstrated.

'Well, you see, Mother, till I can have a *real* horse, I like to have *some* sort of animal about,' had been his quaint answer.

'Do you feel he keeps you company?' she laughed.

'Oh yes! He's very good, he always keeps me company, when I'm there,' said Paul.

So the horse, rather shabby, stood in an arrested prance in the boy's bedroom.

The Derby was drawing near, and the boy grew more and more tense. He hardly heard what was spoken to him, he was very frail, and his eyes were really uncanny. His mother had sudden strange seizures of uneasiness about him. Sometimes, for half an hour, she would feel a sudden anxiety about him that was almost anguish. She wanted to rush to him at once, and know he was safe.

Two nights before the Derby, she was at a big party in town, when one of her rushes of anxiety about her boy, her first-born, gripped her heart till she could hardly speak. She fought with the feeling, might and main, for she believed in common sense. But it was too strong. She had to leave the dance and go downstairs to telephone to the country. The children's nursery-governess was terribly surprised and startled at being rung up in the night.

'Are the children all right, Miss Wilmot?'

'Oh yes, they are quite all right.'

'Master Paul? Is he all right?'

'He went to bed as right as a trivet. Shall I run up and look at him?'

'No,' said Paul's mother reluctantly. 'No! Don't trouble. It's all right. Don't sit up. We shall be home fairly soon.' She did not want her son's privacy intruded upon.

'Very good,' said the governess.

It was about one o'clock when Paul's mother and father drove up to their house. All was still. Paul's mother went to her room and slipped off her white fur cloak. She had told her maid not to wait up for her. She heard her husband downstairs, mixing a whisky and soda.

And then, because of the strange anxiety at her heart, she stole upstairs to her son's room. Noiselessly she went along the upper corridor. Was there a faint noise? What was it?

She stood, with arrested muscles, outside his door, listening. There was a strange, heavy, and yet not loud noise. Her heart stood still. It was a soundless noise, yet rushing and powerful. Something huge, in violent, hushed motion. What was it? What in God's name was it? She ought to know. She felt that she knew the noise. She knew what it was.

Yet she could not place it. She couldn't say what it was. And on and on it went, like a madness.

Softly, frozen with anxiety and fear, she turned the door-handle.

The room was dark. Yet in the space near the window, she heard and saw something plunging to and fro. She gazed in fear and amazement.

Then suddenly she switched on the light, and saw her son, in his green pyjamas, madly surging on the rocking-horse. The blaze of light suddenly lit him up, as he urged the wooden horse, and lit her up, as she stood, blonde, in her dress of pale green and crystal, in the doorway.

'Paul!' she cried. 'Whatever are you doing?'

'It's Malabar!' he screamed in a powerful, strange voice. 'It's Malabar!'

His eyes blazed at her for one strange and senseless second, as he ceased urging his wooden horse. Then he fell with a crash to the ground, and she, all her tormented motherhood flooding upon her, rushed to gather him up.

But he was unconscious, and unconscious he remained, with some brain-fever. He talked and tossed, and his mother sat stonily by his side.

'Malabar! It's Malabar! Bassett, Bassett, I *know*! It's Malabar!'

So the child cried, trying to get up and urge the rocking-horse that gave him his inspiration.

'What does he mean by Malabar?' asked the heart-frozen mother.

'I don't know,' said the father stonily.

'What does he mean by Malabar?' she asked her brother Oscar.

'It's one of the horses running for the Derby,' was the answer.

And, in spite of himself, Oscar Cresswell spoke to Bassett, and himself put a thousand on Malabar: at fourteen to one.

The third day of the illness was critical: they were waiting for a change. The boy, with his rather long, curly hair, was tossing ceaselessly on the pillow. He neither slept nor regained consciousness, and his eyes were like blue stones. His mother sat, feeling her heart had gone, turned actually into a stone.

In the evening, Oscar Cresswell did not come, but Bassett sent a message, saying could he come up for one moment, just one moment? Paul's mother was very angry at the intrusion, but on second thoughts she agreed. The boy was the same. Perhaps Bassett might bring him to consciousness.

The gardener, a shortish fellow with a little brown moustache and sharp little brown eyes, tiptoed into the room, touched his imaginary cap to Paul's mother, and stole to the bedside, staring with glittering, smallish eyes at the tossing, dying child.

'Master Paul!' he whispered. 'Master Paul! Malabar came in first all right, a clean win. I did as you told me. You've made over seventy thousand pounds, you have; you've got over eighty thousand. Malabar came in all right, Master Paul.'

'Malabar! Malabar! Did I say Malabar, Mother? Did I say Malabar? Do you think I'm lucky, Mother? I knew Malabar, didn't I? Over eighty thousand pounds! I call that lucky, don't you, Mother? Over eighty thousand pounds! I knew, didn't I know I knew? Malabar came in all right. If I ride my horse till I'm sure, then I tell you, Bassett, you can go as high as you like. Did you go for all you were worth, Bassett?'

'I went a thousand on it, Master Paul.'

'I never told you, Mother, that if I can ride my horse, and *get there*, then I'm absolutely sure – oh, absolutely! Mother, did I ever tell you? I *am* lucky!'

'No, you never did,' said his mother.

But the boy died in the night.

And even as he lay dead, his mother heard her brother's voice saying to her: 'My God, Hester, you're eighty-odd thousand to the good, and a poor devil of a son to the bad. But, poor devil, poor devil, he's best gone out of a life where he rides his rocking-horse to find a winner.'

Hilda's Letter

L. P. HARTLEY

It may take time to get over an obsession, even after the roots have been pulled out. Eustace was satisfied that 'going away' did not mean that he was going to die; but at moments the fiery chariot still cast its glare across his mind, and he was thankful to shield himself behind the prosaic fact that going away meant nothing worse than going to school. In other circumstances the thought of going to school would have alarmed him; but as an alternative to death it was almost welcome.

Unconsciously he tried to inoculate himself against the future by aping the demeanour of the schoolboys he saw about the streets or playing on the beach at Anchorstone. He whistled, put his hands in his pockets, swayed as he walked, and assumed the serious but detached air of someone who owes fealty to a masculine corporation beyond the ken of his womenfolk: a secret society demanding tribal peculiarities of speech and manner. As to the thoughts and habits of mind which should inspire these outward gestures, he found them in school stories; and if they were sometimes rather lurid they were much less distressing than the fiery chariot.

His family was puzzled by his almost eager acceptance of the trials in store. His aunt explained it as yet another instance of Eustace's indifference to home-ties, and an inevitable consequence of the money he had inherited from Miss Fothergill. She had to remind herself to be fair to him whenever she thought of this undeserved success. But to his father the very fact that it was undeserved made Eustace something of a hero. His son was a dark horse who had romped home, and the sight of Eustace often gave him a pleasurable tingling, an impulse to laugh and make merry, such as may greet the evening paper when it brings news of a win. A lad of such mettle would naturally want to go to school.

To Minney her one-time charge was now more than ever 'Master' Eustace; in other ways her feeling for him remained unchanged by anything that happened to him. He was just her little boy who was obeying the natural order of things by growing up. Barbara was too young to realize that the hair she sometimes pulled belonged to an embryo schoolboy. In any case, she was an egotist, and had she been older she would have regarded her brother's translation to another sphere from the angle of how it affected her. She would have set about finding other strings to pull now that she was denied his hair.

Thus, the grown-ups, though they did not want to lose him, viewed Eustace's metamorphosis without too much misgiving; and moreover they felt that he must be shown the forbearance and accorded the special privileges of one who has an ordeal before him. Even Aunt Sarah, who did not like the whistling or the hands in the pockets or the slang, only rebuked them half-heartedly.

But Hilda, beautiful, unapproachable Hilda, could not reconcile herself to the turn events had taken. Was she not and would she not always be nearly four years older than her brother Eustace? Was she not his spiritual adviser, pledged to make him a credit to her and to himself and to his family?

He was her care, her task in life. Indeed, he was much more than that; her strongest feelings centred in him and at the thought of losing him she felt as if her heart was being torn out of her body.

So while Eustace grew more perky, Hilda pined. She had never carried herself well, but now she slouched along, hurrying past people she knew as if she had important business to attend to, and her beauty, had she been aware of it, might have been a pursuer she was trying to shake off.

Eustace must not go to school, he must not. She knew he would not want to, when the time came; but by then it would be too late. She had rescued him from Anchorstone Hall, the lair of the highwayman, Dick Staveley, his hero and her *bête noire*; and she would rescue him again. But she must act, and act at once.

It was easy to find arguments. School would be bad for him. It would bring out the qualities he shared with other little boys, qualities which could be kept in check if he remained at home.

'What are little boys made of?' she demanded, and looked round in triumph when Eustace ruefully but dutifully answered:

> 'Snips and snails and puppy-dogs' tails
> And *that*'s what *they* are made of.'

He would grow rude and unruly and start being cruel to animals. Schoolboys always were. And he would fall ill; he would have a return of his bronchitis. Anchorstone was a health-resort. Eustace (who loved statistics and had a passion for records) had told her that Anchorstone had the ninth lowest death-rate in England. (This thought had brought him some fleeting comfort in the darkest hours of his obsession.) If he went away from Anchorstone he might die. They did not want him to die, did they?

Her father and her aunt listened respectfully to Hilda. Since her mother's death they had treated her as if she was half grown up, and they often told each other that she had an old head on young shoulders.

Hilda saw that she had impressed them and went on to say how much better Eustace was looking, which was quite true, and how much better behaved he was, except when he was pretending to be a schoolboy (Eustace reddened at this). And, above all, what a lot he knew; far more than most boys of his age, she said. Why, besides knowing that Anchorstone had the ninth lowest death-rate in England, he knew that Cairo had the highest death-rate in the world, and would speedily have been wiped out had it not also had the highest birth-rate. (This double pre-eminence made the record-breaking city one of Eustace's favourite subjects of contemplation.) And all this he owed to Aunt Sarah's teaching.

Aunt Sarah couldn't help being pleased; she was well educated herself and knew that Eustace was quick at his lessons.

'I shouldn't be surprised if he gets into quite a high class,' his father said; 'you'll see, he'll be bringing home a prize or two, won't you, Eustace?'

'Oh, but boys don't always learn much at school,' objected Hilda.

'How do you know they don't?' said Mr Cherrington teasingly. 'She never speaks to any other boys, does she, Eustace?'

But before Eustace had time to answer, Hilda surprised them all by saying: 'Well, I do, so there! I spoke to Gerald Steptoe!'

Everyone was thunderstruck to hear this, particularly Eustace, because Hilda had always had a special dislike for Gerald Steptoe, who was a sturdy, round-faced, knockabout boy with rather off-hand manners.

'I met him near the post office,' Hilda said, 'and he took off his cap, so I had to speak to him, hadn't I?'

Eustace said nothing. Half the boys in Anchorstone, which was only a small place, knew Hilda by sight and took their caps off when they passed her in the street, she was so pretty; and grown-up people used to stare at her, too, with a smile dawning on their faces. Eustace had often seen Gerald Steptoe take off his cap to Hilda, but she never spoke to him if she could help it, and would not let Eustace either.

Aunt Sarah knew this.

'You were quite right, Hilda. I don't care much for Gerald Steptoe, but we don't want to be rude to anyone, do we?'

Hilda looked doubtful.

'Well, you know he goes to a school near the one – St Ninian's – that you want to send Eustace to.'

'Want to! That's good,' said Mr Cherrington 'He *is* going, poor chap, on the seventeenth of January – that's a month from today – aren't you, Eustace? Now don't you try to unsettle him, Hilda.'

Eustace looked nervously at Hilda and saw the tears standing in her eyes.

'Don't say that to her, Alfred,' said Miss Cherrington. 'You can see she minds much more than he does.'

Hilda didn't try to hide her tears, as some girls would have; she just brushed them away and gave a loud sniff.

'It isn't Eustace's feelings I'm thinking about. If he wants to leave us all, let him. I'm thinking of his – his education.' She paused, and noticed that at the word 'education' their faces grew grave. 'Do you know what Gerald told me?'

'Well, what did he tell you?' asked Mr Cherrington airily, but Hilda saw he wasn't quite at his ease.

'He told me they didn't teach the boys *anything* at St Ninian's,' said Hilda. 'They just play games all the time. They're very good at games, he said, better than his school – I can't remember what it's called.'

'St Cyprian's,' put in Eustace. Any reference to a school made him feel self-important.

'I knew it was another saint. But the boys at St Ninian's aren't saints at all, Gerald said. They're all the sons of rich swanky people who go there to do nothing. Gerald said that what they don't know would fill books.'

There was a pause. No one spoke, and Mr Cherrington and his sister exchanged uneasy glances.

'I expect he exaggerated, Hilda,' said Aunt Sarah. 'Boys do exaggerate sometimes. It's a way of showing off. I hope Eustace won't learn to. As you know, Hilda, we went into the whole thing very thoroughly. We looked through twenty-nine prospectuses before we decided, and your father thought Mr Waghorn a very gentlemanly, understanding sort of man.'

'The boys call him "Old Foghorn",' said Hilda, and was rewarded by seeing Miss Cherrington stiffen in distaste. 'And they imitate him blowing his nose, and take bets about how many times he'll clear his throat during prayers. I don't like having to tell you this,' she added virtuously, 'but I thought I ought to.'

'What are bets, Daddy?' asked Eustace, hoping to lead the conversation into safer channels.

'Bets, my boy?' said Mr Cherrington. 'Well, if you think something will happen, and another fellow doesn't, and you bet him sixpence that it will, then if it does he pays you sixpence, and if it doesn't you pay him sixpence.'

Eustace was thinking that this was a very fair arrangement when Miss Cherrington said, 'Please don't say "you", Alfred, or Eustace might imagine that you were in the habit of making bets yourself.'

'Well –' began Mr Cherrington.

'Betting is a very bad habit,' said Miss Cherrington firmly, 'and I'm sorry to hear that the boys of St Ninian's practise it – if they do; again, Gerald may have been exaggerating, and it is quite usual, I imagine, for the boys of one school to run down another. But there is no reason that Eustace should learn to. To be exposed to temptation is one thing, to give way is another, and resistance to temptation is a valuable form of self-discipline.'

'Oh, but they don't resist!' cried Hilda. 'And Eustace wouldn't either. You know how he likes to do the same as everyone else. And if any boy, especially any new boy, tries to be good and different from the rest they tease him and call him some horrid name (Gerald wouldn't tell me what it was), and sometimes punch him, too.'

Eustace, who had always been told he must try to be good in all circumstances, turned rather pale and looked down at the floor.

'Now, now, Hilda,' said her father, impatiently. 'You've said quite enough. You sound as if you didn't want Eustace to go to school.'

But Hilda was unabashed. She knew she had made an impression on the grown-ups.

'Oh, it's only that I want him to go to the right school, isn't it, Aunt Sarah?' she said. 'We shouldn't like him to go to a school where he learned bad habits and – and nothing else, should we? He would be much better off as he is now, with you teaching him and me helping. Gerald said they really knew *nothing*; he said he knew more than the oldest boys at St Ninian's, and he's only twelve.'

'But he does boast, doesn't he?' put in Eustace timidly. 'You used to say so yourself, Hilda.' Hilda had never had a good word for Gerald Steptoe before today.

'Oh, yes, you all boast,' said Hilda sweepingly. 'But I don't think he was boasting. I asked him how much he knew, and he said, the Kings and Queens of England, so I told him to repeat them and he broke down at Richard II. Eustace can say them perfectly, and he's only ten, so you see for the next four years he wouldn't be learning anything, he'd just be forgetting everything, wouldn't he, Aunt Sarah? Don't let him go, I'm sure it would be a mistake.'

Minney, Barbara's nurse, came bustling in. She was rather short and had soft hair and gentle eyes. 'Excuse me, Miss Cherrington,' she said, 'but it's Master Eustace's bedtime.'

Eustace said good-night. Hilda walked with him to the door and when they were just outside she said in a whisper:

'I think I shall be able to persuade them.'

'But I think I want to go, Hilda!' muttered Eustace.

'It isn't what you want, it's what's good for you,' exclaimed Hilda, looking at him with affectionate fierceness. As she turned the handle of the drawing-room door she overheard her father saying to Miss Cherrington: 'I shouldn't pay too much attention to all that, Sarah. If the boy didn't want to go it would be different. As the money's his, he ought to be allowed to please himself. But he'll be all right, you'll see.'

The days passed and Hilda wept in secret. Sometimes she wept openly, for she knew how it hurt Eustace to see her cry. When he asked her why she was crying she wouldn't tell him at first, but just shook her head. Later on she said, 'You know quite well: why do you ask me?' and, of course, Eustace did know. It made him unhappy to know he was making her unhappy and besides, as the time to leave home drew nearer, he became much less sure that he liked the prospect. Hilda saw that he was weakening and she played upon his fears and gave him *Eric or Little by Little* as a Christmas present, to warn him of what he might expect when he went to school. Eustace read it and was extremely worried; he didn't see how he could possibly succeed where a boy as clever, and handsome, and good as Eric had been before he went to school, had failed. But it did not make him want to turn back, for he now felt that if school was going to be an unpleasant business, all the more must he go through with it – especially as it was going to be unpleasant for him, and not for anyone else; which would have been an excuse for backing out. 'You see it won't really matter,' he explained to Hilda, 'they can't kill me – Daddy said so – and he said they don't even roast boys at preparatory schools, only at public schools, and I

189

shan't be going to a public school for a long time, if ever. I expect they will just do a few things to me like pulling my hair and twisting my arm and perhaps kicking me a little, but I shan't really mind that. It was much worse all that time after Miss Fothergill died, because then I didn't know what was going to happen and now I do know, so I shall be prepared.' Hilda was non-plussed by this argument, all the more so because it was she who had told Eustace that it was always good for you to do something you didn't like. 'You say so now,' she said, 'but you won't say so on the seventeenth of January.' And when Eustace said nothing but only looked rather sad and worried she burst into tears. 'You're so selfish,' she sobbed. 'You only think about being good – as if that mattered – you don't think about me at all. I shan't eat or drink anything while you are away, and I shall probably die.'

Eustace was growing older and he did not really believe that Hilda would do this, but the sight of her unhappiness and the tears (which sometimes started to her eyes unbidden the moment he came into the room where she was) distressed him very much. Already, he thought, she was growing thinner, there were hollows in her cheeks, she was silent, or spoke in snatches, very fast and with far more vehemence and emphasis than the occasion called for; she came in late for meals and never apologized; she had never been interested in clothes, but now she was positively untidy. The grown-ups, to his surprise, did not seem to notice.

He felt he must consult someone and thought at once of Minney, because she was the easiest to talk to. But he knew she would counsel patience; that was her idea, that people would come to themselves if they were left alone. Action was needed and she wouldn't take any action. Besides, Hilda had outgrown Minney's influence; Minney wasn't drastic enough to cut any ice with her. Aunt Sarah would be far more helpful because she understood Hilda. But she didn't understand Eustace and would make him feel that he was making a fuss about nothing, or if he did manage to persuade her that Hilda was unhappy she would somehow lay the blame on him. There remained his father. Eustace was nervous of consulting his father, because he never knew what mood he would find him in. Mr Cherrington could be very jolly and treat Eustace almost as an equal; then something Eustace said would upset him and he would get angry and make Eustace wish he had never spoken. But since Miss Fothergill's death his attitude to Eustace had changed. His outbursts of irritation were much less frequent and he often asked Eustace his opinion and drew him out and made him feel more self-confident. It all depended on finding him in a good mood.

Of late Mr Cherrington had taken to drinking a whisky and soda and smoking a cigar when he came back from his office in Ousemouth; this was at about six o'clock, and he was always alone then, in the drawing-room, because Miss Cherrington did not approve of this new habit. When he had finished she would go in and throw open the windows, but she never went in while he was there.

Eustace found him with his feet up enveloped in the fumes of whisky and cigar smoke, which seemed to Eustace the very being and breath of manliness. Mr Cherrington stirred. The fragrant cloud rolled away and his face grew more distinct.

'Hullo,' he said, 'here's the Wild Man.' The Wild Man from Borneo was in those days an object of affection with the general public. 'Sit down and make yourself comfortable. Now, what can I do for you?'

The armchair was too big for Eustace: his feet hardly touched the floor.

'It's about Hilda,' he said.

'Well, Hilda's a nice girl, what about her?' said Mr Cherrington, his voice still jovial. Eustace hesitated and then said with a rush:

'You see, she doesn't want me to go to school.'

Mr Cherrington frowned, and sipped at his glass.

'I know, we've heard her more than once on that subject. She thinks you'll get into all sorts of bad ways.' His voice sharpened; it was too bad that his quiet hour should be interrupted by these nursery politics. 'Have you been putting your heads together? Have you come to tell me you don't want to go either?'

Eustace's face showed the alarm he felt at his father's change of tone.

'Oh, *no*, Daddy. At least – well – I . . .'

'You *don't* want to go. That's clear,' his father snapped.

'Yes, I do. But you see . . .' Eustace searched for a form of words

191

which wouldn't lay the blame too much on Hilda and at the same time excuse him for seeming to shelter behind her. 'You see, though she's older than me she's only a *girl* and she doesn't understand that men have to do certain things' – Mr Cherrington smiled, and Eustace took heart – 'well, like going to school.'

'Girls go to school, too,' Mr Cherrington said. Eustace tried to meet this argument. 'Yes, but it's not the same for them. You see, girls are always nice to each other; why, they always call each other by their Christian names even when they're at school. Fancy that! And they never bet or' (Eustace looked nervously at the whisky decanter) 'or drink, or use bad language, or kick each other, or roast each other in front of a slow fire.' Thinking of the things that girls did not do to each other, Eustace began to grow quite pale.

'All the better for them, then,' said Mr Cherrington robustly. 'School seems to be the place for girls. But what's all this leading *you* to?'

'I don't mind about those things,' said Eustace eagerly. 'I ... I should quite enjoy them. And I shouldn't even mind, well, you know, not being so good for a change, if it was only for a time. But Hilda thinks it might make me ill as well. Of course, she's quite mistaken, but she says she'll miss me so much and worry about me, that she'll never have a peaceful moment, and she'll lose her appetite and perhaps pine away and . . .' He paused, unable to complete the picture. 'She doesn't know I'm telling you all this, and she wouldn't like me to, and at school they would say it was telling tales, but I'm not at school yet, am I? Only I felt I must tell you because then perhaps you'd say I'd better not go to school, though I hope you won't.'

Exhausted by the effort of saying so many things that should (he felt) have remained locked in his bosom, and dreading an angry reply, Eustace closed his eyes. When he opened them his father was standing up with his back to the fireplace. He took the cigar from his mouth and puffed out an expanding cone of rich blue smoke.

'Thanks, old chap,' he said. 'I'm very glad you told me, and I'm not going to say you shan't go to school. Miss Fothergill left you the money for that purpose, so we chose the best school we could find; and why Hilda should want to put her oar in I can't imagine – at least, I can, but I call it confounded cheek. The very idea!' his father went on, working himself up and looking at Eustace as fiercely as if it was his fault, while Eustace trembled to hear Hilda criticized. 'What she needs is to go to school herself. Yes, that's what she needs.' He took a good swig at the whisky, his eyes brightened and his voice dropped. 'Now I'm going to tell you something, Eustace, only you must keep it under your hat.'

'Under my hat?' repeated Eustace, mystified. 'My hat's in the hall. Shall I go and get it?'

His father laughed. 'No, I mean you must keep it to yourself. You mustn't tell anyone, because nothing's decided yet.'

'Shall I cross my heart and swear?' asked Eustace anxiously. 'Of course, I'd rather not.'

'You can do anything you like with yourself as long as you don't tell Hilda,' his father remarked, 'but just see the door's shut.'

Eustace tiptoed to the door and cautiously turned the handle several times, after each turn giving the handle a strong but surreptitious tug. Coming back still more stealthily, he whispered, 'It's quite shut.'

'Very well, then,' said Mr Cherrington. 'Now give me your best ear.'

'My best ear, Daddy?' said Eustace, turning his head from side to side. 'Oh, I see!' and he gave a loud laugh which he immediately stifled. 'You just want me to listen carefully.'

'You've hit it,' and between blue, fragrant puffs Mr Cherrington began to outline his plan for Hilda.

While his father was speaking Eustace's face grew grave, and every now and then he nodded judicially. Though his feet still swung clear of the floor, to be taken into his father's confidence seemed to add inches to his stature.

'Well, old man, that's what I wanted to tell you,' said his father at length. 'Only you mustn't let on, see? Mum's the word.'

'Wild horses won't drag it out of me, Daddy,' said Eustace earnestly.

'Well, don't you let them try. By the way, I hear your friend Dick Staveley's back.'

Eustace started. The expression of an elder statesman faded from his face and he suddenly looked younger than his years.

'Oh, is he? I expect he's just home for the holidays.'

'No, he's home for some time, he's cramming for Oxford or something.'

'Cramming?' repeated Eustace. His mind suddenly received a most disagreeable impression of Dick, his hero, transformed into a turkey strutting and gobbling round a farmyard.

'Being coached for the 'Varsity. It may happen to you one day. Somebody told me they'd seen him, and I thought you might be interested. You liked him, didn't you?'

'Oh, *yes*,' said Eustace. Intoxicating visions began to rise, only to be expelled by the turn events had taken. 'But it doesn't make much difference now, does it? I mean, I shouldn't be able to go there, even if he asked me.'

Meanwhile, Hilda on her side had not been idle. She turned over in her mind every stratagem and device she could think of that might keep Eustace at home. Since the evening when she so successfully launched her bombshell about the unsatisfactory state of education and morals at St Ninian's, she felt she had been losing ground. Eustace did not respond, as he once used to, to the threat of terrors to come; he professed to be quite pleased at the thought of being torn limb from limb by older stronger boys. She didn't believe he was really unmoved by such a prospect, but he successfully pretended to be. When she said that it would make her ill he seemed to care a great deal more; for several days he looked as sad as she did, and he constantly, and rather tiresomely, begged her to eat more – requests which Hilda received with a droop of her long, heavy eyelids and a sad shake of her beautiful head. But lately Eustace hadn't seemed to care so much. When Christmas came he suddenly discovered the fun of pulling crackers. Before this year he wouldn't even stay in the room if crackers were going off; but now he revelled in them and made almost as much noise as they did, and his father even persuaded him to grasp the naked strip of cardboard with the explosive in the middle, which stung your fingers and made even grown-ups pull faces. Crackers bored Hilda; the loudest report did not make her change her expression, and she would have liked to tell Eustace how silly he looked as, with an air of triumph, he clasped the smoking fragment; but she hadn't the heart to. He might be at school already, his behaviour was so unbridled. And he had a new way of looking at her, not unkind or cross or disobedient, but as if he was a gardener tending a flower and watching to see how it was going to turn out. This was a reversal of their rôles; she felt as though a geranium had risen from its bed and was bending over her with a watering-can.

As usual, they were always together and if Hilda did not get the old satisfaction from the company of this polite but aloof little stranger (for so he seemed to her) the change in his attitude made her all the more determined to win him back, and the thought of losing him all the more desolating. She hated the places where they used to play together and wished that Eustace, who was sentimental about his old haunts, would not take her to them. 'I just want to see it once again,' he would plead, and she did not like to refuse him, though his new mantle of authority sat so precariously on him. Beneath her moods, which she expressed in so many ways, was a steadily increasing misery; the future stretched away featureless without landmarks; nothing beckoned, nothing drew her on.

Obscurely she realized that the change had been brought about by Miss Fothergill's money. It had made Eustace independent, not completely independent, not as independent as she was, but it had given a force to his wishes that they never possessed before. It was no good trying to make him not want to go to school; she must make him want to stay at home. In this new state of affairs she believed that if Eustace refused to go to school his father would not try to compel him. But how to go about it? How to make Anchorstone suddenly so attractive, so irresistibly magnetic, that Eustace would not be able to bring himself to leave?

When Eustace told her that Dick Staveley was coming to live at Anchorstone Hall he mentioned this (for him) momentous event as casually as possible. Hilda did not like Dick Staveley, she professed abhorrence of him; she would not go to Anchorstone Hall when Dick had invited her, promising he would teach her to ride. The whole idea of the place was distasteful to her; it chilled and shrivelled her thoughts, just as it warmed and expanded Eustace's. Even to hear it mentioned cast a shadow over her mind, and as to going there, she would rather die; and she had often told Eustace so.

It was a sign of emancipation that he let Dick's name cross his lips. He awaited the explosion, and it came.

'That man!' – she never spoke of him as a boy, though he was only a few years older than she was. 'Well, *you* won't see him, will you?' she added almost vindictively. 'You'll be at school.'

'Oh,' said Eustace, 'that won't make any difference. I shouldn't see him anyhow. You see, he never wanted to be friends with me. It was you he liked. If you had gone, I dare say he would have asked me to go too, just as your – well, you know, to hold the horse, and so on.'

'You and your horses!' said Hilda, scornfully. 'You don't know one end of a horse from the other.' He expected she would let the subject drop, but her eyes grew thoughtful and to his astonishment she said, 'Suppose I *had* gone?'

'Oh, *well*,' said Eustace, 'that would have changed everything. I shouldn't have had time to go to tea with Miss Fothergill – you see we should always have been having tea at Anchorstone Hall. Then she wouldn't have died and left me her money – I mean, she would have died; but she wouldn't have left me any money because she wouldn't have known me well enough. You have to know someone well to do that. And then I shouldn't be going to school now, because Daddy says it's her money that pays for me – and now' (he glanced up, the clock on the Town Hall, with its white face and black hands, said four o'clock) 'you would be coming in from riding with Dick, and I should be sitting on one of those grand sofas in the drawing-room at Anchorstone Hall, perhaps talking to Lady Staveley.'

Involuntarily Hilda closed her eyes against this picture – let it be confounded! Let it be blotted out! But aloud she said:

'Wouldn't you have liked that?'

'Oh, *yes*,' said Eustace fervently.

'Better than going to school?'

Eustace considered. The trussed boy was being carried towards a very large, but slow, fire; other boys, black demons with pitchforks, were scurrying about, piling on coals. His mood of heroism deserted him.

196

'Oh yes, much better.'

Hilda said nothing, and they continued to saunter down the hill, past the ruined cross, past the pierhead with its perpetual invitation, towards the glories of the Wolferton Hotel – winter-gardened, girt with iron fire-escapes – and the manifold exciting sounds, and heavy, sulphurous smells, of the railway station.

'Are we going to Mrs Wrench's?' Eustace asked.

'No, why should we? We had fish for dinner; you never notice. Oh, I know, you want to see the crocodile.'

'Well, just this once. You see, I may not see it again for a long time.'

Hilda sniffed. 'I wish you wouldn't keep on saying that,' she said. 'It seems the only thing you can say. Oh, very well, then, we'll go in and look round and come out.'

'Oh, but we must buy something. She would be disappointed if we didn't. Let's get some shrimps. Aunt Sarah won't mind just for once, and I don't suppose I shall have any at St Ninian's. I expect the Fourth Form gets them, though.'

'Why should they?'

'Oh, didn't you know, they have all sorts of privileges.'

'I expect they have shrimps every day at Anchorstone Hall,' said Hilda, meaningly.

'Oh, I expect they do. What a pity you didn't want to go. We have missed such a lot.'

Cautiously they crossed the road, for the wheeled traffic was thick here and might include a motor car. Fat Mrs Wrench was standing at the door of the fish shop. She saw them coming, went in, and smiled expectantly from behind the counter.

'Well, Miss Hilda?'

'Eustace wants a fillet of the best end of the crocodile.'

'Oh Hilda, I don't!'

They all laughed uproariously, Hilda loudest of all; while the stuffed crocodile (a small one) sprawling on the wall with tufts of bright green foliage glued round it, glared down on them malignantly. Eustace felt the tremor of delighted terror that he had been waiting for.

'I've got some lovely fresh shrimps,' said Mrs Wrench.

* * *

'Turn round, Eustace,' said Miss Cherrington.

'Oh must I again, Aunt Sarah?'

'Yes, you must. You don't want the other boys to laugh at you, do you?'

Reluctantly, Eustace revolved. He hated having his clothes tried on. He felt it was he who was being criticized, not they. It gave him a feeling of being trapped, as though each of the three pairs of eyes fixed on him, impersonal, fault-finding, was attached to him by a silken cord that bound him to the spot. He tried to restrain his wriggles within himself but they broke out and rippled on the surface.

'Do try to stand still, Eustace.'

Aunt Sarah was operating; she had some pins in her mouth with which, here and there, she pinched grooves and ridges in his black jacket. Alas, it was rather too wide at the shoulders and not wide enough round the waist.

'Eustace is getting quite a corporation,' said his father.

'Corporation, Daddy?' Eustace was always interested in words.

'Well, I didn't like to say fat.'

'It's because you would make me feed up,' Eustace complained. 'I was quite thin before. Nancy Steptoe said I was just the right size for a boy.'

No one took this up; indeed, a slight chill fell on the company at the mention of Nancy's name.

'Never mind,' Minney soothed him, 'there's some who would give a lot to be so comfortable looking as Master Eustace is.'

'Would they, Minney?'

Eustace was encouraged.

'Yes, they would, nasty scraggy things. And I can make that quite all right.' She inserted two soft fingers beneath the tight line round his waist.

'Hilda hasn't said anything yet,' said Mr Cherrington. 'What do you think of your brother now, Hilda?'

Hilda had not left her place at the luncheon table, nor had she taken her eyes off her plate. Without looking up she said:

'He'll soon get thin if he goes to school, if that's what you want.'

'*If* he goes?' said Mr Cherrington. 'Of course he's going. Why do you suppose we took him to London to Faith Brothers if he wasn't? All the same, I'm not sure we ought to have got his clothes off the peg . . . Now go and have a look at yourself, Eustace. Mind the glass doesn't break.'

Laughing, but half afraid of what he might see, Eustace tiptoed to the mirror. There stood his new personality, years older than a moment ago. The Eton collar, the black jacket cut like a man's, the dark grey trousers that he could feel through his stockings, caressing his calves, made a veritable mantle of manhood. A host of new sensations, adult, prideful, standing no nonsense, coursed through him. Involuntarily, he tilted his head back and frowned, as though he were considering a leg-break that might dismiss R. H. Spooner.

'What a pity he hasn't got the cap,' said Minney admiringly.

Eustace half turned his head. 'It's because of the crest, the White Horse of Kent. You see, if they let a common public tailor make that, anyone might wear it.'

'Don't call people common, please, Eustace, even a tailor.'

'I didn't mean common in a nasty way, Aunt Sarah. Common just means anyone. It might mean me or even you.'

Hoping to change the subject, Minney dived into a cardboard box, noisily rustling the tissue paper.

'But we've got the straw hat. Put that on, Master Eustace . . . There, Mr Cherrington, doesn't he look nice?'

'Not so much on the back of your head, Eustace, or you'll look like Ally Sloper. That's better.'

'I wish it had a guard,' sighed Eustace, longingly.

'Oh well, one thing at a time.'

'And of course it hasn't got the school band yet. It's blue, you know, with a white horse.'

'What, another?'

'Oh, no, the same one, Daddy. You are silly.'

'Don't call your father silly, please, Eustace.'

'Oh, let him, this once . . . Now take your hat off, Eustace, and bow.'
Eustace did so.

'Now say "Please, sir, it wasn't my fault".'
Eustace did not quite catch what his father said.

'Please, sir, it was my fault.'

'No, no. *Wasn't* my fault.'

'Oh, I see, Daddy. Please, sir, it wasn't my fault. But I expect it would have been really. It nearly always is.'

'People will think it is, if you say so. Now say "That's all very well, old chap, but this time it's my turn".'

Eustace repeated the phrase, imitating his father's intonation and *dégagé* man-of-the-world air; then he said:

'What would it be my turn to do, Daddy?'

'Well, what do you think?' When Eustace couldn't think, his father said: 'Ask Minney.'

Minney was mystified but tried to carry it off.

'They do say one good turn deserves another,' she said, shaking her head wisely.

'That's the right answer as far as it goes. Your Aunt knows what I mean, Eustace, but she won't tell us.'

'I don't think you should teach the boy to say such things, Alfred, even in fun. It's an expression they use in a . . . in a public house, Eustace.'

Eustace gave his father a look of mingled admiration and reproach which Mr Cherrington answered with a shrug of his shoulders.

'Between you, you'll make an old woman of the boy. Good Lord, at his age, I . . .' He broke off, his tone implying that at ten years old he had little left to learn. 'Now stand up, Eustace, and don't stick your tummy out.'

Eustace obeyed.

'Shoulders back.'

'Head up.'

'Don't bend those knees.'

'Don't arch your back.'

Each command set up in Eustace a brief spasm ending in rigidity, and soon his neck, back, and shoulders were a network of wrinkles. Miss Cherrington and Minney rushed forward.

'Give me a pin, please, Minney, the left shoulder still droops.'

'There's too much fullness at the neck now, Miss Cherrington. Wait a moment, I'll pin it.'

'It's the back that's the worst, Minney. I can get my hand and arm up it – stand still, Eustace, one pin won't be enough. Oh, he hasn't buttoned his coat in front, that's the reason –'

Hands and fingers were everywhere, pinching, patting, and pushing; Eustace swayed like a sapling in a gale. Struggling to keep his balance on the chair, he saw intent eyes flashing round him, leaving gleaming streaks like shooting stars in August. He tried first to resist, then to abandon himself to all the pressures. At last the quickened breathing subsided, there were gasps and sighs, and the ring of electric tension round Eustace suddenly dispersed, like an expiring thunderstorm.

'*That's* better.'

'Really, Minney, you've made quite a remarkable improvement.'

'He looks quite a man now, doesn't he, Miss Cherrington? Oh, I *wish* he could be photographed, just to remind us. If only Hilda would fetch her camera –'

'Hilda!'

There was no answer. They all looked round.

The tableau broke up; and they found themselves staring at an empty room.

'Can I get down now, Daddy?' asked Eustace.

'Yes, run and see if you can find her.'

'She can't get used to the idea of his going away,' said Minney when Eustace had gone.

'No, I'm afraid she'll suffer much more than he will,' Miss Cherrington said.

Mr Cherrington straightened his tie and shot his cuffs. 'You forget, Sarah, that she's going to school herself.'

'It's not likely I should forget losing my right hand, Alfred.'

After her single contribution to the problems of Eustace's school outfit, Hilda continued to sit at the table, steadily refusing to look in his direction, and trying to make her disapproval felt throughout the room. Unlike Eustace, she had long ago ceased to think that grown-up people were always right, or that if she was angry with them they possessed some special armour of experience, like an extra skin, that made them unable to feel it. She thought they were just as fallible as she was, more so, indeed; and that in this instance they were making a particularly big mistake. Her father's high-spirited raillery, as if the whole thing was a joke, exasperated her. Again, she projected her resentment through the æther, but they all had their backs to her, they were absorbed with Eustace. Presently his father made him stand on a chair. How silly he looked, she thought, like a dummy, totally without the dignity that every human being should possess. All this flattery and attention was making him conceited, and infecting him with the lax standards of the world, which she despised and dreaded. Now he was chattering about his school crest, as if that was anything to be proud of, a device woven on a cap, such as every little boy wore. He was pluming and preening himself, just as if she had never brought him up to know what was truly serious and worthwhile. A wave of bitter feeling broke against her. She could not let this mutilation of a personality go on; she must stop it, and there was only one way, though that way was the hardest she could take and the thought of it filled her with loathing.

Her aunt and Minney were milling round Eustace like dogs over a bone; sticking their noses into him. It was almost disgusting. To get away unnoticed was easy; if she had fired a pistol they would not have heard her. Taking her pencil box which she had left on the sideboard she slouched out of the room. A moment in the drawing-room to collect some writing paper and then she was in the bedroom which she still shared with Eustace. She locked the door and, clearing a space at the corner of the dressing-table, she sat down to write. It never crossed Hilda's mind that her plan could miscarry; she measured its success entirely by the distaste it aroused in her, and that was absolute – the strongest of her many strong feelings. She no more doubted its success than she doubted that, if she threw herself off the cliff, she would be dashed to pieces on the rocks below. In her mind, as she wrote, consoling her, was the image of Eustace, stripped of all his foolish finery, his figure restored to its proper outlines, his mouth cleansed of the puerilities of attempted schoolboy speech, his mind soft and tractable – forever hers.

But the letter did not come easily, partly because Hilda never wrote letters, but chiefly because her inclination battled with her will, and her sense of her destiny warned her against what she was doing. More

Hilda's Letter

than once she was on the point of abandoning the letter, but in the pauses of her thoughts she heard the excited murmur of voices in the room below. This letter, if she posted it, would still those voices and send those silly clothes back to Messrs Faith Brothers. It could do anything, this letter, stop the clock, put it back even, restore to her the Eustace of pre-Miss Fothergill days. Then why did she hesitate? Was it an obscure presentiment that she would regain Eustace but lose herself?

DEAR MR STAVELEY (she had written),
    Some time ago you asked me and Eustace to visit you, and we were not able to because ... (Because why?)
    Because I didn't want to go, that was the real reason, and I don't want to now except that it's the only way of keeping Eustace at home.

Then he would see where he stood; she had sacrificed her pride by writing to him at all, she wouldn't throw away the rest by pretending she wanted to see him. Instinctively she knew that however rude and ungracious the letter, he would want to see her just the same.

    So we can come any time you like, and would you be quick and ask us because Eustace will go to school, so there's no time to lose.
        Yours sincerely,
            HILDA CHERRINGTON.

Hilda was staring at the letter when there came a loud knock on the door, repeated twice with growing imperiousness before she had time to answer.
'Yes?' she shouted.
'Oh, Hilda, can I come in?'
'No, you can't.'
'Why not?'
'I'm busy, that's why.'
Eustace's tone gathered urgency and became almost menacing as he said:

203

'Well, you've got to come down because Daddy said so. He wants you to take my snapshot.'

'I can't. I couldn't anyhow because the film's used up.'

'Shall I go out and buy some? You see, it's very important, it's like a change of life. They want a record of me.'

'They can go on wanting, for all I care.'

'Oh, Hilda, I shan't be here for you to photograph this time next Thursday week.'

'Yes, you will, you see if you're not.'

'Don't you want to remember what I look like?'

'No, I don't. Go away, go away, you're driving me mad.'

She heard his footsteps retreating from the door. Wretchedly she turned to the letter. It looked blurred and misty, and a tear fell on it. Hilda had no blotting-paper, and soon the tear-drop, absorbing the ink, began to turn blue at the edges.

'He mustn't see that,' she thought, and taking another sheet began to copy the letter out. 'Dear Mr Staveley . . .' But she did not like what she had written; it was out of key with her present mood. She took another sheet and began again:

'Dear Mr Staveley, My brother Eustace and I are now free . . .' That wouldn't do. Recklessly she snatched another sheet, and then another. 'Dear Mr Staveley, Dear Mr Staveley.' Strangely enough, with the repetition of the words he seemed to become almost dear; the warmth of dearness crept into her lonely, miserable heart and softly spread there – 'Dear Richard,' she wrote, and then, 'Dear Dick'. 'Dear' meant something to her now; it meant that Dick was someone of whom she could ask a favour without reserve.

DEAR DICK,

I do not know if you will remember me. I am the sister of Eustace Cherrington who was a little boy then and he was ill at your house and when you came to our house to ask after him you kindly invited us to go and see you. But we couldn't because Eustace was too delicate. And you saw us again last summer on the sands and told Eustace about the money Miss Fothergill had left him but it hasn't done him any good, I'm afraid, he still wants to go to school because other boys do but I would much rather he stayed at home and didn't get like them. If you haven't forgotten, you will remember you said I had been a good sister to him, much better than Nancy Steptoe is to Gerald. You said you would like to have me for a sister even when your own sister was there. You may not have heard but he is motherless and I have been a mother to him and it would be a great pity I'm sure you would agree if at this critical state of his development my influence was taken away. You may not remember but if you do you will recollect that you said you would pretend to be a cripple so that I could come and talk to you and play games with you like Eustace did with Miss Fothergill. There is no need for that because we can both walk over quite easily any day and the sooner the better otherwise Eustace will go to school. He is having his Sunday suit tried on at this moment so there is no time to lose. I shall be very pleased to come any time you want me and so will Eustace and we will do anything you want. I am quite brave Eustace says and do not mind strange experiences as long as they are for someone else's good. That is why I am writing to you now.

> With my kind regards,
> Yours sincerely,
> HILDA CHERRINGTON.

She sat for a moment looking at the letter, then with an angry and despairing sigh she crossed out 'sincerely' and wrote 'affectionately'. But the word 'sincerely' was still legible, even to a casual glance; so she again tried to delete it, this time with so much vehemence that her pen almost went through the paper.

Sitting back, she fell into a mood of bitter musing. She saw the letter piling up behind her like a huge cliff, unscalable, taking away the sunlight, cutting off retreat. She dared not read it through but thrust it into an envelope, addressed and stamped it in a daze, and ran downstairs.

Eustace and his father were sitting together; the others had gone. Eustace kept looking at his new suit and fingering it as though to make sure it was real. They both jumped as they heard the door bang, and exchanged man-to-man glances.

'She seems in a great hurry,' said Mr Cherrington.

'Oh yes, Hilda's always like that. She never gives things time to settle.'

'You'll miss her, won't you?'

'Oh, of *course*,' said Eustace. 'I shall be quite unconscionable.' It was the new suit that said the word; Eustace knew the word was wrong and hurried on.

'Of course, it wouldn't do for her to be with me there, even if she could be, in a boys' school, I mean, because she would see me being, well, you know, tortured, and that would upset her terribly. Besides, the other fellows would think she was bossing me, though I don't.'

'You don't?'

'Oh no, it's quite right at her time of life, but, of course, it couldn't go on always. They would laugh at me, for one thing.'

'If they did,' said Mr Cherrington, 'it's because they don't know Hilda. Perhaps it's a good thing she's going to school herself.'

'Oh, she *is*?' Eustace had been so wrapped up in his own concerns that he had forgotten the threat which hung over Hilda. But was it a threat or a promise? Ought he to feel glad for her sake or sorry? He couldn't decide, and as it was natural for his mind to feel things as either nice or nasty, which meant right or wrong, of course, but one didn't always know that at the time, he couldn't easily entertain a mixed emotion, and the question of Hilda's future wasn't very real to him.

'Yes,' his father was saying, 'we only got the letter this morning, telling us we could get her in. The school is very full but they are making an exception for her, as a favour to Dr Waghorn, your headmaster.'

'Then it must be a good school,' exclaimed Eustace, 'if it's at all like mine.'

'Yes, St Willibald's is a pretty good school,' said his father carelessly. 'It isn't so far from yours, either; just round the North Foreland. I shouldn't be surprised if you couldn't see each other with a telescope.'

Eustace's eyes sparkled, then he looked anxious. 'Do you think they'll have a white horse on their hats?'

Mr Cherrington laughed. 'I'm afraid I couldn't tell you that.' Eustace shook his head, and said earnestly:

'I hope they won't try to copy us too much. Boys and girls should be kept separate, shouldn't they?' He thought for a moment and his brow cleared. 'Of course, there was Lady Godiva.'

'I'm afraid I don't see the connection,' said his father.

'Well, she rode on a white horse.' Eustace didn't like being called on to explain what he meant. 'But only with nothing on.' He paused. 'Hilda will have to get some new clothes now, won't she? She'll have to have them tried on.' His eyes brightened; he liked to see Hilda freshly adorned.

'Yes, and there's no time to lose. I've spoken to your aunt, Eustace, and she agrees with me that you're the right person to break the news to Hilda. We think it'll come better from you. Companions in adversity and all that, you know.'

Eustace's mouth fell open.

'Oh, Daddy, I couldn't. She'd – I don't know what she might not do. She's so funny with me now, anyway. She might almost go off her rocker.'

'Not if you approach her tactfully.'

'Well, I'll try,' said Eustace. 'Perhaps the day after tomorrow.'

'No, tell her this afternoon.'

'Fains I, Daddy. Couldn't *you*? It *is* your afternoon off.'

'Yes, and I want a little peace. Listen, isn't that Hilda coming in? Now run away and get your jumping-poles and go down on the beach.'

They heard the front door open and shut; it wasn't quite a slam but near enough to show that Hilda was in the state of mind in which things slipped easily from her fingers.

Each with grave news to tell the other, and neither knowing how, they started for the beach. Eustace's jumping-pole was a stout rod of bamboo, prettily ringed and patterned with spots like a leopard. By stretching his hand up he could nearly reach the top; he might have been a bear trying to climb up a ragged staff. As they walked across the green that sloped down to the cliff he planted the pole in front of him and took practice leaps over any obstacle that showed itself – a brick it might be, or a bit of fencing, or the cart-track which ran just below the square. Hilda's jumping-pole was made of wood, and much longer than Eustace's; near to the end it tapered slightly and then swelled out again, like a broom-handle. It was the kind of pole used by real pole-jumpers at athletic events, and she did not play about with it but saved her energy for when it should be needed. The January sun still spread a pearly radiance round them; it hung over the sea, quite low down, and was already beginning to cast fiery reflections on the water. The day was not cold for January, and Eustace was well wrapped up, but his bare knees felt the chill rising from the ground, and he said to Hilda:

'Of course, trousers would be much warmer.'

She made no answer but quickened her pace so that Eustace had to run between his jumps. He had never known her so preoccupied before.

In silence they reached the edge of the cliff and the spiked railing at the head of the concrete staircase. A glance showed them the sea was coming in. It had that purposeful look and the sands were dry in front of it. A line of foam, like a border of white braid, was curling round the outermost rocks.

Except for an occasional crunch their black beach shoes made no sound on the sand-strewn steps. Eustace let his pole slide from one to the other, pleased with the rhythmic tapping.

'Oh, don't do that, Eustace. You have no pity on my poor nerves.'

'I'm so sorry, Hilda.'

But a moment later, changing her mind as visibly as if she were passing an apple from one hand to the other, she said, 'You can, if you like. I don't really mind.'

Obediently Eustace resumed his tapping but it now gave him the feeling of something done under sufferance and was not so much fun. He was quite glad when they came to the bottom of the steps and the tapping stopped.

Here, under the cliff, the sand was pale and fine and powdery; it lay in craters inches deep and was useless for jumping, for the pole could get no purchase on such a treacherous foundation; it turned in mid-air and the jumper came down heavily on one side or the other. So they hurried down to the beach proper, where the sand was brown and close and firm, and were soon among the smooth, seaweed-coated rocks which bestrewed the shore like a vast colony of sleeping seals.

Eustace was rapidly and insensibly turning into a chamois or an ibex when he checked himself and remembered that, for the task that lay before him, some other pretence might be more helpful. An ibex *could* break the news to a sister-ibex that she was to go to boarding-school in a few days' time, but there would be nothing tactful, subtle, or imaginative in such a method of disclosure; he might almost as well tell her himself. They had reached their favourite jumping-ground and he took his stand on a rock, wondering and perplexed.

'Let's begin with the Cliffs of Dover,' he said. The Cliffs of Dover, so called because a sprinkling of barnacles gave it a whitish look, was a somewhat craggy boulder about six feet away. Giving a good foothold it was their traditional first hole, and not only Hilda but Eustace could clear the distance easily. When he had alighted on it, feet together, with the soft springy pressure that was so intimately satisfying, he pulled his pole out of the sand and stepped down to let Hilda do her jump. Hilda landed on the Cliffs of Dover with the negligent grace of an alighting eagle; and, as always, Eustace, who had a feeling for style, had to fight back a twinge of envy.

'Now the Needles,' he said. 'You go first.' The Needles was both more precipitous and further away, and there was only one spot on it where you could safely make a landing. Eustace occasionally muffed it, but Hilda never; what was his consternation therefore to see her swerve in mid-leap, fumble for a foothold, and slide off on to the sand.

'Oh, hard luck, sir!' exclaimed Eustace. The remark fell flat. He followed her in silence and made a rather heavy-footed but successful landing.

'You're one up,' said Hilda. They scored as in golf over a course of eighteen jumps, and when Hilda had won usually played the bye before beginning another round on a different set of rocks. Thus, the miniature but exciting landscape of mountain, plain and lake (for many of the rocks stood in deep pools, starfish-haunted), was continually changing.

Eustace won the first round at the nineteenth rock. He could hardly believe it. Only once before had he beaten Hilda, and that occasion was so long ago that all he could remember of it was the faint, sweet feeling of triumph. In dreams, on the other hand, he was quite frequently victorious. The experience then was poignantly delightful, utterly beyond anything obtainable in daily life. But he got a whiff of it now. Muffled to a dull suggestion of itself, like some dainty eaten with a heavy cold, it was still the divine elixir.

Hilda did not seem to realize how momentous her defeat was, nor, happily, did she seem to mind. Could she have lost on purpose? Eustace wondered. She was thoughtful and abstracted. Eustace simply had to say something.

'Your sandshoes are very worn, Hilda,' he said. 'They slipped every time. You *must* get another pair.'

She gave him a rather sad smile, and he added tentatively:

'I expect the ibex sheds its hoofs like its antlers. You're just going through one of those times.'

'Oh, so *that's* what we're playing,' said Hilda, but there was a touch of languor in her manner, as well as scorn.

'Yes, but we can play something else,' said Eustace. Trying to think of a new pretence, he began to make scratches with his pole on the smooth sand. The words 'St Ninian's' started to take shape. Quickly he obliterated them with his foot, but they had given him an idea. They had given Hilda an idea, too.

He remarked as they moved to their new course, 'I might be a boy going to school for the first time.'

'You might be,' replied Hilda, 'but you're not.'

Eustace was not unduly disconcerted.

'Well, let's pretend I am, and then we can change the names of the rocks, to suit.'

The incoming tide had reached their second centre, and its advancing ripples were curling round the bases of the rocks.

'Let's re-christen this one,' said Eustace, poised on the first tee. 'You kick off. It used to be "Aconcagua",' he reminded her.

'All right,' said Hilda, 'call it "Cambo".'

Vaguely Eustace wondered why she had chosen the name of their house, but he was so intent on putting ideas into her head that he did not notice she was trying to put them into his.

'Bags I this one for St Ninian's,' he ventured, naming a not too distant boulder. Hilda winced elaborately.

'Mind you don't fall off,' was all she said.

'Oh, no. It's my honour, isn't it?' asked Eustace diffidently. He jumped.

Perhaps it was the responsibility of having chosen a name unacceptable to Hilda, perhaps it was just the perversity of Fate; anyhow, he missed his aim. His feet skidded on the slippery seaweed and when he righted himself he was standing in water up to his ankles.

'Now we must go home,' said Hilda. In a flash Eustace saw his plan going to ruin. There would be no more rocks to name; he might have to tell her the news outright.

'Oh, please not, Hilda, please not. Let's have a few more jumps. They make my feet warm, they really do. Besides, there's something I want to say to you.'

To his astonishment Hilda agreed at once.

'I oughtn't to let you,' she said, 'but I'll put your feet into mustard and hot water, privately, in the bathroom.'

'Crikey! That would be fun.'

'And I have something to say to you, too.'

'Is it something nice?'

'You'll think so,' said Hilda darkly.

'Tell me now.'

'No, afterwards. Only you'll have to pretend to be a boy who isn't going to school. Now hurry up.'

They were both standing on Cambo with the water swirling round them.

'Say "Fains I" if you'd like me to christen the next one,' said Eustace hopefully. 'It used to be called the Inchcape Rock.'

'No,' said Hilda slowly, and in a voice so doom-laden that anyone less preoccupied than Eustace might have seen her drift. 'I'm going to call it "Anchorstone Hall".'

'Good egg!' said Eustace. 'Look, there's Dick standing on it. Mind you don't knock him off!'

Involuntarily Hilda closed her eyes against Dick's image. She missed her take-off and dropped a foot short of the rock, knee-deep in water.

'Oh, *poor* Hilda!' Eustace cried, aghast.

But wading back to the rock she turned to him an excited, radiant face.

'Now it will be mustard and water for us both.'

'How ripping!' Eustace wriggled with delight. 'That'll be something to tell them at St Ninian's. I'm sure none of the other men have sisters who dare jump into the whole North Sea!'

'Quick, quick!' said Hilda. 'Your turn.'

Anchorstone Hall was by now awash, but Eustace landed easily. The fear of getting his feet wet being removed by the simple process of having got them wet, he felt gloriously free and ready to tell anyone anything. 'All square!' he announced.

'All square and one to play. Do you know what I am going to call this one?' He pointed to a forbiddingly bare, black rock, round which the water surged, and when Hilda quite graciously said she didn't, he added:

'But first you must pretend to be a girl who's going to school.'

'Anything to pacify you,' Hilda said.

'Now I'll tell you. It's St Willibald's. Do you want to know why?'

'Not specially,' said Hilda. 'It sounds such a silly name. Why should Willie be bald?' When they had laughed their fill at this joke, Eustace said:

'It's got something to do with you. It's . . . well, you'll know all about it later on.'

'I hope I shan't,' said Hilda loftily. 'It isn't worth the trouble of a pretence. Was this all you were going to tell me?'

'Yes, you see it's the name of your school.'

Hilda stared at him. 'My school? What do you mean, my school? Me a school-mistress? You must be mad.'

Eustace had not foreseen this complication.

'Not a school-mistress, Hilda,' he gasped. 'You wouldn't be old enough yet. No, a schoolgirl, like I'm going to be a schoolboy.'

'A schoolgirl?' repeated Hilda. 'A schoolgirl?' she echoed in a still more tragic voice. 'Who said so?' she challenged him.

212

'Well, Daddy did. They all did, while you were upstairs. Daddy told me to tell you. It's quite settled.'

Thoughts chased each other across Hilda's face, thoughts that were incomprehensible to Eustace. They only told him that she was not as angry as he thought she would be, perhaps not angry at all. He couldn't imagine why she wasn't, but the relief was overwhelming.

'We shall go away almost on the same day,' he said. 'Won't that be fun? I mean it would be much worse if one of us didn't. And we shall be quite near to each other, in Kent. It's called the Garden of England. That's a nice name. You're glad, aren't you?'

Her eyes, swimming with happy tears, told him she was; but he could hardly believe it, and her trembling lips vouchsafed no word. He felt he must distract her.

'You were going to tell me something, Hilda. What was it?'

She looked at him enigmatically, and the smile playing on her lips restored them to speech.

'Oh, that? That was nothing.'

'But it must have been something,' Eustace persisted. 'You said it was something I should like. Please tell me.'

'It doesn't matter now,' she said, 'now that I am going to school.' Her voice deepened and took on its faraway tone. 'You will never know what I meant to do for you – how I nearly sacrificed *all* my happiness.'

'Will anyone know?' asked Eustace.

He saw he had made a false step. Hilda turned pale and a look of terror came into her eyes, all the more frightening because Hilda was never frightened. So absorbed had she been by the horrors that the letter would lead to, so thankful that the horrors were now removed, that she had forgotten the letter itself. Yes. Someone would know . . .

Timidly Eustace repeated his question.

The pole bent beneath Hilda's weight and her knuckles went as white as her face.

'Oh, don't nag me, Eustace! Can't you see? . . . What's the time?' she asked sharply. 'I've forgotten my watch.'

'But you never forget it, Hilda.'

'Fool, I tell you I *have* forgotten it! What's the time?'

Eustace's head bent towards the pocket in his waistline where his watch was lodged, and he answered with maddening slowness, anxious to get the time exactly right:

'One minute to four.'

'And when does the post go?'

'A quarter past. But you know that better than I do, Hilda.'

'Idiot, they might have changed it.' She stiffened. The skies might fall but Eustace must be given his instructions.

'Listen, I've got something to do. You go straight home, slowly, mind, and tell them to get the bath water hot and ask Minney for the mustard.'

'How topping, Hilda! What fun we shall have.'

'Yes, it must be boiling. I shall hurry on in front of you, and you mustn't look to see which way I go.'

'Oh, no, Hilda.'

'Here's my pole. You can jump with it if you're careful. I shan't be long.'

'But, Hilda –'

There was no answer. She was gone, and he dared not turn round to call her.

A pole trailing from either hand, Eustace fixed his eyes on the waves and conscientiously walked backwards, so that he should not see her. Presently he stumbled against a stone and nearly fell. Righting himself he resumed his crab-like progress, but more slowly than before. Why had Hilda gone off like that? He could not guess, and it was a secret into which he must not pry. His sense of the inviolability of Hilda's feelings was a *sine qua non* of their relationship.

The tracks traced by the two poles, his and Hilda's, made a pattern that began to fascinate him. Parallel straight lines, he knew, were such that even if they were produced to infinity they could not meet. The idea of infinity pleased Eustace, and he dwelt on it for some time. But these lines were not straight; they followed a serpentine course, bulging at times and then narrowing, like a boa-constrictor that has swallowed a donkey. Perhaps with a little manipulation they could be made to meet.

He drew the lines closer. Yes, it looked as though they might

214

converge. But would it be safe to try to make them when a law of Euclid said they couldn't?

A backward glance satisfied Hilda that Eustace was following her instructions. Her heart warmed to him. How obedient he was, in spite of everything. The tumult in her feelings came back, disappointment, relief, and dread struggling with each other. Disappointment that her plan had miscarried; relief that it had miscarried; dread that she would be too late to spare herself an unbearable humiliation.

She ran, taking a short cut across the sands, going by the promenade where the cliffs were lower. She flashed past the Bank with its polished granite pillars, so much admired by Eustace. Soon she was in the heart of the town.

The big hand of the post-office clock was leaning on the quarter. Breathless, she went in. Behind the counter stood a girl she did not know.

'Please can you give me back the letter I posted this afternoon?'

'I'm afraid not, Miss. We're not allowed to.'

'Please do it this once. It's very important that the letter shouldn't go.'

The girl – she was not more than twenty herself – stared at the beautiful, agitated face, imperious, unused to pleading, the tall figure, the bosom that rose and fell, and it scarcely seemed to her that Hilda was a child.

'I could ask the postmaster.'

'No, please don't do that, I'd rather you didn't. It's a letter that I . . . regret having written.' A wild look came into Hilda's eye; she fumbled in her pocket.

'If I pay a fine may I have it back?'

How pretty she is, the girl thought. She seems thoroughly upset. Something stirred in her, and she moved towards the door of the letter-box.

'I oughtn't to, you know. Who would the letter be to?'

'It's a gentleman.' Hilda spoke with an effort.

I thought so, the girl said to herself; and she unlocked the door of the letter-box.

'What would the name be?'

The name was on Hilda's lips, but she checked it and stood speechless.

'Couldn't you let me look myself?' she said.

'Oh, I'm afraid that would be against regulations. They might give me the sack.'

'Oh, please, just this once. I . . . I shall never write to him again.'

The assistant's heart was touched. 'You made a mistake, then,' she said.

'Yes,' breathed Hilda. 'I don't know . . .' she left the sentence unfinished.

'You said something you didn't mean?'

'Yes,' said Hilda.

'And you think he might take it wrong?'

'Yes.'

The assistant dived into the box and brought out about twenty letters. She laid them on the counter in front of Hilda.

'Quick! quick!' she said. 'I'm not looking.'

Hilda knew the shape of the envelope. In a moment the letter was in her pocket. Looking at the assistant she panted; and the assistant panted slightly too. They didn't speak for a moment; then the assistant said:

'You're very young, dear, aren't you?'

Hilda drew herself up. 'Oh, no, I've turned fourteen.'

'You're sure you're doing the right thing? You're not acting impulsive-like? If you're really fond of him . . .'

'Oh, no,' said Hilda. 'I'm not . . . I'm not.' A tremor ran through her. 'I must go now.'

The assistant bundled the letters back into the box. There was a sound behind them: the postman had come in.

'Good afternoon, Miss,' he said.

'Good afternoon,' said the assistant languidly. 'I've been hanging about for you. You don't half keep people waiting, don't you?'

'There's them that works, and them that waits,' said the postman.

The assistant tossed her head.

'There's some do neither,' she said tartly, and then, turning in a business-like way to Hilda:

'Is there anything else, Miss?'

216

'Nothing further today,' said Hilda, rather haughtily. 'Thank you very much,' she added.

Outside the post office, in the twilight, her dignity deserted her. She broke into a run, but her mind outstripped her, surging, exultant.

'I shall never see him now,' she thought, 'I shall never see him now,' and the ecstasy, the relief, the load off her mind, were such as she might have felt had she loved Dick Staveley and been going to meet him.

Softly she let herself into the house. The dining-room was no use: it had a gas fire. She listened at the drawing-room door. No sound. She tiptoed into the fire-stained darkness, crossed the hearthrug and dropped the letter into the reddest cleft among the coals. It did not catch at once so she took the poker to it, driving it into the heart of the heat. A flame sprang up, and at the same moment she heard a movement and, turning, saw the fire reflected in her father's eyes.

'Hullo, Hilda – you startled me. I was having a nap. Burning something?'

'Yes,' said Hilda, poised for flight.

'A love-letter, I expect.'

'Oh, no, Daddy; people don't write love-letters at my age.'

'At your age –' began Mr Cherrington. But he couldn't remember, and anyhow it wouldn't do to tell his daughter that at her age he had already written a love-letter.

'Must be time for tea,' he said, yawning. 'Where's Eustace?'

As though in answer they heard a thud on the floor above, and the sound of water pouring into the bath.

'That's him,' cried Hilda. 'I promised him I would put his feet into mustard and water. He won't forgive me if I don't.'

She ran upstairs into the steam and blurred visibility, the warmth, the exciting sounds and comforting smells of the little bathroom. At first she couldn't see Eustace; the swirls of luminous vapour hid him; then they parted and disclosed him, sitting on the white curved edge of the bath with his back to the water and his legs bare to the knee, above which his combinations and his knickerbockers had been neatly folded back, no doubt by Minney's practised hand.

'Oh, there you are, Hilda!' he exclaimed. 'Isn't it absolutely spiffing!

217

The water's quite boiling. I only turned it on when you came in. I wish it was as hot as boiling oil – boiling water isn't, you know.'

'How much mustard did you put in?' asked Hilda.

'Half a tin. Minney said she couldn't spare any more.'

'Well, turn round and put your feet in,' Hilda said.

'Yes. Do you think I ought to take off my knickers, too? You see I only got wet as far as my ankles. I should have to take off my combinations.'

Hilda considered. 'I don't think you need this time.'

Eustace swivelled round and tested the water with his toe.

'Ooo!'

'Come on, be brave.'

'Yes, but you must put your feet in too. It won't be half the fun if you don't. Besides, you said you would, Hilda.' In his anxiety to share the experience with her he turned round again. 'Please! You got much wetter than I did.'

'I got warm running. Besides, it's only salt water. Salt water doesn't give you a cold.'

'Oh, but my water was salt, too.'

'You're different,' said Hilda. Then, seeing the look of acute disappointment on his face, she added, 'Well, just to please you.'

Eustace wriggled delightedly, and, as far as he dared, bounced up and down on the bath edge.

'Take off your shoes and stockings, then.' It was delicious to give Hilda orders. Standing stork-like, first on one foot, then on the other, Hilda obeyed.

'Now come and sit by me. It isn't very safe, take care you don't lose your balance.'

Soon they were sitting side by side, looking down into the water. The clouds of steam rising round them seemed to shut off the outside world. Eustace looked admiringly at Hilda's long slim legs.

'I didn't fill the bath any fuller,' he said, in a low voice, 'because of the marks. It might be dangerous, you know.'

Hilda looked at the bluish chips in the enamel, which spattered the sides of the bath. Eustace's superstitions about them, and his fears of submerging them, were well known to her.

'They won't let you do that at school,' she said.

'Oh, there won't be any marks at school. A new system of plumbing and sanitarization was installed last year. The prospectus said so. That would mean new baths, of course. New baths don't have marks. Your school may be the same, only the prospectus didn't say so. I expect baths don't matter so much for girls.'

'Why not?'

'They're cleaner, anyway. Besides, they wash.' Eustace thought of washing and having a bath as two quite different, almost unconnected things. 'And I don't suppose they'll let us put our feet in mustard and water.'

'Why not?' repeated Hilda.

'Oh, to harden us, you know. Boys have to be hard. If they did, it would be for a punishment, not fun like this . . . Just put your toe in, Hilda.'

Hilda flicked the water with her toe, far enough to start a ripple, and then withdrew it.

'It's still a bit hot. Let's wait a minute.'

'Yes,' said Eustace. 'It would spoil *everything* if we turned on the cold water.'

They sat for a moment in silence. Eustace examined Hilda's toes. They were really as pretty as fingers. His own were stunted and shapeless, meant to be decently covered.

'Now, both together!' he cried.

In went their feet. The concerted splash was magnificent, but the agony was almost unbearable.

'Put your arm round me, Hilda!'

'Then you put yours round me, Eustace!'

As they clung together their feet turned scarlet, and the red dye ran up far above the water-level almost to their knees. But they did not move, and slowly the pain began to turn into another feeling, a smart still, but wholly blissful.

'Isn't it wonderful?' cried Eustace. 'I could never have felt it without you!'

Hilda said nothing, and soon they were swishing their feet to and fro in the cooling water. The supreme moment of trial and triumph had gone by; other thoughts, not connected with their ordeal, began to slide into Eustace's mind.

'Were you in time to do it?' he asked.

'Do what?'

'Well, what you were going to do when you left me on the sands.'

'Oh, that,' said Hilda indifferently. 'Yes, I was just in time.' She thought a moment, and added: 'But don't ask me what it was, because I shan't ever tell you.'

Wailing Well

M. R. JAMES

In the year 19— there were two members of the Troop of Scouts attached to a famous school, named respectively Arthur Wilcox and Stanley Judkins. They were the same age, boarded in the same house, were in the same division, and naturally were members of the same patrol. They were so much alike in appearance as to cause anxiety and trouble, and even irritation, to the masters who came in contact with them. But oh how different were they in their inward man, or boy!

It was to Arthur Wilcox that the Head Master said, looking up with a smile as the boy entered chambers, 'Why, Wilcox, there will be a deficit in the prize fund if you stay here much longer! Here, take this handsomely bound copy of the *Life and Works of Bishop Ken*, and with it my hearty congratulations to yourself and your excellent parents.' It was Wilcox again, whom the Provost noticed as he passed through the playing fields, and, pausing for a moment, observed to the Vice-Provost, 'That lad has a remarkable brow!' 'Indeed, yes,' said the Vice-Provost. 'It denotes either genius or water on the brain.'

As a Scout, Wilcox secured every badge and distinction for which he competed. The Cookery Badge, the Map-Making Badge, the Life-Saving Badge, the Badge for picking up bits of newspaper, the Badge

221

for not slamming the door when leaving pupil-room, and many others. Of the Life-Saving Badge I may have a word to say when we come to treat of Stanley Judkins.

You cannot be surprised to hear that Mr Hope Jones added a special verse to each of his songs, in commendation of Arthur Wilcox, or that the Lower Master burst into tears when handing him the Good Conduct Medal in its handsome claret-coloured case: the medal which had been unanimously voted to him by the whole of Third Form. Unanimously, did I say? I am wrong. There was one dissentient, Judkins *mi.*, who said that he had excellent reasons for acting as he did. He shared, it seems, a room with his major. You cannot, again, wonder that in after years Arthur Wilcox was the first, and so far the only boy, to become Captain of both the School and of the Oppidans, or that the strain of carrying out the duties of both positions, coupled with the ordinary work of the school, was so severe that a complete rest for six months, followed by a voyage round the world, was pronounced an absolute necessity by the family doctor.

It would be a pleasant task to trace the steps by which he attained the giddy eminence he now occupies; but for the moment enough of Arthur Wilcox. Time presses, and we must turn to a very different matter: the career of Stanley Judkins – Judkins *ma.*

Stanley Judkins, like Arthur Wilcox, attracted the attention of the authorities; but in quite another fashion. It was to him that the Lower Master said, with no cheerful smile, 'What, again, Judkins? A very little persistence in this course of conduct, my boy, and you will have cause to regret that you ever entered this academy. There, take that, and that, and think yourself very lucky you don't get that and that!' It was Judkins, again, whom the Provost had cause to notice as he passed through the playing fields, when a cricket ball struck him with considerable force on the ankle, and a voice from a short way off cried, 'Thank you, cut-over!' 'I think,' said the Provost, pausing for a moment to rub his ankle, 'that that boy had better fetch his cricket ball for himself!' 'Indeed, yes,' said the Vice-Provost, 'and if he comes within reach, I will do my best to fetch him something else.'

As a Scout, Stanley Judkins secured no Badge save those which he was able to abstract from members of other patrols. In the cookery competition he was detected trying to introduce squibs into the Dutch oven of the next-door competitors. In the tailoring competition he succeeded in sewing two boys together very firmly, with disastrous effect when they tried to get up. For the Tidiness Badge he was disqualified because, in the Midsummer schooltime, which chanced to be hot, he could not be dissuaded from sitting with his fingers in the ink: as he said, for coolness' sake. For one piece of paper which he picked up, he must have dropped at least six banana skins or orange peels. Aged women seeing him approaching would beg him with tears in their eyes not to carry their pails of water across the road. They knew too well what the result would inevitably be. But it was in the life-saving competition that Stanley Judkins' conduct was most blameable and had the most far-reaching effects. The practice, as you know, was to throw a selected lower boy, of suitable dimensions, fully dressed, with his hands and feet tied together, into the deepest part of Cuckoo Weir, and to time the Scout whose turn it was to rescue him. On every occasion when he was entered for this competition Stanley Judkins was seized, at the critical moment, with a severe fit of cramp, which caused him to roll on the ground and utter alarming cries. This naturally distracted the attention of those present from the boy in the water, and had it not been for the presence of Arthur Wilcox the death-roll would have been a heavy one. As it was, the Lower Master found it necessary to take a firm line and say that the competition must be discontinued. It was in vain that Mr Beasley Robinson represented to him that in five competitions only four lower boys had actually succumbed. The Lower Master said that he would be the last to interfere in any way with the work of the Scouts; but that three of these boys had been valued members of his choir, and both he and Dr Ley felt that the inconvenience caused by the losses outweighed the advantages of the competitions. Besides, the correspondence with the parents of these boys had become annoying, and even distressing: they were no longer satisfied with the printed form which he was in the habit of sending out, and more than one of them had actually visited E— and taken up much of his valuable time with complaints. So the life-saving competition is now a thing of the past.

In short, Stanley Judkins was no credit to the Scouts, and there was talk on more than one occasion of informing him that his services were no longer required. This course was strongly advocated by Mr Lambart: but in the end milder counsel prevailed, and it was decided to give him another chance.

So it is that we find him at the beginning of the Midsummer holidays of 19— at the Scouts' camp in the beautiful district of W (or X) in the county of D (or Y).

It was a lovely morning and Stanley Judkins and one or two of his friends – for he still had friends – lay basking on the top of the down. Stanley was lying on his stomach with his chin propped on his hands, staring into the distance.

'I wonder what that place is,' he said.

'Which place?' said one of the others.

'That sort of dump in the middle of the field down there.'

'Oh, ah! How should I know what it is?'

'What do you want to know for?' said another.

'I don't know: I like the look of it. What's it called? Nobody got a map?' said Stanley. 'Call yourselves Scouts!'

'Here's a map all right,' said Wilfred Pipsqueak, ever resourceful, 'and there's the place marked on it. But it's inside the red ring. We can't go there.'

'Who cares about a red ring?' said Stanley. 'But it's got no name on your silly map.'

'Well, you can ask this old chap what it's called if you're so keen to find out.' 'This old chap' was an old shepherd who had come up and was standing behind them.

'Good morning, young gents,' he said, 'you've got a fine day for your doin's, ain't you?'

'Yes, thank you,' said Algernon de Montmorency, with native politeness. 'Can you tell us what that clump over there's called? And what's that thing inside it?'

''Course I can tell you,' said the shepherd. 'That's Wailin' Well, that is. But you ain't got no call to worry about that.'

'Is it a well in there?' said Algernon. 'Who uses it?'

The shepherd laughed. 'Bless you,' he said, 'there ain't from a man to a sheep in these parts uses Wailin' Well, nor haven't done all the years I've lived here.'

'Well, there'll be a record broken today, then,' said Stanley Judkins, 'because I shall go and get some water out of it for tea!'

'Sakes alive, young gentleman!' said the shepherd in a startled voice, 'don't you get to talkin' that way! Why, ain't your masters give you notice not to go by there? They'd ought to have done.'

'Yes, they have,' said Wilfred Pipsqueak.

'Shut up, you ass!' said Stanley Judkins. 'What's the matter with it? Isn't the water good? Anyhow, if it was boiled, it would be all right.'

'I don't know as there's anything much wrong with the water,' said the shepherd. 'All I know is, my old dog wouldn't go through that field, let alone me or anyone else that's got a morsel of brains in their heads.'

'More fool them,' said Stanley Judkins, at once rudely and ungrammatically. 'Who ever took any harm going there?' he added.

'Three women and a man,' said the shepherd gravely. 'Now just you listen to me. I know these 'ere parts and you don't, and I can tell you this much: for these ten years last past there ain't been a sheep fed in that field, nor a crop raised off of it – and it's good land, too. You can pretty well see from here what a state it's got into with brambles and suckers and trash of all kinds. *You've* got a glass, young gentleman,' he said to Wilfred Pipsqueak, 'you can tell with that anyway.'

'Yes,' said Wilfred, 'but I see there's tracks in it. Someone must go through it sometimes.'

'Tracks!' said the shepherd. 'I believe you! Four tracks: three women and a man.'

'What d'you mean, three women and a man?' said Stanley, turning over for the first time and looking at the shepherd (he had been talking with his back to him till this moment: he was an ill-mannered boy).

'Mean? Why, what I says: three women and a man.'

'Who are they?' asked Algernon. 'Why do they go there?'

'There's some p'r'aps could tell you who they *was*,' said the shepherd, 'but it was afore my time they come by their end. And why they goes there still is more than the children of men can tell: except I've heard they was all bad 'uns when they was alive.'

'By George, what a rum thing!' Algernon and Wilfred muttered: but Stanley was scornful and bitter.

'Why, you don't mean they're deaders? What rot! You must be a lot of fools to believe that. Who's ever seen them, I'd like to know?'

'*I've* seen 'em, young gentleman!' said the shepherd, 'seen 'em from near by on that bit of down: and my old dog, if he could speak, he'd tell you he've seen 'em, same time. About four o'clock of the day it was, much such a day as this. I seen 'em, each one of 'em, come peerin' out of the bushes and stand up, and work their way slow by them tracks towards the trees in the middle where the well is.'

'And what were they like? Do tell us!' said Algernon and Wilfred eagerly.

'Rags and bones, young gentlemen: all four of 'em: flutterin' rags and whity bones. It seemed to me as if I could hear 'em clackin' as they got along. Very slow they went, and lookin' from side to side.'

'What were their faces like? Could you see?'

'They hadn't much to call faces,' said the shepherd, 'but I could seem to see as they had teeth.'

'Lor!' said Wilfred, 'and what did they do when they got to the trees?'

'I can't tell you that, sir,' said the shepherd. 'I wasn't for stayin' in that place, and if I had been, I was bound to look to my old dog: he'd gone! Such a thing he never done before as leave me; but gone he had, and when I came up with him in the end, he was in that state he didn't know me, and was fit to fly at my throat. But I kep' talkin' to him, and after a bit he remembered my voice and came creepin' up like a child askin' pardon. I never want to see him like that again, nor yet no other dog.'

The dog, who had come up and was making friends all round, looked up at his master, and expressed agreement with what he was saying very fully.

The boys pondered for some moments on what they had heard: after which Wilfred said, 'And why's it called Wailing Well?'

'If you was round here at dusk of a winter's evening, you wouldn't want to ask why,' was all the shepherd said.

'Well, I don't believe a word of it,' said Stanley Judkins, 'and I'll go there next chance I get: blowed if I don't!'

'Then you won't be ruled by me?' said the shepherd. 'Nor yet by your masters as warned you off? Come now, young gentleman, you don't want for sense, I should say. What should I want tellin' you a pack of lies? It ain't sixpence to me anyone goin' in that field: but I wouldn't like to see a young chap snuffed out like in his prime.'

'I expect it's a lot more than sixpence to you,' said Stanley. 'I expect you've got a whisky still or something in there, and want to keep other people away. Rot I call it. Come on back, you boys.'

So they turned away. The two others said, 'Good evening' and 'Thank you' to the shepherd, but Stanley said nothing. The shepherd shrugged his shoulders and stood where he was, looking after them rather sadly.

On the way back to the camp there was great argument about it all, and Stanley was told as plainly as he could be told all the sorts of fools he would be if he went to the Wailing Well.

That evening, among other notices, Mr Beasley Robinson asked if all maps had got the red ring marked on them. 'Be particular,' he said, 'not to trespass inside it.'

Several voices – among them the sulky one of Stanley Judkins – said, 'Why not, sir?'

'Because not,' said Mr Beasley Robinson, 'and if that isn't enough for you, I can't help it.' He turned and spoke to Mr Lambart in a low voice, and then said, 'I'll tell you this much: we've been asked to warn Scouts off that field. It's very good of the people to let us camp here at all, and the least we can do is to oblige them – I'm sure you'll agree to that.'

Everybody said, 'Yes, sir!' except Stanley Judkins, who was heard to mutter, 'Oblige them be blowed!'

Early in the afternoon of the next day, the following dialogue was heard. 'Wilcox, is all your tent there?'

'No, sir, Judkins isn't!'

'That boy is *the* most infernal nuisance ever invented! Where do you suppose he is?'

'I haven't an idea, sir.'

'Does anybody else know?'

'Sir, I shouldn't wonder if he'd gone to the Wailing Well.'

'Who's that? Pipsqueak? What's the Wailing Well?'

'Sir, it's that place in the field by – well, sir, it's in a clump of trees in a rough field.'

'D'you mean inside the red ring? Good heavens! What makes you think he's gone there?'

'Why, he was terribly keen to know about it yesterday, and we were talking to a shepherd man, and he told us a lot about it and advised us not to go there: but Judkins didn't believe him, and said he meant to go.'

'Young ass!' said Mr Hope Jones, 'did he take anything with him?'

'Yes, I think he took some rope and a can. We did tell him he'd be a fool to go.'

'Little brute! What the deuce does he mean by pinching stores like that! Well, come along, you three, we must see after him. Why can't people keep the simplest orders? What was it the man told you? No, don't wait, let's have it as we go along.'

And off they started – Algernon and Wilfred talking rapidly and the other two listening with growing concern. At last they reached that spur of down overlooking the field of which the shepherd had spoken the day before. It commanded the place completely; the well inside the clump of bent and gnarled Scotch firs was plainly visible, and so were the four tracks winding about among the thorns and rough growth.

It was a wonderful day of shimmering heat. The sea looked like a floor of metal. There was no breath of wind. They were all exhausted when they got to the top, and flung themselves down on the hot grass.

'Nothing to be seen of him yet,' said Mr Hope Jones, 'but we must stop here a bit. You're done up – not to speak of me. Keep a sharp look-out,' he went on after a moment, 'I thought I saw the bushes stir.'

'Yes,' said Wilcox, 'so did I. Look ... no, that can't be him. It's somebody though, putting their head up, isn't it?'

'I thought it was, but I'm not sure.'

Silence for a moment. Then:

'That's him, sure enough,' said Wilcox, 'getting over the hedge on the far side. Don't you see? With a shiny thing. That's the can you said he had.'

'Yes, it's him, and he's making straight for the trees,' said Wilfred.

At this moment Algernon, who had been staring with all his might, broke into a scream.

'What's that on the track? On all fours – O, it's a woman. O, don't let me look at her! Don't let it happen!' And he rolled over, clutching at the grass and trying to bury his head in it.

'Stop that!' said Mr Hope Jones loudly – but it was no use. 'Look here,' he said, 'I must go down there. You stop here, Wilfred, and look after that boy. Wilcox, you run as hard as you can to the camp and get some help.'

They ran off, both of them. Wilfred was left alone with Algernon, and did his best to calm him, but indeed he was not much happier himself. From time to time he glanced down the hill and into the field. He saw Mr Hope Jones drawing nearer at a swift pace, and then, to his great surprise, he saw him stop, look up and round about him, and turn quickly off at an angle! What could be the reason? He looked at the field, and there he saw a terrible figure – something in ragged black – with whitish patches breaking out of it, the head, perched on a long thin neck, half hidden by a shapeless sort of blackened sun-bonnet. The creature was waving thin arms in the direction of the rescuer who was approaching, as if to ward him off: and between the two figures the air seemed to shake and shimmer as he had never seen it: and as he looked, he began himself to feel something of a waviness and confusion in his brain, which made him guess what might be the effect on someone within closer range of the influence. He looked away hastily, to see Stanley Judkins making his way pretty quickly towards the clump, and in proper Scout fashion; evidently picking his steps with care to avoid treading on snapping sticks or being caught by arms of brambles. Evidently, though he saw nothing, he suspected some sort of ambush, and was trying to go noiselessly. Wilfred saw all that, and he saw more, too. With a sudden and dreadful sinking at the heart, he caught sight of someone among the trees, waiting: and again of someone – another of the hideous black figures – working slowly along the track from another side of the field, looking from side to side, as the shepherd had described it. Worst of all, he saw a fourth – unmistakably a man this time – rising out of the bushes a few yards behind the wretched Stanley, and painfully, as it seemed, crawling into the track. On all sides the miserable victim was cut off.

Wilfred was at his wits' end. He rushed at Algernon and shook him. 'Get up,' he said. 'Yell! Yell as loud as you can. Oh, if we'd only got a whistle!'

Algernon pulled himself together. 'There's one,' he said, 'Wilcox's: he must have dropped it.'

So one whistled, the other screamed. In the still air the sound carried. Stanley heard: he stopped: he turned round: and then indeed a cry was heard more piercing and dreadful than any that the boys on the hill could raise. It was too late. The crouched figure behind Stanley sprang at him and caught him about the waist. The dreadful one that was standing waving her arms waved them again, but in exultation. The one that was lurking among the trees shuffled forward, and she too stretched out her arms as if to clutch at something coming her way; and the other, farthest off, quickened her pace and came on, nodding gleefully. The boys took it all in in an instant of terrible silence, and they could hardly breathe as they watched the horrid struggle between the man and his victim. Stanley struck with his can, the only weapon he had. The rim of a broken black hat fell off the creature's head and showed a white skull with stains that might be wisps of hair. By this time one of the women had reached the pair, and was pulling at the rope that was coiled about Stanley's neck. Between them they overpowered him in a moment: the awful screaming ceased, and then the three passed within the circle of the clump of firs.

Yet for a moment it seemed as if rescue might come. Mr Hope Jones, striding quickly along, suddenly stopped, turned, seemed to rub his eyes, and then started running *towards* the field. More: the boys glanced behind them, and saw not only a troop of figures from the camp coming over the top of the next down, but the shepherd running up the slope of their own hill. They beckoned, they shouted, they ran a few yards towards him and then back again. He mended his pace.

Once more the boys looked towards the field. There was nothing. Or, was there something among the trees? Why was there a mist about the trees? Mr Hope Jones had scrambled over the hedge, and was plunging through the bushes.

The shepherd stood beside them, panting. They ran to him and clung to his arms. 'They've got him! In the trees!' was as much as they could say, over and over again.

'What? Do you tell me he've gone in there after all I said to him yesterday? Poor young thing! Poor young thing!' He would have said more, but other voices broke in. The rescuers from the camp had arrived. A few hasty words, and all were dashing down the hill.

They had just entered the field when they met Mr Hope Jones. Over his shoulder hung the corpse of Stanley Judkins. He had cut it from the branch on which he found it hanging, waving to and fro. There was not a drop of blood in the body.

On the following day Mr Hope Jones sallied forth with an axe and with the expressed intention of cutting down every tree in the clump, and of burning every bush in the field. He returned with a nasty cut in his leg and a broken axe-helve. Not a spark of fire could he light, and on no single tree could he make the least impression.

I have heard that the present population of the Wailing Well field consists of three women, a man, and a boy.

The shock experienced by Algernon de Montmorency and Wilfred Pipsqueak was severe. Both of them left the camp at once; and the occurrence undoubtedly cast a gloom – if but a passing one – on those who remained. One of the first to recover his spirits was Judkins *mi*.

Such, gentlemen, is the story of the career of Stanley Judkins, and of a portion of the career of Arthur Wilcox. It has, I believe, never been told before. If it has a moral, that moral is, I trust, obvious: if it has none, I do not well know how to help it.

The Visiting Moon

STELLA GIBBONS

The girls were still clapping.

Lucy Rideout sat by the Head Mistress's side, smiling politely, and smoothing with thin, square hands her notes, while she stealthily glanced upwards, to refresh her eyes, at the empty blue square of afternoon sky, subtle with autumn, which she could see through the highest window of the lecture hall.

The Head Mistress was talking to the tiers of young smooth faces:

'. . . such a delightful lecture, and so distinguished a visitor . . . the only disappointment in Miss Rideout's talk had been her silence on the subject of her own work . . . the School was so proud of such a famous Old Girl.'

'How that woman dislikes me,' mused Lucy, bowing and smiling. 'I frighten her, too.' And in spite of her thirty-six years and her fame, Lucy took satisfaction from the thought. It paid off some old scores.

She was wondering, as she sat there, silent and dark in her dark fox furs, whether she could suggest that she should make a solitary tour of the school after tea, 'just to see if it has changed much in twenty-one years.'

Her secret reason was different; she wanted to see once more the old music-rooms at dusk.

'They will think I am mad,' she mused, 'but then, they always did, so what does it matter?'

Achievement was easier than she had expected. During tea, which she took alone with the Prefects, as their guest, she discovered that a rehearsal of a play was to be given in Hall that evening, in preparation for Speech Day, and she gathered, in spite of the attentive courtesy of her hostesses, that they were only longing for the moment when she would get up and go, and leave them to their rehearsal.

She therefore rose as soon after tea as politeness permitted.

'The school hasn't changed much,' she murmured, as she stood in the bleak entry making her adieux. 'I should so like to go over it again some time.' A tiny pause. 'Do you think I might go this evening?'

The Prefects exchanged hopeless glances. The Head Prefect, however, answered politely:

'Oh, yes, Miss Rideout. You can show Miss Rideout over the school, can't you, Monica?'

But this was not at all what Lucy wanted.

'Oh, no – I couldn't dream of it,' she interrupted, in a decided tone which was all the more effective because her normal soft, indolent and fashionably inflected voice seemed incapable of it. 'I will just wander around by myself for a little while, and let myself out. Don't you trouble.'

And she smiled; a brilliant, fashionable smile.

The Prefects were disarmed by this flash, which emphasized in a sentence the chasm of years and achievement lying between themselves and their guest; and though they felt that the situation was most irregular, and would certainly bring a reproof for discourtesy when it came to the ears of the Head Mistress, not one of them had *savoir faire* enough to undertake a protest.

And so, in another two minutes, Lucy found herself mounting the stairs leading to the upper part of the school – alone.

There were five music-rooms, at the very top of the building, huddled under the roof so that the sounds of girls practising and being taught to play might not disturb the classrooms. The sounds in the distant depths of the school grew more remote as Lucy mounted, until they only served to make more intense the silence.

How silent are the upper regions of the school on an autumn evening! The cold sky curves endlessly above a girl's head as she stands dreaming by some half-open window in an empty classroom, looking, with eyes that do not see, between the branches of the great poplar outside the window. Yet she notices that the glossy sides of the twigs nearest the sunken sun reflect a red light.

As Lucy climbed the last stairs she glanced upwards at the nearest window, as she instinctively did when shut away from the clouds and open sky inside a building; and she saw the moon.

Sunset lingered on the panes of the westward-facing houses, the aspens in the playing-field across the railway cutting kept up their ceaseless whisper; and there, lifting above the roofs, was the ghostly pitted moon in the autumn sky.

Lucy turned back to look at it over her shoulder as she crossed the landing, for it had only needed the moon to complete her impression that she was a ghost, returning. Just so, with that comforting suggestion of eternity and peace, the moon had looked when she used to watch it creep up over the roofs twenty-one years ago, and even then she had been calmed by the remoteness of that look, which would have made another kind of child more miserable.

How unhappy her childhood had been, she thought, climbing the narrow uncarpeted stairs between the green walls. In her passionate girlhood, too, her cold manner had repelled or amused the people she most loved.

Now, after thirty-six years in the world, surrounded by the soft prosperity her own brain and fingers had earned, she had realized that all she really cared about was beauty, in its myriad incarnations. But it was only recently that she had surrendered to this secret conviction, and been at peace.

She opened the door of the first music-room; she used to practise here, but it was not this one that she had liked best. The room was full of the soft, unearthly-seeming light which falls from the sky when the

235

day is just beginning to die, and by it the old, shut, brown piano, the ash-pale floor of scrubbed boards, and the silent desks looked beautiful.

Lucy crossed to the window on tip-toe, touched the cold pane with a finger-tip, widened her eyes up at the deepening silver moon. Far below, the long twilit North London road in which the school stood was almost deserted, but a schoolgirl or two lingered under the newly lit lamps by the tramstop, where the dead leaves eddied.

She ran her finger along the piano's breast, and stood there, smiling to herself while her five senses, rather than her brain, faithfully remembered for her certain sounds, certain lights in the sky, which had surrounded her youthful body in this room twenty-one years ago. Now her face was lined, rich with experience, like a rose that has opened right out.

She went back to the window and stood by it, savouring her present deep content by contrasting it with her tortured youth.

She could not take her content for granted.

Living on a planet wrenched from that very sun who gave the moon she watched its clear light, a planet peopled with men developed from animals, and animals that lived by levying their own deaths, content seemed a miracle to Miss Rideout.

The moon was brightening. She turned from the window and went down the stairs to look at her favourite music-room before she left this backwater and went out into the world again.

She was not thinking complacently, 'Here I used to be unhappy, and now I am unhappy no more,' as she turned the handle of her music-room door; her content went far deeper. She saw, as if in a vision, the few crowded years of work and fame left to her, and imagined how she would draw, at last, gently nearer to the secret of death, simple yet answerless. Her life, in memory, seemed like a rich tapestry, and she was grateful.

'This is one of the happiest moments of my life,' she thought, opening the door. (But then, being a poet, she was always having such moments, and seldom fully realized how many of them she had already had.)

As the door opened, and the familiar arrangement of growing shadow and lingering light met her eyes, crowned through the window by the moon, she found that this particular moment, at least, was being shared.

Someone was in her music-room.

On the window-sill, never broad enough to be really comfortable as a seat, yet broad enough to suggest immediately that one must sit there, a schoolgirl was sitting, with the bullet outline of her head, too closely shingled, and her profile, showing hard against the faint evening sky. She was leaning against the window-frame, relaxed, in an attitude strangely graceful for such a sturdy body, and on the window-sill beside her lay a pair of field-glasses.

But Lucy had only two seconds, perhaps, to take the picture in, for, with the mere noise of the opening door the schoolgirl slipped off her seat, dropped her hand casually over the glasses, and let them fall inconspicuously at her side, glided to a desk where a pile of books lay, and bent over them, lifting, at the same moment, a face of the wariest innocence to the door.

The whole manoeuvre was carried out so smoothly that only a schoolmistress or a poet would have attached any importance to that first half-glimpse of another, and more natural, position.

The schoolgirl, therefore, was out of luck. Her face changed when she saw, instead of one of the mistresses, a dark woman in furs, but the wary expression did not relax. For a few seconds they stared at each other in hostile silence. Lucy was disconcerted at finding her music-room invaded, and when at last she spoke it was in her most formal voice, as though she were addressing a grown-up person:

'I beg your pardon; I'm afraid I disturbed you? I am an Old Girl.'

'Oh, it's quite all right, thanks awfully,' said the schoolgirl as politely. 'I was just going, as a matter of fact.'

Her voice had the hard, supercilious yet charming cadence of extreme youth, to which life has as yet done nothing. Lucy found herself remembering, in spite of her irritation, how polite she herself had always been, at fifteen, to grown-up people, because she was so deeply and secretly convinced of their essential wrongheadedness and unimportance.

She crossed to the window, with a murmured apology and leaned out into the dusk air, but she was unable to savour the moment of memory to the full because of the obstinate presence loitering in the room behind her. There were the sighing aspens, the white blouses of the netball team glimmering as they came up across the playing-field to the pavilion, streaked sky, and fiery moon, but her memory was tainted by self-consciousness, and she could experience nothing but irritation.

'Why doesn't she go?' she thought.

A sudden shocking clatter made her turn, with a great nervous start, controlling a cry with difficulty.

'My *dear* child –!'

'I'm awfully sorry –' gasped the schoolgirl from under a desk, where she was groping. 'So stupid of me . . . I dropped them.'

'What is "them"?' Lucy's voice was suddenly friendly. Her irritable moods never lasted more than a few seconds; this time it was the contrast between the Victorian room, slowly growing dark, and the fresh vigour of the young voice coming out of its settled shadows that restored her mood to one of poetry.

A pause. The schoolgirl had found what she had dropped, but did not seem to have heard the question, so Lucy gaily repeated it, her back turned on the cold square of the window. She was ready to be friends.

This time the answer came, too faltering and would-be casual.

'Oh – nothing. That is, I mean, I dropped my field-glasses.'

'*Field-glasses!*' cried Lucy (and twenty-one years, charged to their brims with experience, seemed to flit softly backwards and to stand, surveying what they had made of her, as she heard the word). 'Do *you* come here with field-glasses, too? Why, that's what I used to do, twenty-one years ago!'

She could see by the mingled faintest moonlight and dying daylight on the child's face that she was still hostile. Yet how pretty she was! How could such immature moulding fail to be beautiful, when earliest youth lay over the soft, wide cheeks and close-cropped nape like a bloom – like a perfume?

'Yes – I wasn't allowed to go to the netball match,' was the muttered reply.

'And so you came up here to watch it through the field-glasses – just as I used to!' cried Lucy. 'Was there someone playing you particularly wanted to watch? That's why I used to come here – to watch someone playing netball.'

Silence. Instead of the silly smile which was so likely to have answered her question, a miracle occurred. A blush burned up in the healthy cheeks, recognizable even in the twilight, and Lucy, aghast at her tactlessness, hurried on:

'Why weren't you allowed to go to the match? Who is it against?'

'No one in particular – only Upper Five I playing Upper Five II in the House Matches. But I did want to watch. And then, just because I used my permit last Monday to watch the netball, instead of the hockey (it was a hockey permit, you see), Beaky— Miss Beakman said I wasn't to watch any more netball this term.'

'Beaky?' cried Lucy. 'Is she still here? Why, she must be a hundred! She used to keep me from watching netball matches too, years and years ago. She always seemed to know whenever one particularly wanted to see a match... Does she still talk about "making the punishment fit the crime"?'

An unrestrained gurgling sound invaded the dusk. The schoolgirl was giggling.

'Oh, yes ... and do you rememb— did she used to say "Impertinence is not wit" when you were here?'

'Oh, yes ... and creep about on flat-heeled slippers, so that she could take people by surprise! I should think she did,' said Lucy, with hearty dislike. 'Are her fingers still icy cold? She used to wrap them ve-e-ery slowly round one's wrist, I remember. Heavens, yes! How terrified I was of her ... fancy old Beaky...'

They were laughing together, their clear voices tossed back from wall to wall in the old twilit room.

'Did you manage to see anything of the match? Who won?' she asked.

'Upper Five II. I only saw the second half. I couldn't get up

239

here before. And the trees get in the way so; one can't see much.'

'Yes, they used to when I was here, only, of course, they were smaller then,' murmured Lucy.

And then she added, with the touch of formality which meant that she was nervous, 'May I know your name?'

'Honor King.'

There was a pause, in which Lucy looked at the floor and the schoolgirl frankly stared at her pensive face, with its dark crescents of downcast lashes. She said suddenly and shyly:

'You're Miss Rideout, aren't you?'

'Yes. But how did you know?' asked Lucy, surprised and pleased, for she had never outgrown her pleasure in her fame.

'Oh, I knew you were coming to talk to the Pres. today, and I've seen photographs of you. Is it . . .' she hesitated. 'What does it feel like to be famous?'

Lucy walked restlessly over to the window and leaned out, smelling the cold sooty evening air.

Child, child! she was thinking, how can I expect you to believe me if I tell you that it feels no stranger than to be fifteen, and to watch through field-glasses the love of one's heart playing netball? No stranger, perhaps, but how different!

She began to speak, in a low, reminiscent voice:

'Oh, one gets used to it, I suppose, as a pedlar gets used to his pack . . . Do you know, Honor, when I was at school here I used to come up to this room in the afternoon sometimes, with field-glasses that belonged to my father, and watch a girl I was in lo— a girl I was "cracked" on, playing netball? She was the only beautiful thing in the whole school.'

'What was her name?' asked Honor, in a voice that had lost all its guard of flippancy. It sounded like the very voice of youth, coming soft and moved and eager out of the dusk.

'Myfanwy Price . . . She was Welsh, you see. Heavens, how wretched I used to be! She was very proud-looking, and so graceful and good at games, and I was clumsy and badly dressed and hopeless at games, too–'

240

'Oh, I *know*,' breathed Honor. 'That's exactly how I feel about Molly...'

'I never told anyone. I used to write poems about her (quite good ones, I think) and keep them at home in a little dark-blue velvet box, shaped like a heart.' Her light, carefully modulated voice, with its sudden betraying bursts of over-emphasis, wavered on in a twilight now lessened by the mild beginnings of moonlight.

'And did she ever know about it?'

'Oh, yes! Heavens, yes!' laughed Lucy. 'I told her, after keeping it to myself for two years. Poor lamb, she was so embarrassed and so decent about it.'

'I couldn't bear to do that,' said Honor, very seriously. 'I couldn't bear anyone to know about it, either. I keep a diary, of course, but I wouldn't *dream* of letting anyone read it.'

Lucy looked up suddenly, and stared rather tragically into the child's rounded and delicious face, which was solemn with the effort of sharing a confidence with someone famous. The moon's light made an aura round the sleeves of her white blouse and gave a false pallor to her face – a face so utterly ingenuous, so unimprinted by any experience even approaching reality, that a wave of strong feeling, a mingling of envy and pity, possessed Lucy.

'Honor –' she began impulsively, but she stopped short.

The words would not come in which to warn the child to guard, more fiercely than life, the strength of her feelings, which would so soon broaden into sentiment, be examined inquisitively by other human beings, and replaced by the generalizations and common sense of an adult mind in a maturing body.

Honor was looking at her in polite inquiry.

'I was only going to say,' said Lucy, laughing nervously, 'do try *never* to lose the power of looking at the world as though you were seeing it for the first time, and it was still full of wonder –'

She broke off hopelessly, glanced out of the window at the high-riding moon, shivered, and pulled her furs closer.

The child's face, she could dimly see, was puzzled and a little embarrassed. It was quite useless, of course; children had to grow up. It was like shouting a warning, from one's own desert strand, to a careless traveller wading ankle-deep in fresh flowers and running water.

'Pick them – pick them! Drink, and inhale their scent, so that flowers and water will never, never leave you!'

Sadness and envy possessed her as she gazed into Honor's face, and her own mature content and her fame seemed to wither when she compared it with the force of the dreams behind that smooth childish forehead. The desolate, deliberately pondered words of Cleopatra came into her mind:

> *'And there is nothing left remarkable*
> *Beneath the visiting moon.'*

It was true. Lucy had lived so long with wonder that wonder was her familiar friend. It would never visit her again like a regal guest, as it was visiting Honor King.

'I must go,' said Lucy, abruptly. 'Good night.'

'Good night, Miss Rideout,' said Honor, and her voice was hard and guarded again.

Lucy crossed the room, almost ran over the landing, and down the echoing stairs of stone, and all the way the moon sent its stealthy fingers of light pouring through the tall windows.

Outside the school, waiting in the cold with his coat-collar patiently turned up, she found Roger Ford, whom she was to marry.

'Good Heavens, Lucy, where have you been? I've been waiting half an hour.'

'Darling,' said Lucy, taking his arm and laying her pretty, sallow cheek against his sleeve, 'I'm so sorry, but I went up to look at the old music-rooms – where I used to practise, you know – and I wish I hadn't. I'm so miserable.'

'What else do you expect? You don't know the first thing about your own actions and reactions ... what a child you are,' he grumbled.

But she, thinking of that other child lingering dreaming in the old twilit room high above North London, knew how far she had journeyed from childhood, and shuddered.

ACKNOWLEDGEMENTS

H. E. Bates, 'Great Uncle Crow' from *Seven by Five*, reprinted by permission of Laurence Pollinger Ltd and the Estate of H. E. Bates

Daphne Du Maurier, 'The Pool' from *Echoes from the Macabre*, reprinted by permission of Curtis Brown Ltd on behalf of The Chichester Partnership. Copyright 1959 by Daphne Du Maurier

Stella Gibbons, 'The Visiting Moon' from *The Roaring Tower and Other Stories*, reprinted by permission of Curtis Brown Ltd on behalf of the Estate of Stella Gibbons

L. P. Hartley, 'Hilda's Letter' from *The Complete Short Stories of L. P. Hartley*, reprinted by permission of Hamish Hamilton Ltd

A selection of quality fiction from Headline

THE POSSESSION OF DELIA SUTHERLAND	Barbara Neil	£5.99 ☐
MANROOT	A N Steinberg	£5.99 ☐
DEADLY REFLECTION	Maureen O'Brien	£5.99 ☐
SHELTER	Monte Merrick	£4.99 ☐
VOODOO DREAMS	Jewell Parker Rhodes	£5.99 ☐
BY FIRELIGHT	Edith Pargeter	£5.99 ☐
SEASON OF INNOCENTS	Carolyn Haines	£5.99 ☐
OTHER WOMEN	Margaret Bacon	£5.99 ☐
THE JOURNEY IN	Joss Kingsnorth	£5.99 ☐
SWEET WATER	Christina Baker Kline	£5.99 ☐

All Headline books are available at your local bookshop or newsagent, or can be ordered direct from the publisher. Just tick the titles you want and fill in the form below. Prices and availability subject to change without notice.

Headline Book Publishing, Cash Sales Department, Bookpoint, 39 Milton Park, Abingdon, OXON, OX14 4TD, UK. If you have a credit card you may order by telephone – 01235 400400.

Please enclose a cheque or postal order made payable to Bookpoint Ltd to the value of the cover price and allow the following for postage and packing:

UK & BFPO: £1.00 for the first book, 50p for the second book and 30p for each additional book ordered up to a maximum charge of £3.00.

OVERSEAS & EIRE: £2.00 for the first book, £1.00 for the second book and 50p for each additional book.

Name ....

Address ....

....

....

If you would prefer to pay by credit card, please complete:
Please debit my Visa/Access/Diner's Card/American Express (delete as applicable) card no:

Signature .... Expiry Date..............